HE SEEMED TO GATHER THE DARKNESS ABOUT HIMSELF

"You must know by now that I am at the end of all your paths," Riveda said. "You must know that now, as I have known it for a long time. Deoris, will you come with me—to the Crypt where the God sleeps?"

She caught her hands against her throat. Sacrilege this, for a daughter of Light. And when last she had accompanied Riveda to the Grey Temple, the consequences had been frightening.

Had he commanded, had he pleaded, had he spoken a word of persuasion, Deoris would have fled. But before his silent face she could only say, gravely, "I will come."

Marion Zimmer Bradley
Web of Darkness

A BAEN BOOK

What has gone before . . .

When the daughters of the Arch-priest Talkannon
Domaris and Deoris were young—Domaris only
recently named Acolyte of the Temple of Light and
Deoris not yet consecrated—there came to their
City a man who named himself Micon. He was a
Prince of Atlantis and a figure of wonder and pity
to Domaris, for he had been tortured and maimed
by the dreaded Black-robes, sorcerers of the dark
arts. No man knew their names, and they practised
unmolested in the labyrinthine caves beneath
Domaris's own Temple.

There they had taken Micon and his half-brother
Reio-ta. There Micon suffered tortures whose pain
would never leave him, and there Reio-ta lost his
mind, but not before revealing secrets of magic the
Black-robes would put to dreadful use if not
prevented. Rajasta, Temple Guardian and rescuer of
Micon, sought the Black-robes with the aid of the
Arch-Administrator Talkannon—father to Domaris
and Deoris—but found no clues.

Now Domaris and Deoris, though they could not
be parted as sisters, were different in many ways.
Deoris was, perhaps, the more intelligent, but she
was headstrong and rebellious, enough to cause
her expulsion from the Temple school. Domaris,
the elder, was the steadier and more thoughtful;
she was gentle and loving, and had willingly
pledged herself in marriage to the young priest
Arvath.

But the coming of Micon changed Domaris's life.
Against her own cautiousness she fell in love with the
regal, suffering Prince—though he warned her his

days were ending. He lived for one purpose alone: to father a son, and bequeath the power of Atlantis.

So worthy of love Domaris found Micon that she asked nothing more than to fulfill his last wish, and Micon lived just long enough to bless his son Micail . . .

The tale of Domaris and Micon is told in *Web of Light*. Here now is the story of Deoris—and what befell when she turned from Domaris and the Temple, jealous beyond reason of her sister's love for Micon. Her questing self spurned the thought of a love of her own and sought knowledge instead, and so she became a Priestess of the House of Caratra—and came to know the Healer Riveda. His powers excited and tempted Deoris . . . enough so that she followed him even unto the Grey Temple, dangerous to all of the Temple of Light. There Riveda and the mindless Reio-ta, who had become the Healer's servant, wove magic which would have killed Deoris had her sister not intervened at the risk of her own life. . . .

The Editor

BOOK I—DEORIS

BOOK II—RIVEDA

BOOK III—TIRIKI

Book I
DEORIS

Chapter One

THE PROMISE

I

"Lord Rajasta," Deoris greeted the old Priest anxiously, "I am glad you are come! Domaris is so—so strange!"

Rajasta's lined face quirked into an enquiring glance.

Deoris rushed on impetuously, "I can't understand—she does everything she should, she isn't crying all the time anymore, but—" The words came out as a sort of wail: "She isn't *there!*"

Nodding slowly, Rajasta touched the child's shoulder in a comforting caress. "I feared this—I will see her. Is she alone now?"

"Yes, Domaris wouldn't look at them when they came, wouldn't answer when they spoke, just sat staring at the wall—" Deoris began to cry.

Rajasta attempted to soothe her, and after a few moments managed to discover that "they" referred to Elis and Mother Ysouda. His wise, old eyes looked down into Deoris's small face, white and mournful, and what he saw there made him stroke her hair lingeringly before he said, with gentle insistence, "You are stronger than she, now, though it may not seem so. You must be kind to her. She needs all your love and all your strength, too." Leading the still sniffling Deoris to a nearby couch, and settling her upon it, he said, "I will go to her now."

In the inner room, Domaris sat motionless, her eyes fixed on distances past imagining, her hands idle at her sides. Her face was as a statue's, still and remote.

"Domaris," said Rajasta softly. "My daughter."

Very slowly, from some secret place of the spirit, the woman came back; her eyes took cognizance of her surroundings. "Lord Rajasta," she acknowledged, her voice little more than a ripple in the silence.

"Domaris," Rajasta repeated, with an oddly regretful undertone. "My acolyte, you neglect your duties. This is not worthy of you."

"I have done what I must," Domaris said tonelessly, as if she did not even mean to deny the accusation.

"You mean, you make the gestures," Rajasta corrected her. "Do you think I do not know you are willing yourself to die? You can do that, if you are coward enough. But your son, and Micon's—" Her eyes winced, and seeing even this momentary reaction, Rajasta insisted, "Micon's son needs you."

Now Domaris's face came alive with pain. "No," she said, "even in that I have failed! My baby has been put to a wet nurse!"

"Which need not have happened, had you not let your grief master you," Rajasta charged. "Blind, foolish girl! Micon loved and honored and trusted you above all others—and you fail him like this! You shame his memory, if his trust was misplaced—and you betray yourself—and you disgrace me, who taught you so poorly!"

Domaris sprang to her feet, raising protesting hands, but at Rajasta's imperative gesture she stilled the words rising in her throat, and listened with bent head.

"Do you think you are alone in grieving, Domaris? Do you not know that Micon was more than friend, more than brother to me? I am lonely since I can no longer walk at his side. But I cannot cease to live because one I loved has gone beyond my ability to follow!" He added, more gently, "Deoris, too, grieves for Micon—and she has not even the memory of his love to comfort her."

The woman's head drooped, and she began to weep, stormily, frantically; and Rajasta, his austere face kind again, gathered her in his arms and held her close until the crisis of desolate sobbing worked itself out, leaving Domaris exhausted, but alive.

"Thank you, Rajasta," she whispered, with a smile that almost made the man weep too. "I—I will be good."

II

Restlessly, Domaris paced the floor of her apartments. The weary hours and days that had worn away had only brought the unavoidable nearer, and now the moment of decision was upon her. Decision? No, the decision had been made. Only the time of action had come, when she must grant

the fulfillment of her pledged word. What did it
matter that her promise to Arvath had been given
when she was wholly ignorant of what it entailed?

With a tight smile, she remembered words spoken many years ago: *Yes, my Lords of the Council, I
accept my duty to marry. As well Arvath as another—I
like him somewhat.* That had been long ago, before
she had dreamed that love between man and
woman was more than a romance of pretty words,
before birth and death and loss had become personal to her. She had been, she reflected dryly,
thirteen years old at the time.

Her face, thinner than it had been a month ago,
now turned impassive, for she recognized the step
at the door. She turned and greeted Arvath, and
for a moment Arvath could only stand and stam-
mer her name. He had not seen her since Micon's
death, and the change in her appalled him. Domaris
was beautiful—more beautiful than ever—but her
face was pale and her eyes remote, as if they had
looked upon secret things. From a gay and laughing girl she had changed to a woman—a woman of
marble? Or of ice? Or merely a stilled flame that
burned behind the quiet eyes?

"I hope you are well," he said banally, at last.

"Oh yes, they have taken good care of me,"
Domaris said, and looked at him with tense exas-
peration. She knew what he wanted (she thought
with a faint sarcasm that was new to her); why
didn't he come to the point, why evade the issue
with courtesies?

Arvath sensed that her mood was not entirely
angelic, and it made him even more constrained.
"I have come to ask—to claim—your promise. . . ."

"As is your right," Domaris acknowledged formally, stifling with the attempt to control her breathing.

Arvath's impetuous hands went out and he clasped her close to him. "O beloved! May I claim you tonight before the Vested Five?"

"If you wish," she said, almost indifferently. One time was no worse than another. Then the old Domaris came back for a moment in a burst of impulsive sincerity. "O Arvath, forgive me that I—that I bring you no more than I can give," she begged, and briefly clung to him.

"That you give yourself is enough," he said tenderly.

She looked at him, with a wise sorrow in her eyes, but said nothing.

His arms tightened around her demandingly. "I will make you happy," he vowed. "I swear it!"

She remained passive in his embrace; but Arvath knew, with a nagging sense of futility, that she was unstirred by the torment that swept him. He repeated, and it sounded like a challenge, "I swear it—that I will make you forget!"

After an instant, Domaris put up her hands and freed herself from him; not with any revulsion, but with an indifference that filled the man with apprehension ... Quickly he swept the disturbing thought aside. He would awaken her to love, he thought confidently—and it never occurred to him that she was far more aware of love's nature than he.

Still, he had seen the momentary softening of pity in her eyes, and he knew enough not to press his advantage too far. He whispered, against her hair, "Be beautiful for me, my wife!" Then, brushing her temple with a swift kiss, he left her.

Domaris stood for a long minute, facing the closed door, and the deep pity in her eyes paled gradually to a white dread. "He's—he's *hungry*," she breathed, and a hidden trembling started and would not be stilled through her entire body. "How can I—I can't, I can't! Oh, Micon, *Micon!*"

Chapter Two

THE FEVER

I

That summer, fever raged in the city called the Circling Snake. Within the Temple precincts, where the Healers enforced rigid sanitary laws, it did not strike; but in the city itself it worked havoc, for a certain element of the population was too lazy or too stupid to follow the dictates of the priests.

Riveda and his Healers swept through the city like an invading army, without respect for plague or persons. They burned the stinking garbage heaps and the festering, squalid tenements; burned the foetid slave-huts of cruel or stupid owners who allowed men to live in worse filth than beasts. Invading every home, they fumigated, cleaned, nursed, isolated, condemned, buried or burned, daring even to enter homes where the victims were already rotten with the stink of death. They cremated the corpses—sometimes by force, where caste enjoined burial. Wells suspected of pollution were tested and often sealed, regardless of bribes, threats, and sometimes outright defiance. In short, they made themselves an obnoxious nuisance to the rich and powerful whose neglect or viciousness had permitted the plague to spread in the first place.

Riveda himself worked to exhaustion, nursing cases whom no one else could be persuaded to approach, out-bullying fat city potentates who questioned the value of his destructive mercy, sleeping in odd moments in houses already touched by death. He seemed to walk guarded by a series of miracles.

Deoris, who had served her novitiate in the Healers sponsored by her kinsman Cadamiri, met Riveda one evening as she stepped out for a moment from a house where she, with another Priestess, had been caring for the sick of two families. The woman of the house was out of danger, but four children had died, three more lay gravely ill, and another was sickening.

Seeing her, Riveda crossed the street to give her a greeting. His face was lined and very tired, but he looked almost happy, and she asked why.

"Because I believe the worst is over. There are no new cases in the North Quarter today, and even here—if the rains hold off three days more, we have won." The Adept looked down at Deoris; effort had put years into her face, and her beauty was dimmed by tiredness. Riveda's heart softened, and he said with a gentle smile, "I think you must be sent back to the Temple, my child; you are killing yourself."

She shook her head, fighting temptation. It would

be heavenly comfort to be out of this! But she only said, stubbornly, "I'll stay while I'm needed."

Riveda caught her hands and held them. "I'd take you myself, child, but I'd not be allowed inside the gates, for I go where contagion is worst. I can't return until the epidemic is over, but you. . . ." Suddenly, he caught her against him in a hard, rough embrace. "Deoris, you must go! I won't have you ill, I won't take the chance of losing you too!"

Startled and confused, Deoris was stiff in his arms; then she loosened and clung to him and felt the tickly stubble of his cheek against her face.

Without releasing her, he straightened and looked down, his stern mouth gentle. "Nor should I touch you," he said wryly. "There is danger even in this. You will have to bathe and change your clothing now—but Deoris, you're shivering, you can't be cold in this blistering heat?"

She stirred a little in his arms. "You're hurting me," she protested.

"Deoris!" said Riveda, in swift alarm, as she swayed against him.

The girl shivered with the violent cold that crawled suddenly around her. "I—I am all right," she protested weakly—but then she whispered. "I—I do want to go home," and slipped down, a shivering, limp little huddle in Riveda's arms.

II

It was not the dreaded plague. Riveda diagnosed marsh-fever, aggravated by exhaustion. After a few days, when they were certain there was no danger of contagion, they allowed her to be carried to the Temple in a litter. Once there, Deoris spent weeks that seemed like years, not dangerously ill, but drowsily delirious; even when the fever finally abated, her convalescence was very gradual, and it was a long time before she began to take even the most languid interest in living again.

The days flickered by in brief sleeps and half-waking dreams. She lay watching the play of shadows and sunlight on the walls, listening to the babble of the fountains and to the musical trilling of four tiny blue birds that chirped and twittered in a cage in the sunlight—Domaris had sent them to her. Domaris sent messages and gifts nearly every day, in fact, but Domaris herself did not come near her, though Deoris cried and begged for her for days during her delirium. Elara, who tended Deoris night and day, would say only that Arvath had forbidden it. But when the delirium was gone, Deoris learned from Elis that Domaris was already pregnant, and far from well; they dared not risk the contagion of even this mild fever. At learning this, Deoris turned her face to the wall and lay without speaking for a whole day, and did not mention her sister again.

Arvath himself came often, bringing the gifts and the loving messages Domaris sent. Chedan paid brief, shy, tongue-tied visits almost every day. Once Rajasta came, bearing delicate fruits to tempt her fastidious appetite, and full of commendation for her work in the epidemic.

When memory began to waken in her, and the recollection of Riveda's curious behavior swam out of the bizarre dreams of her delirium, she asked about the Adept of the Grey-robes. They told her Riveda had gone on a long journey, but secretly Deoris believed they lied, that he had died in the

epidemic. Grief died at the source; the well-springs
of her emotions had been sapped by the long illness and longer convalescence, and Deoris went
through the motions of living without much interest in past, present, or future.

It was many weeks before they allowed her to
leave her bed, and months before she was permitted to walk about in the gardens. When, finally,
she was well enough, she returned to her duties in
the Temple of Caratra—more or less, for she found
them all conspiring to find easy and useless tasks
which would not tax her returning strength. She
devoted much of her time to study as she grew
stronger, attending lectures given to the apprentice healers even though she could not accompany
them in their work. Often she would steal into a
corner of the library to listen from afar to the
discussions of the Priests of Light. Moreover, as
the Priestess Deoris, she was now entitled to a
scribe of her own; it was considered more intelligent to listen than to read, for the hearing could
be more completely concentrated than the sight.

On the evening of her sixteenth birthday, one of
the Priestesses had sent Deoris to a hill overlook-
ing the Star Field, to gather certain flowers of
medicinal value. The long walk had taxed her
strength, and she sat down for a moment to rest
before beginning the task when, suddenly, raising
her head, she saw the Adept Riveda walking along
the sunlit path in her direction. For a moment she
could only stare. She had been so convinced of his
death that she thought momentarily that the veil
had thinned, that she saw not him but his spirit
. . . then, convinced she was not having hallucina-
tions after all, she cried out and ran toward him.

Turning, he saw her and held out his arms. "Deoris," he said, and clasped her shoulders with his hands. "I have been anxious about you, they told me you had been dangerously ill. Are you quite recovered?" What he saw as he looked down into her face evidently satisfied him.

"I—I thought you were dead."

His rough smile was warmer than usual. "No, as you can see, I am very much alive. I have been away, on a journey to Atlantis. Perhaps some day I will tell you all about it ... I came to see you before I left, but you were too ill to know me. What are you doing here?"

"Gathering *shaing* flowers."

Riveda snorted. "Oh, a most worthy use of your talents! Well, now I have returned, perhaps I can find more suitable work for you. But at the moment I have errands of my own, so I must return you to your blossoms." He smiled again. "Such an important task must not be interrupted by a mere Adept!"

Deoris laughed, much cheered, and on an impulse Riveda bent and kissed her lightly before going on his way. He could not himself have explained the kiss—he was not given to impulsive actions. As he hastened toward the Temple, Riveda felt curiously disturbed, remembering the lassitude in the girl's eyes. Deoris had grown taller in the months of her illness, although she would never be very tall. Thin and frail, and yet beautiful with a fragile and wraithlike beauty, she was no longer a child, and yet she was hardly a woman. Riveda wondered, annoyed with himself for the direction his thoughts took, how young Chedan stood with his lovemaking. *No*, he decided, *that is not the answer.* Deoris had not the look of a girl mazed by the wakening of passion, nor the consciousness of sex that would have been there in that case. She had *permitted* his kiss, as innocently as a small child.

Riveda did not know that Deoris followed him with her eyes until he was quite out of sight, and that her face was flushed and alive again.

Chapter Three

CHOICE AND KARMA

I

The night was falling, folding like soft and moonless wings of indigo over the towered roofs of the Temple and the ancient city which lay beneath it, smothered in coils of darkness. A net of dim lights lay flung out over the blackness, and far away a pale phosphorescence hung around the heavier darkness of the sea-harbor. Starlight, faint and faulty, flickered around the railings which outlined the roof-platform of the great pyramid and made a ghostly haze around the two cloaked figures who stood there.

Deoris was shivering a little in the chilly breeze, holding, with lifted hands, the folds of her hooded cloak. The wind tugged at them, and finally she threw back the hood and let the short heavy ringlets of her hair blow as they would. She felt a little scared, and very young.

Riveda's face, starkly austere in the pallid light,

brooded with a distant, inhuman calm. He had not spoken a single word since they had emerged onto the rooftop, and her few shy attempts to speak had been choked into silence by the impassive quiet of his eyes. When he made an abrupt movement, she started in sudden terror.

He leaned on the railing, one clenched hand supporting the leaning blackness of his body and said, in tones of command, "Tell me what troubles you, Deoris."

"I don't know," Deoris murmured. "So many new things are coming at once." Her voice grew hard and tight. "My sister Domaris is going to have another baby!"

Riveda stared a moment, his eyes narrowing. "I knew that. What did you expect?"

"Oh, I don't know. . . ." The girl's shoulders drooped. "It was different, somehow, with Micon. He was . . ."

"He was a Son of the Sun," Riveda prompted gently, and there was no mockery in his voice.

Deoris looked up, almost despairing. "Yes. But Arvath—and so soon, like animals—Riveda, why?"

"Who can say?" Riveda replied, and his voice dropped, sorrowful and confiding. "It is a great pity. Domaris could have gone so far. . . ."

Deoris lifted her eyes, eager, mute questions in them.

The Adept smiled, a very little, over her head. "A woman's mind is strange, Deoris. You have been kept in innocence, and cannot yet understand how deeply the woman is in subjugation to her body. I do not say it is wrong, only that it is a great pity." He paused, and his voice grew grim. "So. Domaris has chosen her way. I expected it, and yet. . . ." He looked down at Deoris. "You asked me, *why*. It is for the same reason that so many maidens who enter the Grey Temple are *saji*, and use magic without knowing its meaning. But we of the Magicians would rather have our women free, make them *Sākti Sidhana*—know you what that is?"

She shook her head, dumbly.

"A woman who can use her powers to lead and complement a man's strength. Domaris had that kind of strength, she had the potentiality . . ." A significant pause. "Once."

"Not now?"

Riveda did not answer directly, but mused, "Women rarely have the need, or the hunger, or the courage. To most women, learning is a game, wisdom a toy—attainment, only a sensation."

Timidly, Deoris asked, "But is there any other way for a woman?"

"A woman of your caste?" The Adept shrugged. "I have no right to advise you—and yet, Deoris. . . ."

Riveda paused but a moment—yet the mood was shattered by a woman's cry of terror. The Adept whirled, swift as a hunting-cat; behind him Deoris started back, her hands at her throat. At the corner of the long stairway, she made out two white-robed figures and a crouching, grey and ghostly form which had suddenly risen before them.

Riveda rapped out several words in an alien tongue, then spoke ceremoniously to the white robes: "Be not alarmed, the poor lad is harmless. But his wits are not in their seat."

Clinging to Rajasta's arm, Domaris murmured in little gasps, "He rose out of the shadows—like a ghost."

Riveda's strong warm laughter filled the darkness. "I give you my word he is alive, and harmless." And this last, at least, was proven, for the grey-clad chela had scuttled away into the darkness once again and was lost to their sight. Riveda continued, his voice holding a deep deference exaggerated to the point of mockery, "Lord Guardian, I greet you; this is a pleasure I had ceased to expect!"

Rajasta said with asperity, "You are too courteous, Riveda. I trust we do not interrupt your meditations?"

"No, for I was not alone," Riveda retorted suavely, and beckoned Deoris to come forward. "You are remiss, my lady," he added to Domaris, "your sister has never seen this view, which is not a thing to be missed on a clear night."

Deoris, holding her hood about her head in the wind, looked sullenly at the intruders, and Domaris slipped her arm free of Rajasta's and went to her. "Why, if I had thought, I would have brought you up here long ago," Domaris murmured, her eyes probing her sister's closely. In the instant before the chela had risen up to terrify her, she had seen Riveda and Deoris standing very close together, in what had looked like an embrace. The sight had sent prickles of chill up her spine. Now, taking her sister's hand, she drew Deoris to the railing. "The view from here is truly lovely, you can see the pathway of the moon on the sea. . . ." Lowering her voice almost to a whisper, she murmured, "Deoris, I do not want to intrude on you, but what were you talking about?"

Riveda loomed large beside them, "I have been discussing the Mysteries with Deoris, my lady. I wished to know if she has chosen to walk in the

path which her sister treads with such great honor."
The Adept's words were courteous, even deferential,
but something in their tone made Rajasta frown.

Clenching his fists in almost uncontrollable anger,
the Priest of Light said curtly, "Deoris is an apprenticed Priestess of Caratra."

"Why, I know that," Riveda said, smiling. "Have
you forgotten, it was I who counselled her to seek
Initiation there?"

Forcing his voice to a deliberate calm, Rajasta
answered, "Then you showed great wisdom, Riveda.
May you always counsel as wisely." He glanced
toward the chela, who had reappeared some distance away. "Have you found as yet any key to
what is hidden in his soul?"

Riveda shook his head. "Nor found I anything in
Atlantis which could rouse him. Yet," he paused
and said, "I believe he has great knowledge of
magic. I had him in the Chela's Ring last night."

Rajasta started. "With empty mind?" he accused.
"Without awareness?" His face was deeply troubled.
"Permit me this once to advise you, Riveda, not as
Guardian but as a kinsman or a friend. *Be careful*—
for your own sake. He is—emptied, and a perfect
channel for danger of the worst sort."

Riveda bowed, but Deoris, watching, could see
the ridge of muscle tighten in his jaw. The Grey-
robe bit off his words in little pieces and spat
them at Rajasta. "My Adeptship, cousin, is—suitable
and sufficient—to guard that channel. Do me the
courtesy—to allow me to manage my own affairs
—friend!"

Rajasta sighed, and said, with a quiet patience,
"You could wreck his mind."

Riveda shrugged. "There is not much left to

wreck," he pointed out. "And there is the chance that I might rouse him." He paused, then said, with slow and deadly emphasis, "Perhaps it would be better if I consigned him to the Idiots' Village?"

There was a long and fearful silence. Domaris felt Deoris stiffen, every muscle go rigid, her shoulders taut with trembling horror. Eager to comfort, Domaris held her sister's hand tightly in her own, but Deoris wrenched away.

Riveda continued, completely calm. "Your suspicions are groundless, Rajasta. I seek only to restore the poor soul to himself. I am no black sorcerer; your implication insults me, Lord Guardian."

"You know I meant no insult," Rajasta said, and his voice was weary and old, "but there are those within your Order on whom we cannot lay constraint."

The Grey-robe stood still, the line of his lifted chin betraying an unusual self-doubt; then Riveda capitulated, and joined Rajasta at the railing. "Be not angry," he said, almost contritely. "I meant not to offend you."

The Priest of Light did not even glance at him. "Since we cannot converse without mutual offense, let us be silent," he said coldly. Riveda, stung by the rebuff, straightened and gazed in silence over the harbor for some minutes.

The full moon rose slowly, like a gilt bubble cresting the waves, riding the surf in a fairy play of light. Deoris drew a long wondering breath of delight, looking out in awe and fascination over the moon-flooded waves, the rooftops . . . She felt Riveda's hand on her arm and moved a little closer to him. The great yellow-orange globe moved slowly higher and higher, suspended on the tossing sea, gradually illuminating their faces: Deoris like a wraith against the darkness, Domaris pale beneath the hood of her loose frost-colored robes; Rajasta a luminescent blur against the far railing, Riveda like a dark pillar against the moonlight. Behind them, a dark huddle crouched against the cornice of the stairway, unseen and neglected.

Deoris began to pick out details in the moonlit scene: the shadows of ships, their sails furled, narrow masts lonesome against a phosphorescent sea; nearer, the dark mass of the city called the Circling Snake, where lights flickered and flitted in the streets. Curiously, she raised one hand and traced the outline made by the city and the harbor; then gave a little exclamation of surprise.

"Lord Riveda, look here—to trace the outline of the city from here is to make the Holy Sign!"

"It was planned so, I believe," Riveda responded quietly. "Chance is often an artist, but never like that."

A low voice called, "Domaris?"

The young Priestess stirred, her hand dropping from her sister's arm. "I am here, Arvath," she called.

The indistinct white-robed figure of her husband detached itself from the shadows and came toward them. He looked around, smiling. "Greetings, Lord Rajasta—Lord Riveda," he said. "And you, little Deoris—no, I should not call you that now, should I, kitten? Greetings to the Priestess Adsartha of Caratra's Temple!" He made a deep, burlesque bow.

Deoris giggled irrepressibly, then tossed her head and turned her back on him.

Arvath grinned and put an arm around his wife. "I thought I would find you here," he said, his voice shadowed with concern and reproach as he looked down at her. "You look tired. When you have finished your duties, you should rest, not weary yourself climbing these long steps."

"I am never tired," she said slowly, "not really tired."

"I know, but . . ." The arm around her tightened a little.

Riveda's voice, with its strangely harsh overtones, sounded through the filtered shadows. "No woman will accept sensible advice."

Domaris raised her head proudly. "I am a person before I am a woman."

Riveda let his eyes rest on her, with the strange and solemn reverence which had once before so frightened Domaris. Slowly, he answered, "I think not, Lady Isarma. You are woman, first and always. Is that not altogether evident?"

Arvath scowled and took an angry step forward, but Domaris caught his arm. "Please," she whispered, "anger him not. I think he meant no offense. He is not of our caste, we may ignore what he says."

Arvath subsided and murmured, "It is the woman in you I love, dear. The rest belongs to you. I do not interfere with that."

"I know, I know," she soothed in an undertone.

Rajasta, with an all-embracing kindliness, added, "Have no fear for her, Arvath. I know that she is woman, too, as well as priestess."

Riveda glanced at Deoris, with elaborate mockery. "I think we are two too many here," he murmured, and drew the girl along the railing, toward the southern parapet, where they stood in absorbed silence, looking down into the fires that flickered and danced at the sea-wall.

Arvath turned to Rajasta, half in apology. "I am all too much man where she is concerned," he said, and smiled in wry amusement.

Rajasta returned the smile companionably. "That is readily understood, my son," he said, and looked intently at Domaris. The clear moonlight blurred the wonderful red mantle of her hair to an uneven shining, and softened, kindly, the tiredness in her young face; but Rajasta needed no light to see that. *And why*, he asked himself, *was she so quick to deny that she might be primarily woman?* Rajasta turned away, staring out to sea, reluctantly remembering. *When she bore Micon's son, Domaris was all woman, almost arrogantly so, taking pride and deep joy in that. Why, now, does she speak so rebelliously, as if Riveda had insulted her—instead of paying her the highest accolade he knows?*

With a sudden smile, Domaris flung one arm around her husband and the other around Rajasta, pulling them close. She leaned a little on Arvath, enough to give the effect of submission and affection. Domaris was no fool, and she knew what bitterness Arvath so resolutely stifled. No man would ever be more to Domaris—save the memory she kept with equal resoluteness apart from her life. No woman can be altogether indifferent to the man whose child she carries.

With a secret, wise little smile that did much to reassure the Guardian, Domaris leaned to touch her lips to her husband's cheek. "Soon, now, Rajasta, I shall ask to be released from Temple duties, for I will have other things to think of," she told them, still smiling. "Arvath, take me home, now. I am weary, and I would rest."

Rajasta followed the young couple as Arvath, with tender possessiveness, escorted his wife down the long stairway. He felt reassured: Domaris was safe with Arvath, indeed.

II

As the others disappeared into the shadows, Riveda turned and sighed, a little sorrowfully. "Well, Domaris has chosen. And you, Deoris?"

"No!" It was a sharp little cry of revulsion.

"A woman's mind is strange," Riveda went on reflectively. "She is sensitive to a greater degree; her very body responds to the delicate influence of the moon and the tidewaters. And she has, inborn, all the strength and receptivity which a man must spend years and his heart's blood to acquire. But where man is a climber, woman tends to chain herself. Marriage, the slavery of lust, the brutality of childbearing, the servitude of being wife and mother—and all this without protest! Nay, she seeks it, and weeps if it is denied her!"

A far-off echo came briefly to taunt Deoris— Domaris, so long ago, murmuring, *Who has put these bats into your brain?* But Deoris, hungry for his thoughts, was more than willing to listen to Riveda's justification for her own rebellion, and made only the faintest protest: "But there *must* be children, must there not?"

Riveda shrugged. "There are always more than enough women who are fit for nothing else," he said. "At one time I had a dream of a woman with the strength and hardness of a man but with a woman's sensitivity; a woman who could set aside her self-imposed chains. At one time, I had thought Domaris to be such a woman. And believe me, they are rare, and precious! But she has chosen otherwise." Riveda turned, and his eyes, colorless in the moonlight, stabbed into the girl's uplifted face. His light speaking voice dropped into the rich and resonant baritone in which he sang. "But I think I have found another. Deoris, are you . . . ?"

"What?" she whispered.

"Are *you* that woman?"

Deoris drew a long breath, as fear and fascination tumbled in her brain.

Riveda's hard hands found her shoulders, and he repeated, softly persuasive, "Are you, Deoris?"

A stir in the darkness—and Riveda's chela suddenly materialized from the shadows. Deoris's flesh crawled with revulsion and horror—fear of Riveda, fear of herself, and a sort of sick loathing for the chela. She wrenched herself away and ran, blindly ran, to get away and alone; but even as she fled, she heard the murmur of the Adept's words, re-echoing in her brain.

Are you that woman?

And to herself, more than terrified now, and yet still fascinated, Deoris whispered, "Am I?"

Chapter Four

THE SUMMIT AND THE DEPTHS

I

The opened shutters admitted the incessant flickers of summer lightning. Deoris, unable to sleep, lay on her pallet, her thoughts flickering as restlessly as the lightning flashes. Shc was afraid of Riveda, and yet, for a long time she had admitted to herself that he roused in her a strange, tense emotion that was almost physical. He had grown into her consciousness, he was a part of her imagination. Naive as she was, Deoris realized indistinctly that she had reached, with Riveda, a boundary of no return: their relationship had suddenly and irrevocably changed.

She suspected she could not bear to be closer to him, but at the same time the thought of putting him out of her life—and this was the only alternative—was unbearable. Riveda's swift clarity made even Rajasta seem pompous, fumbling . . . Had she ever seriously thought of following in Domaris's steps?

A soft sound interrupted her thoughts, and Chedan's familiar step crossed the flagstones to her side. "Asleep?" he whispered.

"Oh, Chedan—you?"

"I was in the court, and I could not ..." He dropped to the edge of the bed. "I haven't seen you all day. Your birthday, too—how old?"

"Sixteen. You know that." Deoris sat up, wrapping her thin arms around her knees.

"And I would have a gift for you, if I thought you would take it from me," Chedan murmured. His meaning was unmistakeable, and Deoris felt her cheeks grow hot in the darkness while Chedan went on, teasingly, "Or do you guard yourself virgin for higher ambition? I saw you when Cadamiri carried you, unconscious, from the seance in the Prince Micon's quarters last year! Ah, how Cadamiri was angry! For all of that day, anyone who spoke to him caught only sharp words. *He* would advise you, Deoris—"

"I am not interested in his advice!" Deoris snapped, flicked raw by his teasing.

Again, two conflicting impulses struggled in her: to laugh at him, or to slap him. She had never accepted the easy customs and the free talk of the House of the Twelve; the boys and girls in the Scribes' School were more strictly confined, and Deoris had spent her most impressionable years there. Yet her own thoughts were poor company, confused as they were, and she did not want to be alone.

Chedan bent down and slid his arms around the girl. Deoris, in a kind of passive acquiescence, submitted, but she twisted her mouth away from his.

"Don't," she said sulkily. "I can't breathe."

"You won't have to," he said, more softly than usual, and Deoris made no great protest. She liked the warmth of his arms around her, the way he held her, gently, like something very fragile . . . but tonight there was an urgency in his kisses that had never been there before. It frightened her a little. Warily, she shifted herself away from him, murmuring protesting words—she hardly knew what.

Silence again, and the flickering of lightning in the room, and her own thoughts straying into the borderland of dreams. . . .

Suddenly, before she could prevent him, Chedan was lying beside her and his arms slowly forced themselves beneath her head; then all the strength of his hard young body was pressing her down, and he was saying incoherent things which made no sense, punctuated by frightening kisses. For a moment, surprise and a sort of dreamy lassitude held her motionless . . . then a wave of revulsion sent every nerve in her body to screaming.

She struggled and pulled away from him, scrambling quite to her feet; her eyes burned with shock and shame. "How dare you," she stammered, "how dare you!"

Chedan's mouth dropped open in stupefaction. He raised himself, slowly, and his voice was remorseful. "Deoris, sweet, did I frighten you?" he whispered, and held out his arms.

She jerked away from him with an incongruous little jump. "Don't touch me!"

He was still kneeling on the edge of the bed;

now he rose to his feet, slowly and a little bewildered. "Deoris, I don't understand. What have I done? I am sorry. Please, don't look at me like that," he begged, dismayed and shamed, and angry with himself for a reckless, precipitous fool. He touched her shoulder softly. "Deoris, you're not crying? Don't, please—I'm sorry, sweet. Come back to bed. I promise, I won't touch you again. See, I'll swear it." He added, puzzled, "But I had not thought you so unwilling."

She was crying now, loud shocked sobs. "Go away," she wept, "go away!"

"*Deoris!*" Chedan's voice, still uncertain, cracked into falsetto. "Stop crying like that. Somebody will hear you, you silly girl! I'm not going to touch you, ever, unless you want me to! Why, what in the world did you think I was going to do? I never raped anyone in my life and I certainly wouldn't begin with you! Now stop that, Deoris, stop that!" He put his hand on her shoulder and shook her slightly. "If someone hears you, they'll . . ."

Her voice was high and hysterical. "Go away! Just go away, away!"

Chedan's hands dropped, and his cheeks flamed with wrathful pride. "Fine, I'm going," he said curtly, and the door slammed behind him.

Deoris, shaking with nervous chill, crept to her bed and dragged the sheet over her head. She was ashamed and unhappy and her loneliness was like a physical presence in the room. Even Chedan's presence would have been a comfort.

Restless, she got out of bed and wandered about the room. What had happened? One moment she had been contented, lying in his arms and feeling some emptiness within her heart solaced and filled by his closeness—and in the next instant, a fury of revolt had swept through her whole body. Yet for years she and Chedan had been moving, slowly and inexorably, toward such a moment. Probably everyone in the Temple believed they were already lovers! Why, faced with the prospect itself, had she exploded into this storm of passionate refusal?

Obeying a causeless impulse, she drew a light cape over her night-dress, and went out on the lawn. The dew was cold on her bare feet, but the night air felt moist and pleasant on her hot face. She moved into the moonlight, and the man who was slowly pacing up the path caught his breath, in sharp satisfaction.

"Deoris," Riveda said.

She whirled in terror, and for an instant the Adept thought she would flee; then she recognized his voice, and a long sigh fluttered between her lips.

"Riveda! I was frightened . . . it *is* you?"

"None other," he laughed, and came toward her, his big lean body making a blackness against the stars, his robes shimmering like frost; he seemed to gather the darkness about himself and pour it forth again. She put out a small hand, confidingly, toward his; he took it.

"Why, Deoris, your feet are bare! What brought you to me like this? Not that I am displeased," he added.

She lowered her eyes, returning awareness and shame touching her whole body. "To—you?" she asked, rebellious.

"You always come to me," Riveda said. It was not a statement made in pride, but a casual statement of fact; as if he had said, *the sun rises to the*

East. "You must know by now that I am at the end
of all your paths—you must know that now as I
have known it for a long time. Deoris, will you
come with me?"

And Deoris heard herself say, "Of course," and
realized that the decision had been made long ago.
She whispered, "But where? Where are we going?"

Riveda gazed at her in silence for a moment.
"To the Crypt where the God sleeps," he said at
length.

She caught her hands against her throat. Sacrilege this, for a Daughter of Light—she knew this,
now. And when last she had accompanied Riveda
to the Grey Temple, the consequences had been
frightening. Yet Riveda—he said, and she believed
him—had not been responsible for what had happened then. *What had happened then* . . . she fought
to remember, but it was fogged in her mind. She
whispered, "Must I—?" and her voice broke.

Riveda's hands fell to his sides, releasing her.

"All Gods past, present and future forbid that I
should ever constrain you, Deoris."

Had he commanded, had he pleaded, had he
spoken a word of persuasion, Deoris would have
fled. But before his silent face she could only say,
gravely, "I will come."

"Come, then." Riveda took her shoulder lightly
in his hand, turning her toward the pyramid. "I
took you tonight to the summit; now I will show
you the depths. That, too, is a Mystery." He put
his hand on her arm, but the touch was altogether
impersonal. "Look to your steps, the hill is dangerous in the dark," he cautioned.

She went beside him, docile; he stopped for a

moment, turned to her, and his arm moved; but
she pulled away, panicky with denial.

"So?" Riveda mused, almost inaudibly. "I have
had my question answered without asking."

"What do you mean?"

"You really don't know?" Riveda laughed shortly,
unamused. "Well, you shall learn that, too, perhaps;
but at your own will, always at your own will.
Remember that. The summit—and the depths. You
shall see."

He led her on toward the raised square of
darkness.

II

Steps—uncounted, interminable steps—wound
down, down, endlessly, into dim gloom. The filtered light cast no shadows. Cold, stone steps, as
grey as the light; and the soft pad of her bare feet
followed her in echoes that re-echoed forever. Her
breathing sounded with harsh sibilance, and seemed
to creep after her with the echoes, hounding at her
heels. She forced herself on, one hand thrusting at
the wall. . . . Her going had the feeling of flight,
although her feet refused to change their tempo,
and the echoes had a steady insistence, like heart-
beats.

Another turn; more steps. The greyness curled
around them, and Deoris shivered with a chill not
born altogether of the dank cold. She waded in
grey fog beside grey-robed Riveda, and the fear of
closed places squeezed her throat; the knowledge
of her sacrilege knifed her mind.

Down and down, through eternities of aching
effort.

Her nerves screamed at her to run, run, but the quicksand cold dragged her almost to a standstill. Abruptly the steps came to an end. Another turn led into a vast, vaulted chamber, pallidly lighted with flickering greyness. Deoris advanced with timid steps into the catacomb and stood frozen.

She could not know that the simulacrum of the Sleeping God revealed itself to each seeker in different fashion. She knew only this: Long and long ago, beyond the short memory of mankind, the Light had triumphed, and reigned now supreme in the Sun. But in the everlasting cycles of time—so even the Priests of Light conceded—the reign of the Sun must end, and the Light should emerge back into Dyaus, the Unrevealed God, the Sleeper ... and he would burst his chains and rule in a vast, chaotic Night.

Before her strained eyes she beheld, seated beneath his carven bird of stone, the image of the Man with Crossed Hands ...

She wanted to scream aloud; but the screams died in her throat. She advanced slowly, Riveda's words fresh in her mind; and before the wavering Image, she knelt in homage.

III

At last she rose, cold and cramped, to see Riveda standing nearby, the cowl thrown back from his massive head, his silvered hair shining like an aureole in the pale light. His face was lighted with a rare smile.

"You have courage," he said quietly. "There will be other tests; but for now, it is enough." Unbending, he stood beside her before the great Image, looking up toward what was, to him, an erect image, faceless, formidable, stern but not terrible, a power restricted but not bound. Wondering how Deoris saw the Avatar, he laid a light hand on her wrist, and with a moment of Vision, he caught a brief glimpse in which the God seemed to flow and change and assume, for an instant, the figure of a seated man with hands crossed upon his breast. Riveda shook his head slightly, with a dismissing gesture, and, tightening his grasp upon the girl's wrist, he led her through an archway into a series of curiously furnished rooms which opened out from the great Crypt.

This underground maze was a Mystery forbidden to most of the Temple folk. Even the members of the Grey-robe sect, though their Order and their ritual served and guarded the Unrevealed God, came here but rarely.

Riveda himself did not know the full extent of these caverns. He had never tried to explore more than a little way into the incredible labyrinth of what must, once, have been a vast underground temple in daily use. It honeycombed the entire land beneath the Temple of Light; Riveda could not even guess when or by whom these great underground passages and apartments had been constructed, or for what purpose.

It was rumored that the hidden sect of Black-robes used these forbidden precincts for their secret practice of sorcery; but although Riveda had often wished to seek them out, capture them and try them for their crimes, he had neither the time nor the resources to explore the maze more than a little way. Once, indeed, on the Nadir-night when someone unsanctioned—Black-robes or others—had sought to draw down the awesome thunder-voiced powers of the Lords of Ahtarrath and of the Sea Kingdoms, Riveda had come into these caverns; and there, on that ill-fated night, he had found seven dead men, lying blasted and withered within their black robes, their hands curled and blackened and charred as with fire, their faces unrecognizable, charred skulls. But the dead could neither be questioned nor punished; and when he sought to explore further into the labyrinthine mazes of the underground Temple, he had quickly become lost; it had taken him hours of weary wandering to find his way back to this point, and he had not dared it again. He could not explore it alone, and there was, as yet, no one he could trust to aid him. Perhaps now ... but he cut off the thought, calling years of discipline to his aid. That time had not come. Perhaps it would never come.

He led Deoris into one of the nearer rooms. It was furnished sparsely, in a style ancient beyond belief, and lighted dimly with one of the ever-burning lamps whose secret still puzzled the Priests of Light. In the flickering, dancing illumination, furniture and walls were embellished with ancient and cryptic symbols which Riveda was grateful the girl could not read. He himself had learned their meaning but lately, after much toil and study, and even his glacial composure had been shaken by the obscenity of their meaning.

"Sit here beside me," he bade her, and she obeyed like a child. Behind them the chela ghosted like a wraith through the doorway and stood with empty, unseeing eyes. Riveda leaned forward, his head in his hands, and she looked upon him, a little curious but trusting.

"Deoris," he said at last, "there is much a man can never know. Women like you have certain—awarenesses, which no man may gain; or gain only under the sure guidance of such a woman." He paused, his cold eyes pensive as they met hers. "Such a woman must have courage, and strength, and knowledge, and insight. You are very young, Deoris, you have much to learn but more than ever I believe you could be such a woman." Once again he paused, that pause that gave such a powerful emphasis to his words. His voice deepened as he said, "I am not young, Deoris, and perhaps I have no right to ask this of you, but you are the first I have felt I could trust—or follow." His eyes had flickered away from hers as he said this; now he looked again directly into her face. "Would you consent to this? Will you let me lead you and teach you, guide you to awareness of that strength within you, so that some day you might guide me along that pathway where no man can walk alone, and where only a woman may lead?"

Deoris clasped her hands at her breast, sure that the Adept could hear the pounding of her heart. She felt dazed, sick and weightless with panic—but more, she felt the true emptiness of any other life. She felt a wild impulse to scream, to burst into shattering, hysterical laughter, but she forced her rebellious lips to speak and obey her. "I will, if you think I am strong enough," she whispered, and then emotion choked her with the clamor of her adoration for this man. It was all she desired, all she ever desired, that she might be closer to him, closer than acolyte or chela, closer than any woman might ever be—but she trembled at the knowledge of what she committed herself to; she had some slight knowledge of the bonds the Grey-robes put on their women. She would be—close—to Riveda. What was he like, beneath that cynical, derisive mask he wore? The mask had slipped a little, tonight—

Riveda's mouth moved a little, as if he struggled with strong emotion. His voice was hushed, almost gentle for once. "Deoris," he said, then smiled faintly, "I cannot call you my acolyte—the bonds of that relationship are fixed, and what I wish lies outside those bonds. You understand this?"

"I—think so."

"For a time—I impose obedience on you—and surrender. There must be complete knowledge of one another, and—" He released her hand, and looked at the girl, with the slight, stern pause that gave emphasis to his words, "—and complete intimacy."

"I—know," Deoris said, trying to make her voice steady. "I accept that too."

Riveda nodded, in curt acknowledgement, as if he took no especial notice of her words—but Deoris sensed that he was unsure of himself now; and, in truth, Riveda was unsure, to the point of fear. He was afraid to snap, by some incautious word or movement, the spell of fascination he had, almost without meaning to, woven around the girl. Did she really understand what he demanded of her? He could not guess.

Then, with a movement that startled the Adept, Deoris slid to her knees before him, bending her head in surrender so absolute that Riveda felt his throat tighten with an emotion long unfamiliar.

He drew her forward, gently raising her, until she stood within the circle of his arms. His voice was husky: "I told you once that I am not a good man to trust. But Deoris, may the Gods deal with me as I deal with you!"

And the words were an oath more solemn than her own.

The last remnant of her fear quickened in a protest that was half-instinctive as his hands tightened on her, then died. She felt herself lifted clear of the floor, and cried out in astonishment at the strength in his hands. She was hardly conscious of movement, but she knew that he had laid her down and was bending over her, his head a dark silhouette against the light; she remembered, more than saw, the cruel set of his jaw, the intent strained line of his mouth. His eyes were as cold as the northern lights, and as remote.

No one—certainly not Chedan—had ever touched her like this, no one had ever touched her except gently, and she sobbed in an instant of final, spasmodic terror. *Domaris—Chedan—the Man with Crossed Hands—Micon's death-mask*—these images reeled in her mind in the short second before she felt the roughness of his face against hers, and his strong and sensitive hands moving at the fastenings of her nightdress. Then there was only the dim dancing light, and the shadow of an image— and Riveda.

The chela, muttering witlessly, crouched upon the stone floor until dawn.

Chapter Five

WORDS

I

Beneath a trellised arbor of vines, near the House of the Twelve, lay a deep clear pool which was known as the Mirror of Reflection. Tradition held that once an oracle had stood here; and even now some believed that in moments of soul-stress the answer one's heart or mind most sought might be mirrored in the limpid waters, if the watcher had eyes to see.

Deoris, lying listlessly under the leaves, gazed into the pool in bitter rebellion. Reaction had set in; with it came fear. She had done sacrilege; betrayed Caste and Gods. She felt dreary and deserted, and the faint stab of pain in her body was like the echo and shadow of a hurt already half forgotten. Sharper than the memory of pain was a vague shame and wonder.

She had given herself to Riveda in a dreamy exaltation, not as a maiden to her lover, but in a

surrender as complete as the surrender of a victim
on the altar of a god. And he had taken her—the
thought came unbidden—as a hierophant conduct-
ing an acolyte into a sacred secret; not passion,
but a mystical initiatory rite, all-encompassing in
its effect on her.

Reviewing her own emotions, Deoris wondered
at them. The physical act was not important, but
close association with Domaris had made Deoris
keenly conscious of her own motives, and she had
been taught that it was shameful to give herself
except in love. Did she love Riveda? Did he love
her? Deoris did not know—and she was never to
have more assurance than she had had already.

Even now she did not know whether his mystical and cruel initiatory passion had been ardent,
or merely brutal.

For the time, Riveda had blotted out all else in
her thoughts—and that fact accounted for the
greater part of Deoris's shame. She had counted
on her own ability to keep her emotions aloof from
his domination of her body. *Still*, she told herself
sternly, *I must discipline myself to accept complete
dominance; the possession of my body was only a
means to that end—the surrender of my will to his*.

With all her heart, she longed to follow the path
of psychic accomplishment which Riveda had outlined to her. She knew now that she had always
desired it; she had even resented Micon because he
had tried to hold her back. As for Rajasta—well,
Rajasta had taught Domaris, and she could see the
result of *that*!

She did not hear the approaching steps—for
Riveda could move as noiselessly as a cat when he
chose—until he bent and, with a single flexing of

muscular arms, picked her up and set her on her feet.

"Well, Deoris? Do you consult the Oracle for your fate or mine?"

But she was unyielding in his arms, and after a moment he released her, puzzled.

"What is it, Deoris? Why are you angry with me?"

The last flicker of her body's resentment flared up. "I do not like to be mauled like that!"

Ceremoniously, the Adept inclined his head. "Forgive me. I shall remember."

"Oh Riveda!" She flung her arms about him then, burrowing her head into the rough stuff of his robes, gripping him with a desperate dread. "Riveda, I am afraid!"

His arms tightened around her for a moment, strong, almost passionate. Then, with a certain sternness, he disengaged her clinging clasp. "Be not foolish, Deoris," he admonished. "You are no child, nor do I wish to treat you as one. Remember—I do not admire weakness in women. Leave that for the pretty wives in the back courts of the Temple of Light!"

Stung, Deoris lifted her chin. "Then we have both had a lesson today!"

Riveda stared at her a moment, then laughed aloud. "Indeed!" he exclaimed. "That is more like it. Well then. I have come to take you to the Grey Temple." As she hung back a little, he smiled and touched her cheek. "You need not fear—the foul sorcerer who threw you into illusion that previous time has been exorcized; ask, if you dare, what befell him! Be assured, no one will dare to meddle with the mind of my chosen novice!"

Reassured, she followed him, and he continued, abridging his long stride to correspond with her steps, "You have seen one of our ceremonies, as an outsider. Now you shall see the rest. Our Temple is mostly a place of experiment, where each man works separately, as he will, to develop his own powers."

Deoris could understand this, for in the Priest's Caste great emphasis was placed on self-perfection. But she wondered for what aims the Magicians strove. . . .

He answered her unspoken question. "For absolute self-mastery, first of all; the body and mind must be harnessed and brought into subjugation by—certain disciplines. Then each man works alone, to master sound, or color, or light, or animate things—whatever he chooses—with the powers inherent in his own body and mind. We call ourselves Magicians, but there is no magic; there is only vibration. When a man can attune his body to any vibration, when he can master the vibrations of sound so that rock bursts asunder, or think one color into another, that is not magic. He who masters himself, masters the Universe."

As they passed beneath the great archway which spanned the bronze doors of the Grey Temple, he motioned to her to precede him; the bodiless voice challenged in unknown syllables, and Riveda called back. As they stepped through the doors, he added, in an undertone, "I will teach you the words of admission, Deoris, so that you will have access here even in my absence."

*   *   *

II

The great dim room seemed more vast than before, being nearly empty. Instinctively, Deoris looked for the niche where she had seen the Man with Crossed Hands—but the recess in the wall was hidden with grey veils. Nevertheless she recalled another shrine, deep in the bowels of the earth, and could not control a shudder.

Riveda said in her ear, "Know you why the Temple is grey, why we wear grey?"

She shook her head, voiceless.

"Because," he went on, "color is in itself vibration, each color having a vibration of its own. Grey allows vibration to be transmitted freely, without the interference of color. Moreover, black absorbs light into itself, and white reflects light and augments it; grey does neither, it merely permits the true quality of the light to be seen as it is." He fell silent again, and Deoris wondered if his words had been symbolic as well as scientific.

In one corner of the enormous chamber, five young chelas were grouped in a circle, standing in rigidly unnatural poses and intoning, one by one, sounds that made Deoris's head ache. Riveda listened for a moment, then said, "Wait here. I want to speak to them."

She stood motionless, watching as he approached the chelas and spoke to them, vehemently but in a voice pitched so low that she could not distinguish a word. She looked around the Temple.

She had heard horrible tales about this place—tales of self-torture, the *saji* women, licentious rites—but there was nothing fearful here. At a little distance from the group of chelas, three young girls sat watching, all three younger than Deoris, with loose short hair, their immature bodies saffron-veiled and girdled with silver. They sat cross-legged, looking weirdly graceful and relaxed.

Deoris knew that the *saji* were recruited mostly from the outcastes, the nameless children born unacknowledged, who were put out on the city wall to die of exposure—or be found by the dealers in girl slaves. Like all the Priest's Caste, Deoris believed that the *saji* were harlots or worse, that they were used in rituals whose extent was limited only by the imagination of the teller. But these girls did not look especially vicious or degenerate. Two, in fact, were extremely lovely; the third had a hare-lip which marred her young face, but her body was dainty and graceful as a dancer's. They talked among themselves in low chirping tones, and they all used their hands a great deal as they spoke, with delicately expressive gestures that be-spoke long training.

Looking away from the *saji* girls, Deoris saw the woman Adept she had seen before. From Karahama she had heard this woman's name: *Maleina*. In the Grey-robe sect she stood second only to Rivéda, but it was said that Rivéda and Maleina were bitter enemies for some reason still unknown to Deoris.

Today, the cowl was thrown back from Maleina's head; her hair, previously concealed, was flaming red. Her face was sharp and gaunt, with a strange, ascetic, fine-boned beauty. She sat motionless on the stone floor. Not an eyelash flickered, nor a hair stirred. In her cupped hands she held something bright which flickered light and dark, light and dark, as regularly as a heartbeat; it was the only thing about her that seemed to live.

Not far away, a man clad only in a loincloth stood gravely on his head. Deoris had to stifle an uncontrollable impulse to giggle, but the man's thin face was absolutely serious.

And not five feet from Deoris, a little boy about seven years old was lying on his back, gazing at the vaulted ceiling, breathing with deep, slow regularity. He did not seem to be doing anything except breathing; he was so relaxed that it made Deoris sleepy to look at him, although his eyes were wide-open and clearly alert. He did not appear to move a single muscle ... After several minutes, Deoris realized that his head was several inches off the floor. Fascinated, she continued to watch until he was sitting bolt upright, and yet at no instant had she actually seen the fraction of an inch's movement, or seen him flex a single muscle. Abruptly, the little boy shook himself like a puppy and, bounding to his feet, grinned widely at Deoris, a gamin, little boyish grin very much at variance with the perfect control he had been exercising. Only then did Deoris recognize him: the silver-gilt hair, the pointed features were those of Demira. This was Karahama's younger child, Demira's brother.

Casually, the little boy walked toward the group of chelas where Riveda was still lecturing. The Adept had pulled his grey cowl over his head and was holding a large bronze gong suspended in midair. One by one, each of the five chelas intoned a curious syllable; each made the gong vibrate faintly, and one made it emit a most peculiar ringing sound. Riveda nodded, then handed the gong to one of the boys, and turning toward it, spoke a single deep-throated syllable.

The gong began to vibrate; then clamored a long, loud brazen note as if struck repeatedly by a bar of steel. Again Riveda uttered the bass syllable; again came the gong's metallic threnody. As the chelas stared, Riveda laughed, flung back his cowl and walked away, pausing a moment to put his hand on the small boy's head and ask him some low-voiced questions Deoris could not hear.

The Adept returned to Deoris. "Well, have you seen enough?" he asked, and drew her along until they were in the grey corridor. Many, many doors lined the hallway, and at the centers of several of them a ghostly light flickered. "Never enter a room where a light is showing," Riveda murmured; "it means someone is within who does not wish to be disturbed—or someone it would be dangerous to disturb. I will teach you the sound that causes the light; you will need to practice uninterrupted sometimes."

Finding an unlighted door, Riveda opened it with the utterance of an oddly unhuman syllable, which he taught her to speak, making her repeat it again and again until she caught the double pitch of it, and mastered the trick of making her voice ring in both registers at once. Deoris had been taught singing, of course, but she now began to realize how very much she still had to learn about sound. She was used to the simply-sung tones which produced light in the Library, and other places in the Temple precincts, but *this*—!

Riveda laughed at her perplexity. "These are not used in the Temple of Light in these days of decadence," he said, "for only a few can master them. In the old days, an Adept would bring his chela here and leave him enclosed in one of these cells—to starve or suffocate if he could not speak the word that would free him. And so they assured that no unfit person lived to pass on his inferiority or stupidity. But now—" He shrugged and smiled. "I would never have brought you here, if I did not believe you could learn."

She finally managed to approximate the sound which opened the door of solid stone, but as it swung wide, Deoris faltered on the threshold. "This—this room," she whispered, "it is horrible!"

He smiled, noncommitally. "All unknown things are fearful to those who do not understand them. This room has been used for the initiation of *saji* while their power is being developed. You are sensitive, and sense the emotions that have been experienced here. Do not be afraid, it will soon be dispelled."

Deoris raised her hands to her throat, to touch the crystal amulet there; it felt comfortingly familiar.

Riveda saw, but misinterpreted the gesture, and with a sudden softening of his harsh face he drew her to him. "Be not afraid," he said gently, "even though I seem at times to forget your presence. Sometimes my meditations take me deep into my mind, where no one else can reach. And also—I have been long alone, and I am not used to the presence of—one like you. The women I have known—and there have been many, Deoris—have been *saji*, or they have been—just women. While you, you are . . ." He fell silent, gazing at her intently, as if he would absorb her every feature into him.

Deoris was, at first, only surprised, for she had

never before known Riveda to be so obviously at a
loss for words. She felt her whole identity softening,
pliant in his hands. A flood of emotion overwhelmed
her and she began softly to cry.

With a gentleness she had never known he
possessed, Riveda took her to him, deliberately,
not smiling now. "You are altogether beautiful,"
he said, and the simplicity of the words gave them
meaning and tenderness all but unimaginable. "You
are made of silk and fire."

III

Deoris was to treasure those words secretly in
her heart during the many bleak months that
followed, for Riveda's moods of gentleness were
more rare than diamonds, and days of surly re-
moteness inevitably followed. She was to gather
such rare moments like jewels on the chain of her
inarticulate and childlike love, and guard them
dearly, her only precious comfort in a life that left
her heart solitary and yearning, even while her
questing mind found satisfaction.

Riveda, of course, took immediate steps to regu-
larize her position in regard to himself. Deoris,
who had been born into the Priest's Caste, could
not formally be received into the Grey-robe sect;
also she was an apprenticed Priestess of Caratra
and had obligations there. The latter obstacle
Riveda disposed of quite easily, in a few words
with the High Initiates of Caratra. Deoris, he told
them, had already mastered skills far beyond her
years in the Temple of Birth; he suggested it might
be well for her to work exclusively among the
Healers for a time, until her competence in all

such arts equalled her knowledge of midwifery. To this the Priestesses were glad to agree; they were proud of Deoris, and it pleased them that she had attracted the attention of a Healer of such skill as Riveda.

So Deoris was legitimately admitted into the Order of Healers, as even a Priest of Light might be, and recognized there as Riveda's novice.

Soon after this, Domaris fell ill. In spite of every precaution she went into premature labor and, almost three months too soon, gave painful birth to a girl child who never drew breath. Domaris herself nearly died, and this time, Mother Ysouda, who had attended her, made the warning unmistakable: Domaris must never attempt to bear another child.

Domaris thanked the old woman for her counsel, listened obediently to her advice, accepted the protective runes and spells given her, and kept enigmatic silence. She grieved long hours in secret for the baby she had lost, all the more bitterly because she had not really wanted this child at all. . . . She was privately certain that her lack of love for Arvath had somehow frustrated her child's life. She knew the conviction to be an absurd one, but she could not dismiss it from her mind.

She recovered her strength with maddening slowness. Deoris had been spared to nurse her, but their old intimacy was gone almost beyond recall. Domaris lay silent for hours, quiet and sad, tears sliding weakly down her white face, often holding Micail with a hungry tenderness. Deoris, though she tended her sister with an exquisite competence, seemed abstracted and dreamy. Her absentmindedness puzzled and irritated Domaris, who had protested vigorously against allowing Deoris to work with Riveda in the first place but had only succeeded in alienating her sister more completely.

Only once Domaris tried to restore their old closeness. Micail had fallen asleep in her arms, and Deoris bent to take him, for the heavy child rolled about and kicked in his sleep, and Domaris still could not endure careless handling. She smiled up into the younger girl's face and said, "Ah, Deoris, you are so sweet with Micail, I cannot wait to see you with a child of your own in your arms!"

Deoris started and almost dropped Micail before she realized Domaris had spoken more or less at random; but she could not keep back her own overflowing bitterness. "I would rather die!" she flung at Domaris out of her disturbed heart.

Domaris looked up reproachfully, her lips trembling. "Oh, my sister, you should not say such wicked things—"

Deoris threw the words at her like a curse: "On the day I know myself with child, Domaris, I will throw myself into the sea!"

Domaris cried out in pain, as if her sister had struck her—but although Deoris instantly flung herself to her knees beside Domaris, imploring pardon for her thoughtless words, Domaris said no more; nor did she again speak to Deoris except with cool, reserved formality. It was many years before the impact of those wounding, bitter words left her heart.

Chapter Six

CHILDREN OF THE UNREVEALED GOD

I

Within the Grey Temple, the Magicians were dispersing. Deoris, standing alone, dizzy and light-headed after the frightening rites, felt a light touch upon her arm and looked down into Demira's elfin face.

"Did not Riveda tell you? You are to come with me. The Ritual forbids that they speak to, or touch, a woman for a night and a day after this ceremony; and you must not leave the enclosure until sundown tomorrow." Demira slipped her hand confidently into Deoris's arm and Deoris, too bewildered to protest, went with her. Riveda had told her this much, yes; sometimes a chela who had been in the Ring suffered curious delusions, and they must remain where someone could be summoned to minister to them. But she had expected to remain near Riveda. Above all, she had not expected Demira.

"Riveda told me to look after you," Demira said

pertly, and Deoris recalled tardily that the Grey-robes observed no caste laws. She went acquiescently with Demira, who immediately began to bubble over, "I have thought about you so much, Deoris! The Priestess Domaris is your sister, is she not? She is so beautiful! You are pretty, too," she added as an afterthought.

Deoris flushed, thinking secretly that Demira was the loveliest little creature she had ever seen. She was very fair, all the same shade of silvery gold: the long straight hair, her lashes and level brows, even the splash of gilt freckles across her pale face. Even Demira's eyes looked silver, although in a different light they might have been grey, or even blue. Her voice was very soft and light and sweet, and she moved with the heedless grace of a blown feather and just as irresponsibly.

She squeezed Deoris's fingers excitedly and said, "You were frightened, weren't you? I was watching, and I felt so sorry for you."

Deoris did not answer, but this did not seem to disturb Demira at all. *Of course*, Deoris thought, *she is probably used to being ignored! The Magicians and Adepts are not the most talkative people in the world!*

The cold moonlight played on them like sea-spray, and other women, singly and in little groups, surrounded them on the path. But no one spoke to them. Several of the women, indeed, came up to greet Demira, but something—perhaps only the childlike way the two walked, hand in hand—prevented them. Or perhaps they recognized Deoris as Riveda's novice, and that fact made them a little nervous. Deoris had noted something of the sort on other occasions.

They passed into an enclosed court where a fountain spouted cool silver into a wide oval pool. All around, sheltering trees, silvery black, concealed all but the merest strips of the star-dusted sky. The air was scented with many flowers.

Opening on this court were literally dozens of tiny rooms, hardly more than cubicles, and into one of these Demira led her. Deoris glanced round fearfully. She wasn't used to such small, dim rooms, and felt as if the walls were squeezing inward, suffocating her. An old woman, crouched on a pallet in the corner, got wheezily to her feet and shuffled toward them.

"Take off your sandals," Demira said in a reproving whisper, and Deoris, surprised, bent to comply. The old woman, with an indignant snort, took them and set them outside the door.

Once more Deoris peered around the little room. It was furnished sparsely with a low, rather narrow bed covered with gauzy canopies, a brazier of metal that looked incredibly ancient, an old carved chest, and a divan with a few embroidered cushions; that was all.

Demira noted her scrutiny and said proudly, "Oh, some of the others have nothing but a straw pallet, they live in stone cells and practice austerities like the young priests, but the Grey Temple does not force such things on anyone, and I do not care. Well, you will know that later. Come along, we must bathe before we sleep; and you've been in the Ring! There are some things—I'll show you what to do." Demira turned to the old woman suddenly and stamped her foot. "Don't stand there staring at us! I can't stand it!"

The crone cackled like a hen. "And who is this

one, my missy? One of Maleina's little pretties
who grows lonely when the woman has gone to
the rites with—" She broke off and ducked, with
surprising nimbleness, as one of Demira's sandals
came flying at her head.

Demira stamped her bare foot again furiously.
"Hold your tongue, you ugly witch!"

The old woman's cackling only grew louder.
"She's sure too old for the Priests to take in and—"

"I said hold your tongue!" Demira flew at the
old woman and cuffed her angrily. "I will tell
Maleina what you have said about her and she
will have you crucified!"

"What I *could* say about Maleina," the old witch
mumbled, unhumbled, "would make little missy
turn to one big blush forever—if she has not already lost that talent here!" Abruptly she grasped
Demira's shoulders in her withered claws and held
the girl firmly for an instant, until the angry light
faded from Demira's colorless eyes. Giggling, the
girl slid free of the crone's hands.

"Get us something to eat, then take yourself
off," Demira said carelessly, and as the hag hus-
tled away she sank down languidly on the divan,
smiling at Deoris. "Don't listen to her, she's old
and half-witted, but phew! she should be more
careful, what Maleina would do if she heard her!"
The light laughter bubbled up again. "I'd not want
to be the one to mock Maleina, no not even in the
deepest chambers of the labyrinth! She might strike
me with a spell so I walked blind for three days, as
she did to the priest Nadastor when he laid lewd
hands on her." Suddenly she leaped to her feet
and went to Deoris, who still stood as if frozen.
"You look as if struck with a spell yourself!" she

laughed; then, sobering, she said kindly, "I know you are afraid, we are all afraid at first. You should have seen me staring about and squalling like a legless cat when they first brought me here, five years ago! No one will hurt you, Deoris, no matter what you have heard of us! Don't be afraid. Come to the pool."

II

Around the edge of the great stone basin, women lounged, talking and splashing in the fountain. A few seemed preoccupied and solitary, but the majority were chirping about as heedlessly and sociably as a flock of winter sparrows. Deoris peered at them with frightened curiosity, and all the horror-tales of the *saji* flooded back into her mind.

They were a heterogenous group: some of the brown-skinned pygmy slave race, a few fair, plump and yellow-haired like the commoners of the city, and a very few like Deoris herself—tall and light-skinned, with the silky black or reddish curls of the Priest's Caste. Yet even here Demira stood out as unusual.

They were all immodestly stripped, but that was nothing new to Deoris except for the careless mingling of castes. Some wore curious girdles or pectorals on their young bodies, engraved with symbols that looked vaguely obscene to the still relatively innocent Deoris; one or two were tattooed with even odder symbols, and the scraps of conversation which she caught were incredibly frank and shameless. One girl, a dark beauty with something about her eyes that reminded Deoris of traders from Kei-Lin, glanced at Deoris as she shyly di-

vested herself of the saffron veils Riveda had asked
her to wear, then asked Demira an indecent question which made Deoris want to sink through the
earth; suddenly she realized what the old slave
woman had meant by her taunts.

Demira only murmured an amused negative,
while Deoris stared, wanting to cry, not understanding that she was simply being teased in the
traditional fashion for all newcomers. *Why did
Riveda throw me in with these—these harlots! Who
are they to mock me?* She set her lips proudly, but
she felt more like bursting into tears.

Demira, ignoring the teasing, bent over the edge
of the pool and, dipping up water in her palms,
with murmured words, began swiftly to go through
a stylized and conventional ritual of purification,
touching lips and breasts, in a ritual so formal-
ized that the symbols had all but lost their original form and meaning, and done swiftly, as if from
habit. Once finished, however, she led Deoris to
the water and in an undertone explained the symbolic gestures.

Deoris cut her short in surprise: it was similar
in form to the purification ceremonies imposed on
a Priestess of Caratra—but the Grey-robe version
seemed an adaptation so stylized that Demira herself did not seem to understand the meaning of the
words and gestures involved. Still, the similarity
did a great deal to reassure Deoris. The symbolism
of the Grey-robe ceremonies was strongly sexual,
and now Deoris understood even more. She went
through the brief lustral rite with a thoroughness
that somehow calmed and assuaged her feeling of
defilement.

Demira looked on with respect, struck into a

brief gravity by the evident deep meaning Deoris gave to what was, for Demira, a mere form repeated because it was required.

"Let's go back at once," Demira said, once Deoris had finished. "You were in the Ring, and that can exhaust you terribly. I know." With eyes too wise for her innocent-seeming face, she studied Deoris. "The first time I was in the Ring, I did not recover my strength for days. They took me out tonight because Riveda was there."

Deoris eyed the child curiously as the old slave woman came and wrapped Demira in a sheetlike robe; enveloped Deoris in another. Had not Riveda himself flung Demira out of the Ring, that first time, that faraway and disastrous visit to the Grey Temple? *What has Riveda to do with this nameless brat?* She felt almost sick with jealousy.

III

Demira smiled, a malicious, quirky smile as they came back into the bare little room. "Oho, now I know why Riveda begged me to look after you! Little innocent Priestess of Light, you are not the first with Riveda, nor will you be the last," she murmured in a mocking sing-song. Deoris angrily pulled away, but the child caught her coaxingly and hugged her close with an astonishing strength— her spindly little body seemed made of steel springs. "Deoris, Deoris," she crooned, smiling, "be not jealous of me! Why, I am of all women the *one* forbidden Riveda! Little silly! Has Karahama never told you that I am Riveda's daughter?"

Deoris, unable to speak, looked at Demira with new eyes—and now she saw the resemblance: the same fair hair and strange eyes; that impalpable, indefinable alienness.

"That is why I am placed so that I may never come near him in the rites," Demira went on. "He is a Northman of Zaiadan, and you know how they regard incest—or do you?"

Deoris nodded, slowly, understanding. It was well known that Riveda's countrymen not only avoided their sisters, but even their half-sisters, and she had heard it said that they even refused to marry their cousins, though Deoris found this last almost beyond belief.

"And with the symbols there—oh!" Demira bubbled on confidingly, "It has not been easy for Riveda to be so scrupulous!"

As the old woman dressed them and brought them food—fruits and bread, but no milk, cheese, or butter—Demira continued, "Yes, I am daughter to the great Adept and Master Magician Riveda! Or at least it pleases him to claim me, unofficially, for Karahama will almost never admit she knows my father's name . . . she was *saji* too, after all, and I am a child of ritual." Demira's eyes were mournful. "And now she is Priestess of Caratra! I wish—I wish . . ." She checked herself and went on swiftly, "I shamed her, I think, by being born nameless, and she does not love me. She would have had me exposed on the city wall, there to die or be found by the old women who deal in girl-brats, but Riveda took me the day I was born and gave me to Maleina; and when I was ten, they made me *saji*."

"*Ten!*" Deoris repeated, shocked despite her resolve not to be.

Demira giggled, with one of her volatile shifts of mood. "Oh, they tell some awful stories about us,

don't they? At least we *saji* know everything that
goes on in the Temple! More than some of your
Guardians! We knew about the Atlantean Prince,
but we did not tell. We never tell but a particle of
what we know! Why should we? We are only the
no people, and who would listen to us but ourselves,
and we can hardly surprise one another anymore.
But I know," she said, casually but with a mischie-
vous glance, "who threw the Illusion on you, when
you first came to the Grey Temple." She bit into a
fruit and chewed, watching Deoris out of the corner of her eye.

Deoris stared at her, frozen, afraid to ask but
half desperate to know, even as she dreaded the
knowledge.

"It was Craith—a Black-robe. They wanted Domaris killed. Not because of Talkannon, of course."

"Talkannon?" Deoris whispered in mute shock.
What had her father to do with this?

Demira shrugged and looked away nervously.
"Words, words, all of it—only words. I'm glad you
didn't kill Domaris, though!"

Deoris was by now utterly aghast. "You know
all this?" she said, and her voice was an unrecognizable, rasping whisper in her own ears.

Whatever slight malice had motivated Demira,
it was vanished now. She put out a tiny hand and
slipped it into Deoris's nerveless one. "Oh, Deoris,
when I was only a little girl I used to steal into
Talkannon's gardens and peep at you and Domaris
from behind the bushes! Domaris is *so* beautiful,
like a Goddess, and she loved you so much—how I
used to wish I were you! I think—I think if Domaris
ever spoke kindly to me—or at all!—I would die of
joy!" Her voice was lonely and wistful, and Deoris,

more moved than she knew, drew the blonde head down on her shoulder.

Tossing her feathery hair, Demira shook off the moment of soberness. The gleam came back to her eyes as she went on, "So I wasn't sorry for Craith at all! You don't know what Riveda was like before that, Deoris—he was just quiet and scholarly and didn't come among us for months at a time—but that turned him into a devil! He found out what Craith had done and accused him of meddling with your mind, and of a crime against a pregnant girl." She glanced quickly at Deoris and added, in explanation, "Among the Grey-robes, you know, that is the highest of crimes."

"In the Temple of Light, too, Demira."

"At least they have some sense!" Demira exclaimed. "Well, Riveda said, 'These Guardians let their victims off too easily!' And then he had Craith scourged—whipped almost to death before he ever delivered him over to the Guardians. When they met to judge him, I slipped a grey smock over my *saji* dress, and went with Maleina—" She gave Deoris another wary little glance. "Maleina is an Initiate of some high order, I know not what, but none can deny her anywhere, I think she could walk into the chapel of Caratra and draw dirty pictures on the wall if she wanted to, and no one would dare to do anything! It was Maleina, you know, who freed Karahama from her bondage and arranged for her to enter the Mother's Temple. . . ." Demira shuddered suddenly. "But I was speaking of Craith. They judged him and condemned him to death; Rajasta was terrible! He held the mercy-dagger, but did not give it to Craith. And so they burned him alive to avenge Domaris—and Micon!"

Trembling, Deoris covered her face with her hands. *Into what world have I, by my own act, come?*

IV

But the world of the Grey Temple was soon familiar to Deoris. She continued, occasionally, to serve in the House of Birth, but most of her time was spent now among the Healers, and she soon began to think of herself almost exclusively as a Grey-robe priestess.

She was not accepted among them very soon, however, or without bitter conflict. Although Riveda was their highest Adept, the titular head of their Order, his protection hindered more than helped her. In spite of his surface cordiality, Riveda was not a popular man among his own sect; he was withdrawn and remote, disliked by many and feared by all, especially the women. His stern discipline was over-harsh; the touch of his cynical tongue missed no one, and his arrogance alienated all but the most fanatic.

Of the whole Order of Healers and Magicians, only Demira, perhaps, really loved him. To be sure, others revered him, respected him, feared him— and heartily avoided him when they could. To Demira, however, Riveda showed careless kindness—entirely devoid of paternal affection, but still the closest to it that the motherless and fatherless child had ever known. In return, Demira gave him a curious worshipping hate, that was about the deepest emotion she ever wasted on anything.

In the same mixed way, she championed Deoris among the *saji*. She quarrelled constantly and bitterly with Deoris herself, but would permit no one else to speak a disrespectful word. Since everyone was afraid of Demira's unpredictable temper and her wild rages—she was quite capable of choking a girl breathless or of clawing at her eyes in one of these blind fits of fury—Deoris won a sort of uneasy tolerance. Also, for some reason, Deoris became very fond of Demira in quite a short time, though she realized that the girl was incapable of any very deep emotion, and that it would be safer to trust a striking cobra than the volatile Demira at her worst.

Riveda neither encouraged nor disparaged this friendship. He kept Deoris near him when he could, but his duties were many and varied, and there were times when the Ritual of his Order forbade this; Deoris began to spend more and more time in the curious half-world of the *saji* women.

She soon discovered that the *saji* were not shunned and scorned without good reason. And yet, as Deoris came to know them better, she found them pathetic rather than contemptible. A few even won her deep respect and admiration, for they had strange powers, and these had not been lightly won.

Once, off-handedly, Riveda had told Deoris that she could learn much from the *saji*, although she herself was not to be given the *saji* training.

Asked why, he had responded, "You are too old, for one thing. A *saji* is chosen before maturity. And you are being trained for quite a different purpose. And—and in any case I would not risk it for you, even if I were to be your sole Initiator. One in every four . . ." He broke off and shrugged, dismiss-

ing the subject; and Deoris recalled, with a start of
horror, the tales of madness.

The *saji*, she knew now, were not ordinary harlots.
In certain rituals they gave their bodies to the
priests, but it was by rite and convention, under
conditions far more strict, although very different,
than the codes of more honored societies. Deoris
never understood these conventions completely, for
on this one subject Demira was reticent, and Deoris
did not press her for details. In fact, she felt she
would rather not be too certain of them.

This much Demira did tell her: in certain grades
of initiation, a magician who sought to develop
control over the more complex nervous and invol-
untary reactions of his body must practice certain
rites with a woman who was clairvoyantly aware
of these psychic nerve centers; who knew how to
receive and return the subtle flow of psychic energy.

So much Deoris could understand, for she herself was being taught awareness like these magicians, and in much the same way. Riveda was an
Adept, and his own mastery was complete; his full
awareness worked like a catalytic force in Deoris,
awakening clairvoyant powers in her mind and
body. She and Riveda were physically intimate—
but it was a strange and almost impersonal intimacy. Through the use of controlled and ritualistic
sex, a catalyst in its effects on her nerves, he was
awakening latent forces in her body, which in turn
reacted on her mind.

Deoris underwent this training in full maturity,
safe-guarded by his concern for her, guarded also
by his insistence on discipline, moderation, careful
understanding and lengthy evaluation of every experience and sensation. Her early training as a

Priestess of Caratra, too, had played no small part in her awakening; had prepared her for the balanced and stable acquisition of these powers. How much less and more this was than the training of a *saji*, she learned from Demira.

Saji were, indeed, chosen when young—sometimes as early as in their sixth year—and trained in one direction and for one purpose: the precocious and premature development along psychic lines.

It was not entirely sexual; in fact, that came last in their training, as they neared maturity. Still, the symbolism of the Grey-robes ran like a fiercely phallic undercurrent through all their training. First came the stimulation of their young minds, and excitement of their brains and spirits, as they were subjected to richly personal spiritual experiences which would have challenged a mature Adept. Music, too, and its laws of vibration and polarity, played a part in their training. And while these seeds of conflict flourished in the rich soil of their untrained minds—for they were purposely kept in a state little removed from ignorance—various emotions and, later, physical passions were skillfully and precociously roused in their still-immature minds and bodies. Body, mind, emotion, and spirit—all were roused and kept keyed to a perpetual pitch, restless, over-sensitized to a degree beyond bearing for many. The balance was delicate, violent, a potential of suppressed nervous energy.

When the child so trained reached adolescence, she became *saji*. Literally overnight, the maturing of her body freed the suppressed dynamic forces. With terrifying abruptness the latent potentials became awareness in all the body's reflex centers;

a sort of secondary brain, clairvoyant, instinctive, entirely psychic, erupted into being in the complicated nerve ganglions which held the vital psychic centers: the throat, solar plexus, womb.

The Adepts too had this kind of awareness, but they were braced for the shock by the slow struggle for self-mastery, by discipline, careful austerities, and complete understanding. In the *saji* girls it was achieved by violence, and through the effort of others. The balance, such as it was, was forced and unnatural. One girl in four, when she reached puberty, went into raving madness and died in convulsive nerve spasms. The sudden awakening was an inconceivable thing, referred to, among those who had crossed it, as *The Black Threshold*. Few crossed that threshold entirely sane. None survived it unmarred.

Demira was a little different from the others; she had been trained not by a priest, but by the woman Adept Maleina. Deoris was to learn, in time, something of the special problems confronting a woman who travelled the Magician's path, and to discount as untrue most of the tales told of Maleina—untrue because imagination can never quite keep pace with a truth so fantastic.

The other girls trained by Maleina had exploded, at puberty, into a convulsive madness which soon lapsed into drooling, staring idiocy . . . but Demira, to everyone's surprise, had crossed The Black Threshold not only sane, but relatively stable. She had suffered the usual agonies, and the days of focusless delirium—but she had awakened sane, alert, and quite her normal self . . . on the surface.

She had not escaped entirely unscathed. The days of that fearful torment had made of her a fey

thing set apart from ordinary womanhood. Close
contact with Maleina, as well—and Deoris learned
this only slowly, as the complexity of human psychic awareness, in its complicated psycho-chemical
nervous currents, became clear to her—had partially reversed, in Demira, the flow of the life
currents. Deoris saw traces of this return each
month, as the moon waned and dwindled: Demira
would grow silent, her volatile playfulness disap-
pear; she would sit and brood, her catlike eyes
veiled, and sometimes she would explode into un-
provoked furies; other times she would only creep
away like a sick animal and curl up in voiceless,
inhuman torture. No one dared go near Demira at
such times; only Maleina could calm the child into
some semblance of reason. At such times, Maleina's
face held a look so dreadful that men and women
scattered before her; a haunted look, as if she were
torn by some emotion which no one of lesser awareness could fathom.

Deoris, with the background of her intuitive
knowledge, and what she had learned in the Temple of Caratra about the complexity of a woman's
body, eventually learned to foresee and to cope
with, and sometimes prevent these terrible out-
bursts; she began to assume responsibility for
Demira, and sometimes could ward off or lighten
those terrible days for the little girl—for Demira
was not yet twelve years old when Deoris entered
the Temple. She was hardened and precocious, a
pitifully wise child—but for all that, only a child;
a strange and often suffering little girl. And Deoris
warmed to this little girl in a way that was eventually to prove disastrous for them all.

Chapter Seven

THE MERCY OF CARATRA

I

A young girl of the *saji*, whom Deoris knew very slightly, had absented herself for many weeks from the rituals, and it finally became evident that she was pregnant. This was an exceedingly rare occurrence, for it was believed that the crossing of The Black Threshold so blighted the *saji* that the Mother withdrew from their spirit. Deoris, aware of the extremely ritualistic nature of the sexual rites of the Grey-robes, had become a bit more skeptical of this explanation.

It was a fact, however, that the *saji* women—alone in the whole social structure of the Temple-city—served not Caratra's temple; nor could they claim the privilege granted even to slaves and prostitutes—to bear their children within the Temple of Birth.

Outlawed from the rites of Caratra, the *saji* had to rely on the good graces of the women around them, or their slaves, or—in dire extremity—some Healer-priest who might take pity on them. But even to the *saji*, a man at a childbed was fearful disgrace; they preferred the clumsier ministrations of a slave.

The girl had a difficult time; Deoris heard her cries most of the night. Deoris had been in the Ring, she was exhausted and wanted to sleep, and the tortured moaning, interspersed with hoarse screams, rubbed her nerves raw. The other girls, half fascinated and half horrified, talked in frightened whispers—and Deoris listened, thinking guiltily of the skill Karahama had praised.

At last, maddened and exasperated by the tormented screaming, and the thought of the clumsy treatment the *saji* girl must be getting, Deoris managed to gain access to the room. She knew she risked terrible defilement—but had not Karahama herself been *saji* once?

By a combination of coaxing and bullying, Deoris managed to get rid of the others who had bungled the business, and after an hour of savage effort she delivered a living child, even contriving to correct some of the harm already done by the ignorant slave-women. She made the girl swear not to tell who had attended her, but somehow, either through the insulted and foolish talk of the slaves, or those invisible undercurrents which run deep and intractable within any large and closely-knit community, the secret leaked out.

When next Deoris went to the Temple of Caratra, she found herself denied admission; worse, she was confined and questioned endlessly about what she had done. After a day and a night spent in solitary confinement, during which time Deoris worked herself almost into hysteria, she was sternly informed that her case must be handled by the Guardians.

Word had reached Rajasta of what had happened. His first reaction had been disgust and shock, but he had rejected several plans which occurred to him, and many that were suggested; nor did Deoris ever become aware of what she so narrowly avoided. The most logical thing was to inform Riveda, for he was not only an Adept of the Greyrobe sect but Deoris's personal initiator, and could be relied upon to take appropriate action. This idea, too, Rajasta dismissed without a second thought.

Domaris was also a Guardian, and Rajasta might reasonably have referred the matter to her, but he knew that Domaris and Deoris were no longer friendly, and that such a thing might easily have done far more harm than good. In the end, he called Deoris into his own presence, and after talking to her gently of other matters for a little while, he asked why she had chanced such a serious violation of the laws of Caratra's Temple.

Deoris stammered her answer: "Because—because I could not bear her suffering. We are taught that at such a time all women are one. It might have been Domaris! I mean . . ."

Rajasta's eyes were compassionate. "My child, I can understand that. But why do you think the priestesses of Caratra's Temple are guarded with such care? They work among the women of the Temple and the entire city. A woman in childbirth is vulnerable, sensitive to the slightest psychic disturbance. Whatever bodily danger there may be to her is not nearly so grave as this; her mind and spirit are open to great harm. Not long ago, Domaris lost her child in great suffering. Would you expose others to such misery?"

Deoris stared mutely at the flagstoned floor.

"You yourself are guarded when you go among the *saji*, Deoris," said Rajasta, sensing her mood. "But you attended a *saji* woman at her most vulnerable moment—and had that *not* been discoverd, *any pregnant girl you attended would have lost her child!*"

Deoris gasped, horrified but still half disbelieving.

"My poor girl," said Rajasta gently, shaking his head slowly. "Such things are generally not known; but the laws of the Temple are not mere superstitious prohibitions, Deoris! Which is why the Adepts and Guardians do not permit young novices and acolytes to use their own ignorant judgment; for you know not how to protect yourself from carrying contamination—and I do not mean physical contamination, but something far, far worse: a contamination of the life currents themselves!"

Deoris pressed her fingers over her trembling mouth and did not speak.

Rajasta, moved in spite of himself by her submission—for he had not looked forward to this interview, thinking back upon her younger days— went on, "Still, perhaps they were to blame who did not warn you. And as there was no malice in your infraction of the law, I am going to recommend that you not be expelled from Caratra's Temple, but only suspended for two years." He paused. "You yourself ran great danger, my child. I still think you are somewhat too sensitive for the Magician's Order, but—"

Passionately, Deoris interrupted, "So I am al-

ways to deny aid to a woman who needs it? To
refuse the knowledge taught to me—to a sister
woman—because of caste? Is that the mercy of
Caratra? For lack of my skill a woman must scream
herself to death?"

With a sigh, Rajasta took her small shaking hands
into his own and held them. A memory of Micon
came to him, and softened his reply. "My little
one, there are those who forsake the paths of Light,
to aid those who walk in darkness. If such a path
of mercy is your karma, may you be strong in
walking it—for you will need strength to defy the
simple laws made for ordinary men and women.
Deoris, Deoris! I do not condemn, yet I cannot
condone, either. I only guard, that the forces of
evil may not touch the sons and daughters of Light.
Do what you must, little daughter. You are sensitive—but make that your servant, not your master.
Learn to guard yourself, lest you carry harm to
others." He laid one hand gently on her curls for a
moment. "May you err always on the side of mercy!
In your years of penance, my child, you can turn
this weakness into your strength."

They sat in silence a few moments, Rajasta gazing tenderly on the woman before him, for he
knew, now, that Deoris was a child no longer.
Sadness and regret mingled with a strange pride in
him then, and he thought again of the name she had
been given: Adsartha, child of the Warrior Star.

"Now go," he said gently, when at last she raised
her head. "Come not again into my presence until
your penance is accomplished." And, unknown to
her as she turned away, Rajasta traced a symbol
of blessing in the air between them, for he felt that
she would need such blessings.

II

As Deoris, miserable and yet secretly a little pleased, went slowly along the pathway leading down toward the Grey Temple, a soft, deep contralto voice came at her from nowhere, murmuring her name. The girl raised her eyes, but saw no one. Then there seemed a little stirring and shimmering in the air, and suddenly the woman Maleina stood before her. She might have only stepped from the shrubbery that lined the path, but Deoris believed, then and always, that she had simply appeared out of thin air.

The deep, vibrant voice said, "In the name of Ni-Terat, whom you call Caratra, I would speak with you."

Timidly, Deoris bent her head. She was more afraid of this woman than of Rajasta, Riveda, or any priest or priestess in the entire world of the Temple precincts. Almost inaudibly, she whispered, "What is your will, O Priestess?"

"My lovely child, be not afraid," said Maleina quickly. "Have they forbidden you the Temple of Caratra?"

Hesitantly, Deoris raised her eyes. "I have been suspended for two years."

Maleina took a deep breath, and there was a jewel-like glint in her eyes as she said, "I shall not forget this."

Deoris blinked, uncomprehending.

"I was born in Atlantis," Maleina said then, "where the Magicians are held in more honor than here. I like not these new laws which have all but prohibited magic." The Grey-robed woman paused again, and then asked, "Deoris—what are you to Riveda?"

Deoris's throat squeezed under that compelling stare, forbidding speech.

"Listen, my dear," Maleina went on, "the Grey Temple is no place for you. In Atlantis, one such as you would be honored; here, you will be shamed and disgraced—not this time alone, but again and again. Go back, my child! Go back to the world of your fathers, while there is still time. Complete your penance and return to the Temple of Caratra, while there is still time!"

Tardily, Deoris found her voice and her pride. "By what right do you command me thus?"

"I do not command," Maleina said, rather sadly. "I speak—as to a friend, one who has done me a great service. Semalis—the girl you aided without thought of penalty—she was a pupil of mine, and I love her. And I know what you have done for Demira." She laughed, a low, abrupt, and rather mournful sound. "No, Deoris, it was not I who betrayed you to the Guardians—but I would have, had I thought it would bring sense into your stubborn little head! Deoris, *look at me*."

Unable to speak, Deoris did as she was told.

After a moment, Maleina turned away her compelling gaze, saying gently, "No, I would not hypnotize you. I only want you to see what I am, child."

Deoris studied Maleina intently. The Atlantean woman was tall and very thin, and her long smooth hair, uncovered, flamed above a darkly-bronzed face. Her long slim hands were crossed on her breast, like the hands of a beautiful statue; but the delicately molded face was drawn and haggard, the body beneath the grey robe was flat-breasted, spare and oddly shapeless, and there was a little sag of age in the poised shoulders. Suddenly Deoris saw white strands, cunningly combed, threading the bright hair.

"I too began my life in Caratra's Temple," Maleina said gravely, "and now when it is too late, I would I had never looked beyond. Go back, Deoris, before it is too late. I am an old woman, and I know of what I warn you. Would you see your womanhood sapped before it has fully wakened in you? Deoris, know you *yet* what I am? You have seen what I have brought on Demira! Go back, child."

Fighting not to cry, her throat too tight for speech, Deoris lowered her head.

The long thin hands touched her head lightly. "You cannot," Maleina murmured sadly, "can you? Is it already too late? Poor child!"

When Deoris could look up again, the sorceress was gone.

Chapter Eight

THE CRYSTAL SPHERE

I

Now, sometimes for days at a time, Deoris never left the enclosure of the Grey Temple. It was a lazy and hedonistic life, this world of the Grey-robe women, and Deoris found herself dreamily enjoying it. She spent much of her time with Demira, sleeping, bathing in the pool, chattering idly and endlessly—sometimes childish nonsense, sometimes oddly serious and mature talk. Demira had a quick, though largely neglected intelligence, and Deoris delighted in teaching her many of the things she herself had learned as a child. They romped with the little-boy chelas who were too young for life in the men's courts, and listened avidly—and surreptitiously—to the talk of the older priestesses and more experienced *saji*; talk that often outraged the innocent Deoris, reared among the Priesthood of Light. Demira took a wicked delight in explaining the more cryptic allusions to Deoris, who was first shocked, then fascinated.

She got on well, all told, with Riveda's daughter. They were both young, both far too mature for their years, both forced into a rebellious awareness by tactics—though Deoris never realized this—almost equally unnatural.

She and Domaris were almost strangers now; they met rarely, and with constraint. Nor, strangely enough, had her intimacy with Riveda progressed much further; he treated Deoris almost as impersonally as Micon had, and rarely as gently.

Life in the Grey Temple was largely nocturnal. For Deoris these were nights of strange lessons, at first meaningless; words and chants of which the exact intonation must be mastered, gestures to be practiced with almost mechanical, mathematical precision. Occasionally, with a faintly humoring air, Riveda would set Deoris some slight task as his scribe; and he often took her with him outside the walls of the Temple precincts, for although he was scholar and Adept, the role of Healer was still predominant in Riveda. Under his tuition, Deoris developed a skill almost worthy of her teacher. She also became an expert hypnotist: at times, when a broken limb was to be splinted, or a deep wound opened and cleansed, Riveda would call upon her to hold the patient in deep, tranced sleep, so that he could work slowly and thoroughly.

He had not often allowed her to enter the Chela's Ring. He gave no reason, but she found it easy to guess at one: Riveda did not intend that any man of the Grey-robes should have the slightest excuse for approaching Deoris. This puzzled the girl; no one could have been less like a lover, but he exercised over her a certain jealous possessiveness, tempered just enough with menace that Deoris never felt tempted to brave his anger.

In fact, she never understood Riveda, nor caught a glimmering of the reasons behind his shifting moods—for he was changeable as the sky in raintime. For days at a time he would be gentle, even lover-like. These days were Deoris's greatest joy; her adoration, however edged with fear, was too innocent to have merged completely into passion— but she came close to truly loving him when he was like this, direct and simple, with the plainness of his peasant forefathers. . . . Still, she could never take this for granted. Overnight, with a change of personality so complete that it amounted to sorcery, it would become remote, sarcastic, as icy to her as to any ordinary chela. In these moods he rarely touched her, but when he did, ordinary brutality would have seemed a lover's caress; and she learned to avoid him when such a mood had taken him.

Nevertheless, on the whole, Deoris was happy. The idle life left her mind—and it was a keen and well-trained mind—free to concentrate on the strange things he taught her. Time drifted, on slow feet, until a year had gone by, and then another year.

II

Sometimes Deoris wondered why she had never had even the hope of a child by Riveda. She asked him why more than once. His answer was sometimes derisive laughter, or a flare of exasperated annoyance, occasionally a silent caress and a distant smile.

She was almost nineteen when his insistence on ritual gesture, sound, and intonation, grew exacting—almost fanatical. He had re-trained her voice himself, until it had tremendous range and an incredible flexibility; and Deoris was beginning, now, to grasp something of the significance and power of sound: words that stirred sleeping consciousness, gestures that wakened dormant senses and memories . . .

One night, toward the low end of the year, he brought her to the Grey Temple. The room lay deserted beneath its cold light, the greyness burning dimly like frost around the stone walls and floors. The air was flat and fresh and still, soundless and insulated from reality. At their heels the chela Reio-ta crept, a voiceless ghost in his grey robes, his yellow face a corpse-like mask in the icy light. Deoris, shivering in thin saffron veils, crouched behind a pillar, listening fearfully to Riveda's terse, incisive commands. His voice had dropped from tenor to resonant baritone, and Deoris knew and recognized this as the first storm-warning of the hurricane loose in his soul.

Now he turned to Deoris, and placed between her trembling hands a round, silvery sphere in which coiled lights moved sluggishly. He cupped the fingers of her left hand around it, and motioned her to her place within the mosaiced sign cut into the floor of the Temple. In his own hand was a silvered metal rod; he extended it toward the chela, but at its touch Reio-ta made a curious, inarticulate sound, and his hand, outstretched to receive it, jerked convulsively and refused to take the thing, as if his hand bore no relation to its owner's will. Riveda, with an exasperated

˜hrug, retained it, motioning the chela to the third position.

They were standing by then in a precise triangle, Deoris with the shining sphere cradled in her raised hand, the chela braced defensively as if he held an uplifted sword. There was something defensive in Riveda's own attitude; he was not sure of his own motives. It was partly curiosity that had led him to this trial, but mainly a desire to test his own powers, and those of this girl he had trained—and those of the stranger, whose mind was still a closed book to Riveda.

With a slight shrug, the Adept shifted his own position somewhat, completing a certain pattern of space between them ... instantly he felt an almost electric tension spring into being. Deoris moved the sphere a very little; the chela altered the position of only one hand.

The patterned triangle was complete!

Deoris began a low crooning, a chant, less sung than intoned, less intoned than spoken, but musical, rising and falling in rhythmic cadences. At the first note of the chant, the chela sprang to life. A start of recognition leaped in his eyes, although he did not move the fraction of an inch.

The chant went into a weird minor melody; stopped. Deoris bent her head and slowly, with a beautiful grace and economy of motion, her balanced gestures betraying her arduous practices, sank to her knees, raising the crystal sphere between her hands. Riveda elevated the rod ... and the chela bent forward, automatic gestures animating his hands, so slowly, like something learned in childhood and forgotten.

The pattern of figures and sound altered subtly;

changed. Amber lights and shadows drifted in the
crystal sphere.

Riveda began to intone long phrases that rose
and fell with a sonorous, pulsating rhythm; Deoris
added her voice in subtle counterpoint. The chela,
his eyes aware and alert for the first time, his
motions automatic, like the jerky gestures of a
puppet, was still silent. Riveda, tautly concentrated
on his own part in the ritual, flickered only the
corner of a glance at him.

Would he remember enough? Would the stimulus of the familiar ritual—and that it was familiar
to him, the Adept had no doubts—be sufficient to
waken what was dormant in the chela's memory?
Riveda was gambling that Reio-ta actually possessed the secret.

The electric tension grew, throbbed with the res-
onance of sound in the high and vaulted archway
overhead. The sphere glowed, became nearly transparent at the surface to reveal the play of coiled
and jagged flickers of color; darkened; glowed again.

The chela's lips opened. He wet them, convulsively, his eyes haunted prisoners in the waxen
face. Then he was chanting too, in a hoarse and
gasping voice, as if his very brain trembled with
the effort, rocking in its cage of bone.

No, Deoris reflected secretly, with the scrap of
her consciousness not entirely submerged in the
ceremonial, *this rite is not new to him*.

Riveda had gambled, and won. Two parts of this
ritual were common knowledge, known to all; but
Reio-ta knew the third and hidden part, which
made it an invocation of potent power. Knew it—
and, forced by Riveda's dominant will and the

stimulus of the familiar chant on his beclouded mind, was using it—openly!

Deoris felt a little tingle of exultation. They had broken through an ancient wall of secrecy, they were hearing and witnessing what no one but the highest Initiates of a certain almost legendary secret sect had ever seen or heard—and then only under the most solemn pledges of silence until death!

She felt the magical tension deepen, felt her body prickling with it and her mind being wedged open to accept it. The chela's voice and movements were clearer now, as memory flooded back into his mind and body. The chela dominated now: his voice was clear and precise, his gestures assured, perfect. Behind the mask of his face his eyes lived and burned. The chant rushed on, bearing Deoris and Riveda along on its crest like two straws in a seething torrent.

Lightning flickered within the sphere; flamed out from the rod Riveda held. A vibrant force throbbed between the triangled bodies, an almost visible pulsing of power that brightened, darkened, spasmodically. Lightning flared above them; thunder snapped the air apart in a tremendous crashing.

Riveda's body arched backward, rigid as a pillar, and sudden terror flooded through Deoris. The chela was being *forced* to do this—this secret and sacred thing! And for what? It was sacrilege—it was black blasphemy—somehow it must be stopped! Somehow she must stop it—but it was no longer in her power even to stop herself. Her voice disobeyed her, her body was frozen, the restless sweep of tyrant power bore them all along.

The unbearable chanting slowly deepened to a

single long Word—a Word no one throat could
encompass, a Word needing three blended voices
to transform it from a harmless grouping of syllables into a dynamic rhythm of space-twisting power.
Deoris felt it on her tongue, felt it tearing at her
throat, vibrating the bones of her skull as if to tear
them to scattering atoms . . .

Red-hot fire lashed out with lightning shock.
White whips of flame splayed out as the Word
thundered on, and on, and on . . . Deoris shrieked
in blind anguish and pitched forward, writhing.
Riveda leaped forward, snatching her to him with
a ferocious protectiveness; but the rod clung to his
fingers, twisting with a life of its own, as if it had
grown to the flesh there. The pattern was broken,
but the fire played on about them, pallid, searing,
uncontrollable; a potent spell unleashed only to
turn on its blasphemers.

The chela, frozenly, was sinking, as if forced
down by intense pressure. His waxen face convulsed as his knees buckled beneath him, and then
he jumped forward, clutching at Deoris. With a
savage yell, Riveda lashed out with the rod to
ward him away, but with the sudden strength of a
madman, Reio-ta struck the Adept hard in the
face, narrowly avoiding the crackling nimbus of
the rod. Riveda fell back, half-conscious; and
Reio-ta, moving through the darting lights and
flames as if they were no more than reflections in
a glass, caught Deoris's clawed hands in his own
and tore the sphere from them. Then, turning, he
gave the staggering Riveda another swift blow and
wrenched the rod from him, and with a single
long, low, keening cry, struck rod and sphere

together, then wrenched them apart and flung them viciously into separate ends of the room.

The sphere shattered. Harmless fragments of crystal patterned the stone tiles. The rod gave a final crackle, and darkened. The lightning died.

Reio-ta straightened and faced Riveda. His voice was low, furious—and sane. *"You filthy, damned, black sorcerer!"*

III

The air was void and empty, cold grey again. Only a faint trace of ozone hovered. Silence prevailed, save for Deoris's voice, moaning in delirious agony, and the heavy breathing of the chela. Riveda held the girl cradled across his knees, though his own shaking, seared hands hung limply from his wrists. The Adept's face had gone bone-white and his eyes were blazing as if the lighting had entered into them.

"I will kill you for that someday, Reio-ta."

The chela, his dark face livid with pain and rage, stared down darkly at the Adept and the insensible girl. His voice was almost too low for hearing. "You have killed me already, Riveda—and yourself."

But Riveda had already forgotten Reio-ta's existence. Deoris whimpered softly, unconsciously, making little clawing gestures at her breast as he let her gently down onto the cold stone floor. Carefully Riveda loosened the scorched veils, working awkwardly with the tips of his own injured hands. Even his hardened Healer's eyes contracted with horror at what he saw—then her moans died out; Deoris sighed and went limp and slack against the floor, and for a heart-stopping instant Riveda was sure that she was dead.

Reio-ta was standing very still now, shaken by fine tremors, his head bent and his mind evidently on the narrow horizon between continued sanity and a relapse into utter vacuity.

Riveda flung his head up to meet those darkly condemning eyes with his own compelling stare. Then the Adept made a brief, imperative gesture, and Reio-ta bent and lifted Deoris into Riveda's outstretched arms. She lay like a dead weight against his shoulder, and the Adept set his teeth as he turned and bore her from the Temple.

And behind him, the only man who had ever cursed Riveda and lived followed the Adept meekly, muttering to himself as idiots will . . . but there was a secret spark deep in his eyes that had not been there before.

Chapter Nine

THE DIFFERENCE

I

For the first two years of their marriage, Arvath had deceived himself into believing that he could make Domaris forget Micon. He had been kind and forbearing, trying to understand her inward struggle, conscious of her bravery, tender after the loss of their child.

Domaris was not versed in pretense, and in the last year a tension had mounted between them despite all their efforts. Arvath was not entirely blameless, either; no man can quite forgive a woman who remains utterly untouched by emotion.

Still, in all outward things, Domaris made him a good wife. She was beautiful, modest, conventional, and submissive; she was the daughter of a highly-placed priest and was herself a priestess. She managed their home well, if indifferently, and when she realized that he resented her small son, she arranged to keep Micail out of Arvath's sight.

When they were alone, she was compliant, affectionate, even tender. Passionate she was not, and would not pretend.

Frequently, he saw a curious pity in her grey eyes—and pity was the one thing Arvath would not endure. It stung him into jealous, angry scenes of endless recrimination, and he sometimes felt that if she would but once answer him hotly, if she would ever protest, they would at least have some place for a beginning. But her answers were always the same; silence, or a quiet, half-shamed murmur—"I am sorry, Arvath. I told you it would be like this."

And Arvath would curse in frustrated anger, and look at her with something approaching hate, and storm out to walk the Temple precincts alone and muttering for hour after hour. Had she ever refused him anything, had she ever reproached him, he might in time have forgiven her; but her indifference was worse, a complete withdrawal to some secret place where he could not follow. She simply was not there in the room with him at all.

"I'd rather you made a cuckold of me in the court with a garden slave, where everyone could see!" he shouted at her once, in furious frustration. "At least then I could kill the man, and be satisfied!"

"*Would* that satisfy you?" she asked gently, as if she only awaited his word to pursue exactly the course of action he had outlined; and Arvath felt the hot bitter taste of hate in his mouth and slammed out of the room with fumbling steps, realizing sickly that if he stayed he would kill her, then and there.

Later he wondered if she were trying to goad him to do just that. . . .

He found that he could break through her indifference with cruelty, and he even began to take a certain pleasure in hurting her, feeling that her hot words and her hatred were better than the indifferent tolerance which was the most his tenderness had ever won. He came to abuse her shamefully, in fact, and at last Domaris, hurt past enduring, threatened to complain to the Vested Five.

"*You* will complain!" Arvath jeered. "Then *I* will complain, and the Vested Five will throw us out to settle it ourselves!"

Bitterly, Domaris asked, "Have I ever refused you anything?"

"You've never done anything else, you . . ." The word he used was one which had no written form, and hearing it from a member of the Priest's Caste made Domaris want to faint with sheer shame. Arvath, seeing her turn white, went on pouring out similar abuse with savage enjoyment. "Of course I shouldn't talk this way, you're an Initiate," he sneered. "You know the Temple secrets—one of which allows you to deliberately refuse to conceive my child!" He made a little mocking bow. "All the while protesting your innocence, of course, as befits one so elevated."

The injustice of this—for Domaris had hidden Mother Ysouda's warning in her heart and forgotten her counsel as soon as it was given—stung her into unusual denial. "You lie!" she said shakily, raising her voice to him for the first time. "You lie, and you know you lie! I don't know why the Gods have denied us children, but *my* child bears my name—and the name of his father!"

Arvath, raging, advanced to loom over her threateningly. "I don't see what that has to do with it! Except that you thought more of that Atlantean swine-prince than of me! Don't you think I know that you yourself frustrated the life of the child you almost gave me? And all because of that— that . . ." He swallowed, unable to speak, and caught her thin shoulders in his hands, roughly dragging her to her feet. "Damn you, tell me the truth! Admit what I say is true or I will kill you!"

She let herself go limp between his hands. "Kill me, then," she said wearily. "Kill me at once, and make an end of this."

Arvath mistook her trembling for fear; genuinely frightened, he lowered her gently, releasing her from his harsh clasp. "No, I didn't mean it," he said contritely; then his face crumpled and he flung himself to his knees before her, throwing his arms around her waist and burying his head in her breast. "Domaris, forgive me, forgive me, I did not mean to lay rough hands on you! Domaris, Domaris, Domaris . . ." He kept on saying her name over and over in incoherent misery, sobbing, the tight terrible crying of a man lost and bewildered.

The woman leaned over him at last, clasping him close, her eyes dark with heartbroken pity, and she, too, wept as she rocked his head against her breast. Her whole body, her heart, her very being ached with the wish that she could love him.

II

Later, full of dread and bitter conflict, she was tempted to speak at last of Mother Ysouda's warnings; but even if he believed her—if it did not start the whole awful argument over again—the thought that he might pity her was intolerable. And so she said nothing of it.

Shyly, wanting fatherly advice and comfort, she went to Rajasta, but as she talked with him, she began to blame herself: it had not been Arvath who was cruel, but she who shirked sworn duty. Rajasta, watching her face as she spoke, could find no comfort to offer, for he did not doubt that Domaris had made a deliberate display of her passivity, flaunted her lack of emotion in the man's face. What wonder if Arvath resented such an assault on his manhood? Domaris obviously did not enjoy her martyrdom; but, equally certainly, she took a perverse satisfaction in it. Her face was drawn with shame, but a soft light glowed in her eyes, and Rajasta recognized the signs of a self-made martyr all too easily.

"Domaris," he said sadly, "do not hate even yourself, my daughter." He checked her reply with a raised hand. "I know, you make the gestures of your duty. But are you *his wife*, Domaris?"

"What do you mean?" Domaris whispered; but her face revealed her suspicions.

"It is not I who ask this of you," said Rajasta, relentlessly, "but you who demand it of yourself, if you are to live with yourself. If your conscience were clean, my daughter, you would not have come to me! I know what you have given Arvath, and at what cost; *but what have you withheld?*" Pausing, he saw that she was stricken, unable to meet his gaze. "My child, do not resent that I give you the counsel which you, yourself, know to be right." He reached to her and picked up one of her tautly clenched and almost bloodlessly white hands in his own and stroked it gently, until her fingers relaxed a little. "You are like this hand of yours, Domaris. You clasp the past too tightly, and so turn the knife in your own wounds. Let go, Domaris!"

"I—I cannot," she whispered.

"Nor can you will yourself to die anymore, my child. It is too late for that."

"Is it?" she asked, with a strange smile.

III

Rajasta's heart ached for Domaris; her stilled, bitter smile haunted him day after day, and at last he came to see things more as she did, and realized that he had been remiss. In his innermost self he knew that Domaris was widowed; she had been wife in the truest sense to Micon, and she would never be more than mistress to Arvath. Rajasta had never asked, but he *knew* that she had gone to Micon as a virgin. Her marriage to Arvath had been but a travesty, a mockery, a weary duty, a defilement—and for nothing.

One morning, in the library, unable to concentrate, Rajasta thought in sudden misery, *It is my doing. Deoris warned me that Domaris should not have another child, and I said nothing of it! I could have stopped them from forcing her into marriage. Instead I have sanctimoniously crushed the life from the girl who was child to me in my childless old age—the daughter of my own soul. I have sent my daughter into the place of harlots! And my own light is darkened in her shame.*

Throwing aside the scroll he had ineffectually been perusing, Rajasta rose up and went in search of Domaris, intending to promise that her marriage should be dissolved; that he would move heaven and earth to have it set aside.

He told her nothing of the kind—for before he could speak a word she told him, with a strange, secret, and not unhappy smile, that once again she was bearing Arvath a child.

Chapter Ten

IN THE LABYRINTH

I

Failure was, of all things, the most hateful to Riveda. Now he faced failure; and a common chela, his own chela, in fact, had had the audacity to protect him! The fact that Reio-ta's intervention had saved all their lives made no difference to Riveda's festering hate.

All three had suffered. Reio-ta had escaped most lightly, with blistering burns across shoulders and arms; easily treated, easily explained away. Riveda's hands were seared to the bone—maimed, he thought grimly, for life. But the *dorje* lightning had struck Deoris first with its searing lash; her shoulders, arms and sides were blistered and scorched, and across her breasts the whips of fire had eaten deep, leaving their unmistakable pattern—a cruel sigil stamped with the brand of the blasphemous fire.

Riveda, with his almost-useless hands, did what he could. He loved the girl as deeply as it was in his nature to love anyone, and the need for secrecy maddened him, for he knew himself incapable now of caring for her properly; he lacked proper remedies, lacked—with his hands maimed—the skill to use them. But he dared not seek assistance. The Priests of Light, seeing the color and the fearful form of her wounds, would know instantly what had made them—and then swift, sure and incontrovertible, punishment would strike. Even his own Grey-robes could not be trusted in this; not even they would dare to conceal any such hideous tampering with the forces rightly locked in nature. His only chance of aid lay among the Black-robes; and if Deoris were to live, he must take that chance. Without care, she might not survive another night.

With Reio-ta's assistance, he had taken her to a hidden chamber beneath the Grey Temple, but he dared not leave her there for long. To still her continual moans he had mixed a strong sedative, as strong as he dared, and forced her to swallow it; she had fallen into restless sleep, and while her fretful whimperings did not cease, the potion blurred her senses enough to dull the worst of the agony.

With a sting of guilt Riveda found himself thinking again what he had thought about Micon: *Why did they not confine their hell's play to persons of no importance, or having dared so far, at least make certain their victims did not escape to carry tales?*

He would have let Reio-ta die without compunction. As Prince of Ahtarrath, he had been legally dead for years; and what was one crazy chela more or less? Deoris, however, was the daughter of a powerful priest; her death would mean full and merciless investigation. Talkannon was not one to be trifled with, and Rajasta would almost certainly suspect Riveda first of all.

The Adept felt some shame at his weakness, but he still would not admit, even to himself, that he loved Deoris, that she had become necessary to him. The thought of her death made a black aching within him, an ache so strong and gnawing that he forgot the agonies in his seared hands.

II

After a long, blurred nightmare when she seemed to wander through flames and lightning and shadows out of half-forgotten awful legends, Deoris opened her eyes on a curious scene.

She was lying upon a great couch of carven stone, in a heap of downy cushions. Above was fixed one of the ever-burning lamps, whose flame, leaping and wavering, made the carved figures on the rails of the couch into shapes of grotesque horror. The air was damp and rather chilly, and smelled musty, like cold stone. She wondered at first if she were dead and laid in a vault, and then became aware that she was swathed in moist, cool bandages. There was pain in her body, but it was all very far away, as if that swaddled mass of bandages belonged to someone else.

She turned her head a little, with difficulty, and made out the shape of Riveda, familiar even with his back to her; and before him a man Deoris recognized with a little shiver of terror—Nadastor, a Grey-robe Adept. Middle-aged, gaunt and ascetic in appearance, Nadastor was darkly handsome and yet forbidding. Nor was he robed now in the grey robe of a Magician, but in a long black tabard, embroidered and blazoned with strange emblems; on his head was a tall, mitered hat, and between his hands he held a slight glass rod.

Nadastor was speaking, in a low, cultured voice that reminded Deoris vaguely of Micon's: "You say she is not *saji*?"

"Far from it," Riveda answered dryly. "She is Talkannon's daughter, and a Priestess."

Nadastor nodded slowly. "I see. That does make a difference. Of course, if it were mere personal sentiment, I would still say you should let her die. But . . ."

"I have made her *sākti sidhāna*."

"Within the restraints you have always burdened yourself with," Nadastor murmured, "you have dared much. I knew that you had a great power, of course; that was clear from the first. Were it not for the coward's restrictions imposed by the Ritual . . ."

"I am done with restraints!" Riveda said savagely. "I shall work as I, and I alone, see fit! I have not spared myself to gain this power and no one—now—shall curtail my right to use it!" He raised his left hand, red and raw and horribly maimed, and slowly traced a gesture that made Deoris gasp despite herself. There could be no return from that; that sign, made with the left hand, was blasphemy punishable by death, even in the Grey Temple. It seemed to hang in the air between the Adepts for a moment.

Nadastor smiled. "So be it," he said. "First we must save your hands. As for the girl—"

"Nothing about the girl!" Riveda interrupted violently.

Nadastor's smile had become mockery. "For every strength, a weakness," he said, "or you would not be here. Very well, I will attend her."

Deoris suddenly felt violently sick; Riveda had mocked Micon and Domaris just that way.

"If you have taught her as you say, she is too valuable to let her womanhood be sapped and blasted by—that which has touched her." Nadastor came toward the bed; Deoris shut her eyes and lay like death as the Black-robe drew away the clumsy bandages and skillfully dressed the hurts with a touch as cold and impersonal as if he handled a stone image. Riveda stood close by throughout, and when Nadastor had ended his ministrations, Riveda kenlt and stretched one heavily bandaged hand to Deoris.

"Riveda!" she whispered, weakly.

His voice was hardly any stronger as he said, "This was not failure. We shall make it success, you and I—we have invoked a great power, Deoris, and it is ours to use!"

Deoris longed only for some word of tenderness. This talk of power sickened and frightened her; she had seen that power invoked and wished only to forget it. "An—an evil power!" she managed to whisper, dry-mouthed.

He said, with the old concentrated bitterness, "Always babbling of good and evil! Must everything come in ease and beauty? Will you run away the first time you see something which is not encompassed in your pretty dreams?"

Shamed and defensive as always, she whispered, "No. Forgive me."

Riveda's voice became gentle again. "No, I should not blame you if you are fearful, my own Deoris! Your courage has never failed when there was need for it. Now, when you are so hurt, I should not make things any worse for you. Try to sleep now, Deoris. Grow strong again."

She reached toward him, sick for his touch, for some word of love or reassurance—but suddenly, with a terrifying violence, Riveda burst into a fit of raving blasphemy. He cursed, shouting, straining with an almost rabid wrath, calling down maledictions in a foul litany in which several languages seemed to mix in a pidgin horrible to hear, and Deoris, shocked and frightened beyond her limits, began to weep wildly. Riveda only stopped when his voice failed him hoarsely, and he flung himself down on the couch beside her, his face hidden, his shoulders twitching, too exhausted to move or speak another word.

After a long time Deoris stirred painfully, curving her hand around his cheek which rested close to hers. The movement roused the man a little; he turned over wearily and looked at Deoris from wide, piteous eyes in which steaks of red showed where tiny veins had burst.

"Deoris, Deoris, what is it that I've done to you? How can I hold you to me, after this? Flee while you can, desert me if you will—I have no right to ask anything more of you!"

She tightened her clasp a little. She could not raise herself, but her voice was trembling with passion. "I gave you that right! *I go where you go!* Fear or no fear. Riveda, don't you know yet that I love you?"

The bloodshot eyes flickered a little, and for the first time in many months he drew her close and kissed her, with concentrated passion, hurting her in his fierce embrace. Then, recollecting himself, he drew carefully away—but she closed her weak fingers around his right arm, just above the bandage.

"I love you," she whispered weakly. "I love you enough to defy gods and demons alike!"

Riveda's eyes, dulled with pain and sorrow, dropped shut for a moment. When he opened them, his face was once again composed, a mask of unshakeable calm. "I may ask you to do just that," he said, in a low, tense voice, "but I will be just one step behind you all the way."

And Nadastor, unseen in the shadows beyond the arched door of the room, shook his head and laughed softly to himself.

III

For some time Deoris alternated between brief lucid moments and days of hellish pain and delirious, drugged nightmares. Riveda never left her side; at whatever hour she awakened, he would be there, gaunt and impassive; deep in meditation, or reading from some ancient scroll.

Nadastor came and went, and Deoris listened to all they said to one another—but her intervals of conciousness were so brief and painful at first that she never knew where reality ended and dreams began. She remembered once waking to see Riveda fondling a snake which writhed around his head like a pet kitten—but when she spoke of it days later, he stared blankly and denied it.

Nadastor treated Riveda with courtesy and respect, as an equal; but an equal whose education has been uncouthly remiss and must be remedied. After Deoris was out of danger and could stay awake for more than a few minutes undrugged,

Riveda read to her—things that made her blood run cold. Now and again Riveda demonstrated his new skill with these manipulations of nature, and gradually Deoris lost her personal fear; never again would Revida allow any rite to get out of control through lack of knowledge!

With only one thing was Deoris at odds: Riveda had suddenly become ambitious; his old lust for knowledge had somehow muted into a lust for power. But she did not voice her misgivings over this, lying quiet and listening when he talked, too full of love to protest and sure in any case that if she protested he would not listen.

Never had Riveda been so kind to her. It was as if his whole life had been spent in some tense struggle between warring forces, which had made him stern and rigid and remote in the effort to cleave to a line of rectitude. Now that he had finally abandoned himself to sorcery, this evil and horror absorbed all his inborn cruelty, leaving the man himself free to be kind, to be tender, to show the basic simplicity and goodness that was in him. Deoris felt her old childlike adoration slowly merging into something deeper, different . . . and once, when he kissed her with that new tenderness, she clung to him, in sudden waking of an instinct as old as womanhood.

He laughed a little, his face relaxing into humorous lines. "My precious Deoris . . ." Then he murmured doubtfully, "But you are still in so much pain."

"Not much, and I—I want to be close to you. I want to sleep in your arms and wake there—as I have never done."

Too moved to speak, Riveda drew her close to

him. "You shall lie in my arms tonight," he whispered at last. "I—I too would have you close."

He held her delicately, afraid to hurt by a careless touch, and she felt his physical presence—so familiar to her, so intimately known to her body, and yet alien, altogether strange, after all these years a stranger to her—so that she found herself shy of the lover as she had never been of the initiator.

Riveda made love to her softly, with a sensitive sincerity she had not dreamed possible, at first half fearful lest he bring her pain; then, when he was certain of her, drawing on some deep reserve of gentleness, giving himself up to her with the curious, rare warmth of a man long past youth: not passionate, but very tender and full of love. In all her time with Riveda she had never known him like this; and for hours afterward she lay nestled in his arms, happier than she had ever been in her life, or would ever be again, while in a muted, hoarse, hesitant voice he told her all the things every woman dreams of hearing from her lover, and his shaking scarred hands moved softly on her silky hair.

Chapter Eleven

THE DARK SHRINE

I

Deoris remained within the subterranean labyrinth for a month, cared for by Riveda and Nadastor.
She saw no other person, save an old deaf-mute
who brought her food. Nadastor treated Deoris
with a ceremonious deference which astonished
and terrified the girl—particularly after she heard
one fragment of conversation ...

She and Riveda had grown by degrees into a
tender companionship like nothing the girl had
ever known. He had no black, surly moods now.
On this day he had remained near her for some
time, translating some of the ancient inscriptions
with an almost lewd gaiety, coaxing her to eat
with all sorts of playful little games, as if she
were an ailing child. After a time, for she still
tired quickly, he laid her down and drew a blanket of woven wool over her shoulders, and left
her; she slept until she was wakened by a voice,

raised a little as if he had forgotten her in his annoyance.

"... *all my life* have I held that in abhorrence!"

"Even within the Temple of Light," Nadastor was saying, "brothers and sisters marry sometimes; their line is kept pure, they want no unknown blood which might bring back those traits they have bred out of the Priest's Caste. Children of incest are often natural clairvoyants."

"When they are not mad," said Riveda cynically.

Deoris closed her eyes again as the voices fell to a murmur; then Riveda raised his voice angrily again.

"*Which* of Talkannon's ... ?"

"You will wake the girl," Nadastor rebuked; and for minutes they spoke so softly that Deoris could hear nothing. The next thing she caught was Nadastor's flat statement, "Men breed animals for what they want them to become. Should they scatter the seed of their own bodies?" The voice fell again, then surged upward: "I have watched you, Riveda, for a long time. I knew that one day you would weary of the restraints laid on you by the Ritual!".

"Then you knew more than I," Riveda retorted. "Well, I have no regrets—and whatever you may think, no scruples in that line. Let us see if I understand you. The child of a man past the age of passion, and a girl just barely old enough to conceive, can be—almost outside the laws of nature ..."

"And as little bound by them," Nadastor added. He rose and left the room, and Riveda came to look down at Deoris. She shut her eyes, and after a moment, thinking her still sleeping, he turned away.

II

The burns on her back and shoulders had healed quickly, but the cruel brand on her breasts had bitten deep; even by the time she was able to be up again, they were still swathed in bandages which she could not bear to touch. She was growing restless; never had she been so long absent from the Temple of Light, and Domaris must be growing anxious about her—at the very least, she might make inquiries.

Riveda soothed her fear a little.

"I have told a tale to account for you," he said. "I told Cadamiri that you had fallen from the sea-wall and been burned at one of the beacon fires; that also explained my own hurt." He held out his hands, free now of bandages, but terribly scarred, too stiff even to recover their old skill.

"No one questions my ability as Healer, Deoris, so they did not protest when I said you must be left in peace. And your sister—" His eyes narrowed slightly. "She waylaid me today in the library. She *is* anxious about you; and in all truth, Deoris, I could give no reason why she should not see you, so tomorrow it would be well if you left this place. You must see her, and reassure her, else. . . ." he laid a heavy hand on her arm, "the Guardians may descend on us. Tell Domaris—whatever you like, I care not, but—whatever you do, Deoris, unless you want me to die like a dog, Let not even Domaris see the scars on your breasts until they are wholly healed. And Deoris, if your sister insists, you may have to return to the Temple of Light. I—I grieve to send you from me, and would not have it so, but—the Ritual forbids any maiden of the Light-born to live among Grey-robes. It is an old law, and seldom invoked; it has been ignored time and time again. But Domaris reminded me of it, and—I dare not endanger you by angering her."

Deoris nodded without speaking. She had known that this interlude could not last forever. In spite of all the pain, all the terror, her new dread of Riveda, this had been a sort of idyll, suspended in nothingness and wrapped in an unexpected certainty of Riveda's nearness and his love; and now, already it was part of the past.

"You will be safest under your sister's protection. She loves you, and will ask no questions, I think." Riveda clasped her hand in his own and sat without moving or speaking for a long time; at last, he said, "I told you, once, Deoris, that I am not a good man to trust. By now I imagine I have proved that to you." The bitter and despondent tone was back in his voice. Then, evenly and carefully, he asked, "Are you still—my Priestess? I have forfeited the right to command you, Deoris. I offer to release you, if you wish it."

As she had done years ago, Deoris let go of his hand, dropped to her knees and pressed her face to his robes in surrender. She whispered, "I have told you I will defy all for you. Why will you never believe me?"

After a moment, Riveda raised her gently, his touch careful and light. "One thing remains," he said in a low voice. "You have suffered much, and I—I would not force this on you, but—but if not tonight, a year's full cycle must go by before we can try again. This is the Night of Nadir, and the only night on which I can complete this."

Deoris did not hesitate even a moment, although her voice shook a little. "I am at your command," she whispered, in the ritual phrase of the Grey-robes.

III

Some few hours later, the old deaf-mute woman came. She stripped Deoris, bathed and purified her, and robed her in the curious garments Riveda had sent. First a long, full robe of transparent linen, and over this a tabard of stiffly embroidered silk, decorated with symbols of whose meaning Deoris was not wholly certain. Her hair, now grown thick and long, was confined in a silver fillet, and her feet stained with dark pigment. As the deaf-mute completed this final task, Riveda returned— and Deoris forgot her own unusual garb in amazement at the change in him.

She had never seen him clothed in aught but the voluminous grey robe, or a simpler grey smock for magical work. Tonight he blazed in raw colors that made him look crude, sinister—frightening. His silver-gilt hair shone like virgin gold beneath a horned diadem which partially concealed his face; he wore a tabard of crimson like her own, with symbols worked in black from which Deoris turned away shamed eyes: the emblems were legitimate magical symbols, but in company with the ornaments of her clothing they seemed obscene. Under the crimson surcoat, Riveda wore a close-fitting tunic dyed blue—and this to Deoris was the crowning obscenity, for blue was the color sacred to Caratra, and reserved for women; she found she could not look at it on his body, and her face was aflame. Over all, he wore the loose magician's cloak which could be drawn about him to form the Black Robe. Seeing her blushes slowly whiten, Riveda smiled sternly.

"You are not *thinking*, Deoris! You are reacting to your childhood's superstitions. Come, what have I taught you about vibration and color?"

She felt all the more shamed and foolish at the reminder. "Red vitalizes and stimulates," she muttered, reciting, "where blue produces calmness and peace, mediating all inflamed and feverish conditions. And black absorbs and intensifies vibrations."

"That's better," he approved, smilingly. He then surveyed her costume critically, and once satisfied, said, "One thing remains; will you wear this for me, Deoris?"

He held out a girdle to her. Carved of wooden links, it was bound with crimson cords knotted in odd patterns. Runes were incised in the wood, and for a moment some instinct surged up in Deoris, and her fingers refused to touch the thing.

Riveda, more sternly, said, "Are you afraid to wear this, Deoris? Must we waste time with a lengthy explanation?"

She shook her head, chastened, and began to fasten it about her body—but Riveda bent and prevented her. With his strong, scarred hands he cinctured it carefully about her waist, tying the cords into a firm knot and ending with a gesture incomprehensible to her.

"Wear this until I give you leave to take it off," he told her. "Now come."

She almost rebelled again when she saw where he was taking her—to the terrible shrouded Crypt of the Avatar, where the Man with Crossed Hands lay, continually bound. Once within, she watched, frozen, as Riveda kindled ritual fire upon the altar which had been dark for a million years.

In his deepest voice, blazing in his symbolic robes, he began to intone the invocatory chant and Deoris, recognizing it, knew in trembling terror what it invoked. Was Riveda mad indeed? Or splendidly, superbly courageous? This was blackest blasphemy—*or was it?* And for what?

Shivering, she had no real choice but to add her own voice to the invocation. Voice answered voice in dark supplication, strophe and antistrophe, summoning . . . entreating. . . .

Riveda turned abruptly to the high stone altar where a child lay, and with a surge of horror Deoris saw what Riveda held in his hands. She clasped her own hands over her mouth so that she would not scream aloud as she recognized the child: *Larmin.* Karahama's son, Demira's little brother—Riveda's own son . . .

The child watched with incurious drugged eyes. The thing was done with such swiftness that the child gave only a single smothered whimper of apprehension, then fell back into the drugged sleep. Riveda turned back to the terrible ceremony which had become, to Deoris, a devil's rite conducted by a maniac.

Nadastor glided from the shadows, unbound the little boy, lifted the small senseless figure from the altar-stone and bore it from the Crypt. Deoris and Riveda were alone in the Dark Shrine—the very shrine where Micon had been tortured, alone with the Unrevealed God.

Her mind reeling with the impact of sound and

sight, she began to comprehend if not the whole, then the drift of the blasphemous ritual: Riveda meant nothing less than to loose the terrible chained power of the Dark God, to bring the return of the Black Star. But there was something more, something she could not quite understand . . . or was it that she dared not understand?

She sank to her knees; a deathly intangible horror held her by the throat, and though her mind screamed *No! No-no-no-no!* in the grip of that hypnotic dream she could not move or cry out. With a single word or gesture of protest she could so distort and shatter the pattern of the ritual that Riveda must fail—but sound was beyond her power, and she could not raise a hand or move her head so much as a fraction to one side or the other . . . and because in this crisis she could not summon the courage to defy Riveda, her mind slid off into incoherence, seeking an escape from personal guilt.

She could not—she *dared* not understand what she was hearing and seeing; her brain refused to seize on it. Her eyes became blank, blind and though Riveda saw the last remnant of sanity fade from her wide eyes, it was with only the least of his attention; the rest of him was caught up in what he did.

The fire on the shrine blazed up.

The chained and faceless image stirred . . .

Deoris saw the smile of the Man with Crossed Hands leering from the distorted shadows. Then, for an instant, she saw what Riveda saw, a chained and faceless figure standing upright—but that too swam away. Where they had been a great and fearful form hulked, recumbent and swathed in corpse-windings—an image that stirred and fought its bonds.

Then Deoris saw only an exploding pinwheel of lights into which she fell headlong. She barely knew it when Riveda seized her; she was inert, half-conscious at best, her true mind drowned in the compassionate stare of the Man with Crossed Hands, blinded by the spinning wheel of lights that whirled blazing above them. She knew, dimly, that Riveda lifted and laid her on the altar, and she felt a momentary shock of chill awareness and fear as she was forced back onto the wet stone. Not here, not here, not on the stone stained with the child's blood . . .

But he isn't dead! she thought with idiotic irrelevance, *he isn't dead, Riveda didn't kill him, it's all right if he isn't dead . . .*

IV

As if breaking the crest of a deep dark wave, Deoris came to consciousness suddenly, sensible of cold, and of pain from her half-healed burns. The fire on the shrine was extinguished; the Man with Crossed Hands had become but a veiled darkness.

Riveda, the frenzy gone, was lifting her carefully from the altar. With his normal, composed severity, he assisted her to rearrange her robes. She felt bruised and limp and sick, and leaned heavily on Riveda, stumbling a little on the icy stones—and she guessed, rightly, that he was remembering another night in this crypt, years before.

Somewhere in the labyrinth she could hear a child's distant sobs of pain and fright. They seemed to blend with her own confusion and terror that she put her hands up to her face to be sure that she was not crying, whether the sounds came from within or without.

At the door of the room where she had lain all during her long illness, Riveda paused, beckoning the deaf-mute woman and giving her some orders in sign-language.

He turned to Deoris again, and spoke with a cold formality that chilled her to the bone: "To-morrow you will be conducted above ground. Do not fear to trust Demira, but be very careful. Re-member what I have told you, especially in regard to your sister Domaris!" He paused, for once at a loss for words; then, with sudden and unexpected reverence, the Adept dropped to his knees before the terrified girl and taking her icy hand in his, he pressed it to his lips, then to his heart.

"Deoris," he said, falteringly. "O, my love—"

Quickly he let go her hand, rose to his feet and was gone before the girl could utter a single word.

Book II
RIVEDA

". . . common wisdom has it that Good has a tendency to grow and preserve itself, whereas Evil tends to grow until it destroys itself. But perhaps there is a flaw in our definitions—for would it be evil for Good to grow until it crowded Evil out of existence?

". . . everyone is born with a store of knowledge he doesn't know he possesses. . . . The human body of flesh and blood, which has to feed itself upon plants and their fruits, and upon animal meats, is not a fit habitation for the eternal spirit that moves us—and for this, we must die—but somewhere in the future is the assurance of a new body-type which can outlast the stones which do not die. . . . The things we learn strike sparks, and the sparks light fires; and the firelight reveals strange things moving in the darkness. . . . The darkness can teach you things that the light has never seen, and will never be able to see. . . .

"Unwilling to continue a merely mineral existence, plants were the first rebels; but the pleasures of a plant are limited to the number of ways in which it can circumvent the laws governing the mineral world. . . . There are poisonous minerals that can kill plants or animals or men. There are poisonous plants that can kill animals or men. There are poisonous animals (mostly reptiles) which can kill men—but man is unable to continue the poisonous chain, poison other creatures though he may, because he has never developed a means for poisoning the gods. . . ."

—from *The Codex of the Adept Riveda*

Chapter One

A WORLD OF DREAMS

I

"But Domaris, why?" Deoris demanded. "Why do you hate him so?"

Domaris leaned against the back of the stone bench where they sat, idly fingering a fallen leaf from the folds of her dress before casting it into the pool at their feet. Tiny ripples fanned out, winking in the sunlight.

"I don't believe that I do hate Riveda," Domaris mused, and shifted her swollen body awkwardly, as if in pain. "But I disturst him. There is—something about him that makes me shiver." She looked at Deoris, and what she saw in her sister's pale face made her add, with a deprecating gesture, "Pay not too much attention to me. You know Riveda better than I. And—oh, it may all be my imagination! Pregnant women have foolish fancies."

At the far end of the enclosed court, Micail's tousled head popped up from behind a bush and as quickly ducked down again; he and Lissa were playing some sort of hiding game.

The little girl scampered across the grass. "I see you, M'cail!" she cried shrilly, crouching down beside Domaris's skirt. "Pe-eep!"

Domaris laughed and petted and the little girl's shoulder, looking with satisfaction at Deoris. The last six months had wrought many changes in the younger girl; Deoris was not now the frail, huge-eyed wraith bound in bandages and weak with pain, whom Domaris had brought from the Grey Temple. Her face had begun to regain its color, though she was still paler than Domaris liked, if no longer so terribly thin . . . Domaris frowned as another, persistent suspicion came back to her. *That change I can recognize!* Domaris never forced a confidence, but she could not keep herself from wondering, angrily, just *what* had been done to Deoris. That story of falling from the sea-wall into a watch-fire . . . did not ring true, somehow.

"*You* don't have foolish fancies, Domaris," the girl insisted. "Why do you distrust Riveda?"

"Because—because he doesn't feel *true* to me; he hides his mind from me, and I think he has lied to me more than once." Domaris's voice hardened to ice. "But mostly because of what he is doing to you! The man is using you, Deoris . . . Is he your lover?" she asked suddenly, her eyes searching the young face.

"No!" The denial was angry, almost instinctive.

Lissa, forgotten at Domaris's knee, stared from one sister to the other for a moment, confused and a little worried; then she smiled slightly, and ran to chase Micail. Grown-ups had these exchanges. It didn't usually mean anything, as far as Lissa could tell, and so she rarely paid attention to such talk—though she had learned not to interrupt.

Domaris moved a little closer to Deoris and asked, more gently, "Then—who?"

"I—I don't know what you mean," Deoris said; but the look in her eyes was that of a trapped and frightened creature.

"Deoris," her sister said kindly, "be honest with me, kitten; do you think you can hide it forever? I have served Caratra longer than you—if not as well."

"I am *not* pregnant! It isn't possible—I *won't*!" Then, controlling her panic, Deoris took refuge in arrogance. "I have no lover!"

The grave grey eyes studied her again. "You may be sorceress," Domaris said deliberately, "but all your magic could not compass *that* miracle." She put her arm around Deoris, but the girl flung it petulantly away.

"Don't! I'm not!"

The response was so immediate, so angry, that Domaris only stared, open-mouthed. How could Deoris lie with such conviction, unless—unless . . . *Has that damned Grey-robe, then, taught her his own deceptive skills?* The thought troubled her. "Deoris," she said, half-questioning, "it *is* Riveda?"

Deoris edged away from her, sullenly, scared. "And if it were so—which it is not!—it is my right! You claimed yours!"

Domaris sighed; Deoris was going to be tiresome. "Yes," the older woman said tiredly, "I have no right to blame. Yet—" She looked away across the garden to the tussling children, her brows contracting in a half-troubled smile. "I *can* wish it were any other man."

"You do hate him!" Deoris cried, "I think you're —I hate *you!*" She rose precipitately to her feet, and ran from the garden, without a backward glance. Domaris half rose to follow her, then sank back heavily, sighing.

What's the use? She felt weary and worn, not at all inclined to soothe her sister's tantrums. Domaris felt unable to deal with her own life at present— how could she handle her sister's?

When she had carried Micon's child, Domaris had felt an odd reverence for her body; not even the knowledge that Micon's fate followed them like a shadow had dimmed her joy. Bearing Arrath's was different; this was duty, the honoring of a pledge. She was resigned, rather than rejoicing. Vised in pain, she walked with recurrent fear, and Mother Ysouda's words whispering in her mind. Domaris felt a guilty, apologetic love for Arvath's unborn son—as if she had wronged him by conceiving him.

And now—why is Deoris like that? Perhaps it isn't Riveda's child, and she's afraid of what he'll do . . . ? Domaris shook her head, unable to fathom the mystery.

From certain small but unmistakable signs, she was certain of her sister's condition; the girl's denial saddened and hurt Domaris. The lie itself was not important to her, but the reason for it was of great moment.

What have I done, that my own sister denies me her confidence?

She got up, with a little sigh, and went heavily toward the archway leading into the building, blaming herself bitterly for her neglect. She had been lost in grief for Micon—and then had come her marriage, and the long illness that followed the loss of her other child—and her Temple duties were onerous. Yet, somehow, Deoris's needs should have been met.

Rajasta warned me, years ago, Domaris thought sadly. Was it this he foresaw? Would that I had listened to him! If Deoris has ceased to trust me— Pausing, Domaris tried to reassure herself. *Deoris is a strange girl; she has always been rebellious. And she's been so ill, perhaps she wasn't really lying; maybe she really doesn't know, hasn't bothered to think about the physical aspects of the thing. That would be just like Deoris!*

For a moment, Domaris saw the garden rainbowed through sudden tears.

II

In the last months, Deoris had abandoned herself to the moment, not thinking ahead, not letting herself dwell on the past. She drifted on the surface of events; and when she slept, she dreamed obsessively of that night in the Crypt—so many terrifying nightmares that she almost managed to convince herself that the blood-letting, the blasphemous invocation, all that had transpired there, had been only another, more frightening dream.

This had been reinforced by the ease with which she had been able to pick up most of the broken threads of her life. Riveda's story had been accepted without question.

At her sister's insistence, Deoris had returned to Domaris's home. It was not the same. The House of the Twelve now contained a new group of Acolytes; Domaris and Arvath, with Elis and Chedan and another young couple, occupied pleasant apartments in a separate dwelling. Into this home Deoris had been welcomed, made a part of their family life. Until this moment, Domaris had never once questioned the past years.

But I should have known! Deoris thought superstitiously, and shivered. Only last night, very late, Demira had stolen secretly into the courts and into her room, whispering desperately, "Deoris—oh, Deoris, I shouldn't be here, I know, but don't send me away, I'm so terribly, terribly frightened!"

Deoris had taken the child into her bed and held her until the scared crying quieted, and then asked, incredulously, "But what is it, Demira, what's happened? I won't send you away, darling, no matter what it was, you can tell me what's the matter!" She looked at the thin, huddled girl beside her with troubled eyes, and said, "It's not likely Domaris would come into my rooms at this hour of the night, either; but if she did, I'll tell her—tell her something."

"Domaris," said Demira, slowly, and smiled—that wise and sad smile which always saddened Deoris; it seemed such an old smile for the childlike face. "Ah, Domaris doesn't know I exist, Deoris. Seeing me wouldn't change that." Demira sat up then, and looked at Deoris a moment before her silvery-grey eyes slid away again, blank and unseeing, the white showing all around the pupil. *"One of us three will die very soon,"* she said suddenly, in a strange, flat voice as unfocussed as her eyes. "One of us three will die, and her child with her. The second will walk beside Death, but it will take only her child. And the third will pray for Death to come for herself and her child, and both will live to curse the very air they breathe."

Deoris grabbed the slim shoulders and shook Demira, hard. "Come out of it!" she commanded, in a high, scared voice. *"Do you even know what you are saying?"*

Demira smiled queerly, her face lax and distorted. "Domaris, and you, and I—Domaris, Deoris, Demira; if you say the three names very quickly it is hard to tell which one you are saying, no? We are bound together by more than that, though, we are all three linked by our fates, all three with child."

"No!" Deoris cried out, in a denial as swift as it was vehement. *No, no, not from Riveda, not that cruelty, not that betrayal . . .*

She bent her head, troubled and afraid, unable to face Demira's wise young eyes. Since the night when she and Riveda and the chela had been trapped in the ritual which had loosed the Firespirit on them, scarring her with the blasting seal of the *dorje*, Deoris had not once had to seclude herself for the ritual purifications . . . She had thought about that, remembering horror-tales heard among the *saji*, of women struck and blasted barren, remembering Maleina's warnings long ago. Secretly, she had come to believe that, just as her breasts were scarred past healing, so she had been blasted in the citadel of her womanhood and become a sapped and sexless thing, the mere shell of a woman. Even when Domaris had suggested a simpler explanation—that she might be pregnant—she could not accept it. Surely if she were capable of conception, she would have borne Riveda's child long before this time!

Or would she? Riveda was versed in the mysteries, able to prevent conception if it pleased him. With a flash of horrified intuition, the thought came, to be at once rejected. *Oh no, not from that night in the Crypt—the mad invocation—the girdle, even now concealed beneath my nightdress . . .*

With a desperate effort, she snapped shut her mind on the memory. *It never happened, it was a dream . . . except for the girdle. But if that's real—no. There must be some explanation . . .*

Then her mind caught up with the other thing Demira had said, seizing on it almost with relief. *"You!"*

Demira looked up plaintively at Deoris. "You'll believe me," she said pitifully. "You will not mock me?"

"Oh, no, Demira, no, of course not." Deoris looked down into the pixyish face that now laid itself confidingly on her shoulder. Demira, at least, had not changed much in these three years; she was still the same, strange, suffering, wild little girl who had excited first Deoris's distrust and fear, and later her pity and love. Demira was now fifteen, but she seemed essentially the same, and she looked much as she had at twelve: taller than Deoris but slight, fragile, with the peculiar, deceptive appearance of immaturity and wisdom intermingled.

Demira sat up and began to reckon on her fingers. "It was like an awful dream. It happened, oh, perhaps one change of the moon after you left us."

"Five months ago," Deoris prompted gently.

"One of the little children had told me I was wanted in a sound-chamber. I thought nothing of it, I had been working with one of Nadastor's chelas. But it was empty. I waited there and then—and then a priest came in, but he was—he was masked, *and in black*, with horns across his face! He didn't say anything, he only—caught at me, and—*oh Deoris!*" The child collapsed in bitter sobbing.

"Demira, no!"

Demira made an effort to stifle her tears, murmuring, "You do believe me—you will not mock me?"

Deoris rocked her back and forth like a baby. "No, no, darling, no," she soothed. She knew very well what Demira meant. Outside the Grey Temple, Demira and her like were scorned as harlots or worse; but Deoris, who had lived in the Grey Temple, knew that such as Demira were held in high honor and respect, for she and her kind were sacred, indispensible, under protection of the highest Adepts. The thought of a *saji* being raped by an unknown was unthinkable, fantastic ... Almost unbelieving, Deoris asked, "Have you *no* idea who he was?"

"No—oh, I should have told Riveda, I should have told, but I couldn't, I just couldn't! After the—the Black-robe went away, I—I just lay there, crying and crying, I couldn't stop myself, I—it was Riveda who heard me, he came and found me there. He was ... for once he was kind, he picked me up and held me, and—and scolded me until I stopped crying. He—he tried to make me tell him what had happened, but I—I was afraid he wouldn't believe me ..."

Deoris let Demira go, remaining as still as if she had been turned to a statue. Scraps of a half-heard conversation had returned to float through her mind; her intuition now turned them to knowledge, and almost automatically she whispered the invocation, *"Mother Caratra! Guard her,"* for the first time in years.

It couldn't be, it simply was not possible, not thinkable . . . She sat motionless, afraid her face would betray her to the child.

At last Deoris said, frozenly, "But you have told Maleina, child? Surely you know she would protect you. I think she would kill with her own hands anyone who harmed you or caused you pain."

Demira shook her head mutely; only after several moments did she whisper, "I am afraid of Maleina. I came to you because—because of Domaris. She has influence with Rajasta . . . When last the Black-robes came into our temple, there was much terror and death, and now, if they have returned—the Guardians should know of it. And Domaris is—is so kind, and beautiful—she might have pity, even on me—"

"I will tell Domaris when I can," Deoris promised, her lips stiff; but conflict tore at her. "Demira, you must not expect too much."

"Oh, you are good, Deoris! Deoris, how I love you!" Demira clung to the older girl, her eyes bright with tears. "And Deoris, if Riveda must know—will you tell him? He will allow you anything, but no one else dares approach him now, since you left us no one dares speak to him unless he undresses them, and even then . . ." Demira broke off. "He was kind, when he found me, but I was so afraid."

Deoris stroked the little girl's shoulder gently, and her own face grew stern. Her last shred of doubt vanished. *Riveda heard her crying? In a sealed sound-chamber? That I'll believe when the sun shines at midnight!*

"Yes," said Deoris grimly, "I will talk to Riveda."

III

"She did not even guess, Deoris. I did not mean that you should know, either, but since you are so shrewd, yes, I admit it." Riveda's voice was as deep and harsh as winter surf; in the same icy bass he went on, "Should you seek to tell her, I—Deoris, much as you mean to me, I think I would kill you first!"

"Take heed lest you be the one killed," Deoris said coldly. "Suppose Maleina makes the same wise guess I did?"

"Maleina!" Riveda practically spat the woman Adept's name. "She did what she could to ruin the child—nevertheless, I am not a monster, Deoris. What Demira does not know will not torment her. It is—unfortunate that she knows I am her father; fool that I was to let it be guessed even in the Grey Temple. I will bear the responsibility; it is better that Demira know nothing more than she does now."

Sickened, Deoris cried out, "And this you will confess to me?"

Slowly, Riveda nodded. "I know now that Demira was begotten and reared for this one purpose alone. Otherwise, why should I have stretched out my hand to save her from squalling to death on the city wall? I knew not what I did, not then. But is it not miraculous, you see, how all things fall together to have meaning? The girl is worthless for anything else—she made Karahama hate me, just by being born." And for the first time Deoris sensed a weak spot in the Adept's icy armor, but he went on swiftly, "But now you see how it all makes a part of the great pattern? I did not know when she was born, but Karahama's blood is one with yours, and so is Demira's, that strain of the Priest's Line, sensitive—and so even this unregarded nothing shall serve some part in the Great work."

"Do you care for nothing else?" Deoris looked at Riveda as if he were a stranger; at this moment he seemed as alien as if he had come from far beyond the unknown seas. This talk of patterns, as if he had planned that Demira should be born for this . . . was he mad, then? Always Deoris had believed that the strangeness of his talk hid some great and lofty purpose which she was too young and ignorant to understand. But this, this she *did* understand for the corrupt madness it was, and of this he spoke as if it were more of the same high purpose. Was it all madness and illusion then, had she been dragged into insanity and corruption under the belief that she was the chosen of the great Adept? Her mouth was trembling; she fought not to break down.

Riveda's mouth curved in a brutal smile. "Why, you little fool, I believe you're jealous!"

Mutely, Deoris shook her head. She did not trust herself to speak. She turned away, but Riveda caught her arm with a strong hand. "Are you going to tell Demira this?" he demanded.

"To what purpose?" Deoris asked coldly, "To make her sick, as I am? No, I will keep your secret. Now take your hands from me!"

His eyes widened briefly, and his hand dropped

to his side. "Deoris," he said in a more persuasive voice, "you have always understood me before."

Tears gathered at her eyelids. "Understood you? No, never. Nor have you been like this before! This is—sorcery, distortion—black magic!"

Riveda bit off his first answer unspoken, and only muttered, rather despondently, "Well, call me Black Magician then, and have done with it." Then, with the tenderness which was so rare, he drew her stiff and unresponsive form to him. "Deoris," he said, and it was like a plea, "you have always been my strength. Don't desert me now! Has Domaris so quickly turned you against me?"

She could not answer; she was fighting back tears.

"Deoris, the thing is done, and I stand by it. It is too late to crawl out of it now, and repentance would not undo it in any case. Perhaps it was— unwise; it may have been cruel. *But it is done.* Deoris, you are the only one I dare to trust: make Demira your care, Deoris, let her be your child. Her mother has long forsworn her, and I—I have no rights anymore, if ever I did." He stopped, his face twisted. Lightly he touched the fearful scars hidden by her clothing; then his hands strayed gently to her waist, to touch the wooden links of the carved symbolic girdle with a curiously tentative gesture. He raised his eyes, and she saw in his face a painful look of question and fear which she did not yet understand as he murmured, "You do not yet know—the Gods save you, the Gods protect you all! I have forfeited their protection; I have been cruel to you—Deoris, help me! Help me, help me—"

And in a moment the melting of his icy reserve was complete—and with it fled all Deoris's anger. Choking, she flung her arms about him, saying half incoherently, "I will, Riveda, always—I will!"

Chapter Two

THE BLASPHEMY

I

Somewhere in the night the sound of a child's sudden shrill wailing shredded the silence into ribbons, and Deoris raised her head from the pillow, pressing her hands to her aching eyes. The room was filled with heavy blackness barred by shuttered moonlight. She was so used to the silence of the *saji* courts—she had been dreaming—then memory came back. She was not in the Grey Temple, nor even in Riveda's austere habitation, but in Domaris's home; it must be Micail crying . . .

She slid from the bed, and barefoot, crossed the narrow hall into her sister's room. At the sound of the opening door, Domaris raised her head; she was half-clad, her unbound hair a coppery mist streaming over the little boy who clung to her, still sobbing.

"Deoris, darling, did he wake you? I'm sorry." She stroked Micail's tangled curls as she rocked the child gently against her shoulder. "There now, there now, hush, hush you," she murmured.

Micail hiccoughed sleepily with the subsidence of his sobs. His head dropped onto Domaris's shoulder, then perked up momentarily. "De'ris," he murmured.

The younger girl came quickly to him. "Domaris, let me take Micail, he's too heavy for you to lift now," she rebuked softly. Domaris demurred, but gave the heavy child into her sister's arms. Deoris looked down at the drooping eyes, darkly blue, and the smudge of freckles across the turned-up nose.

"He will be very like ..." she murmured; but Domaris put out her hands as if to ward off a physical blow, and the younger woman swallowed Micon's name. "Where shall I put him?"

"Into my bed; I'll take him to sleep with me, and perhaps he will be quiet. I am sorry he woke you, Deoris. You look—so tired." Domaris gazed into her sister's face, pale and pinched, with a strange look of weary lethargy. "You are not well, Deoris."

"Well enough," said Deoris indifferently. "You worry too much. You're not in the best health yourself," she accused, suddenly frightened. With the eyes of a trained Healer-priestess, Deoris now saw what her self-absorption had hidden: how thin Domaris was in spite of her pregnancy; how the fine bones of her face grew sharp beneath the white skin, how swollen and blue the veins in her forehead were, and those in her thin white hands ...

Domaris shook her head, but the weight of her unborn child was heavy on her, and her drawn features betrayed the lie. She knew it and smiled, running her hands down her swollen sides with a resigned shrug. "Ill-will and pregnancy grow never less," she quoted lightly. "See—Micail's already asleep."

Deoris would not be distracted. "Where is Arvath?" she asked firmly.

Domaris sighed. "He is not here, he . . ." Her thin face crimsoned, the color flooding into the neck of her shapeless robe. "Deoris, I—I have fulfilled my bargain now! Nor have I complained, nor stinted duty! Nor did I use what Elis . . ." She bit her lip savagely, and went on, "This will be the son he desires! And that should content him!"

Deoris, though she knew nothing of Mother Ysouda's warning, remember her own; and intuition told her the rest. "He is cruel to you, Domaris?"

"The fault is mine, I think I have killed kindness in the man. Enough! I should not complain. But his love is like a punishment! I cannot endure it anymore!" The color had receded from her face, leaving a deathly pallor.

Deoris mercifully turned away, bending to tuck a cover around Micail. "Why don't you let Elara take him nights?" she protested. "You'll get no sleep at all!"

Domaris smiled. "I would sleep still less if he were away from me," she said, and looked tenderly at her son. "Remember when I could not understand why Elis kept Lissa so close to her? Besides, Elara attends even me only in the days, now. Since her marriage I would have freed her entirely, but she says she will not leave me to a strange woman while I am like this." Her laugh was a tiny ghost of its normal self. "*Her* child will be born soon after mine! Even in that she serves me!"

Deoris said sulkily, "I think every woman in this Temple must be bearing a child!" With a guilty start, she silenced herself.

Domaris appeared not to notice. "Childbearing is a disease easily caught," she quoted lightly, then straightened and came close to her sister. "Don't go, Deoris—stay and talk to me a little. I've missed you."

"If you want me," Deoris said ungraciously; then, penitent, she came to Domaris and the two sat on a low divan.

The older woman smiled. "I always want you, little sister."

"I'm not little anymore," Deoris said irritably, tossing her head. "Why must you treat me like a baby?"

Domaris suppressed a laugh and lifted her sister's slender, beringed hand. "Perhaps—because you were my baby, before Micail was born." Her glance fell on the narrow, carven girdle with Deoris wore cinctured loosely over her night-dress. "Deoris, what is that?" she asked softly. "I don't believe I've seen you wearing it before."

"Only a girdle."

"How stupid of me," said Domaris dryly. Her slim fingers touched the crimson cord which knotted the links together, strangely twined through the carven wooden symbols. Clumsily, she bent to examine it more closely—and with a sharply indrawn breath, counted the links. The cord, twined into oddly knotted patterns, was treble; thrice sevenfold the flat carved emblems. It was beautiful, and yet, somehow . . .

"*Deoris!*" she breathed, her voice holding sudden sharpness. "Did Riveda give you *this*?"

Scared by her tone, Deoris went sulky and defensive. "Why not?"

"Why not indeed?" Domaris's words were edged with ice; her hand closed hard around Deoris's thin wrist. "And why should he bind you with a—a thing like that? Deoris, answer me!"

"He has the right . . ."

"No lover has that right, Deoris."

"He is *not*—"

Domaris shook her head. "You lie, Deoris," she said wearily. "If your lover were any other man, he would kill Riveda before he let him put that—that *thing* on you!" She made a queer sound that was almost a sob. "Please—don't lie to me anymore, Deoris. Do you think you can hide it forever? How long must I pretend not to see that you are carrying a child beneath that—that—" Her voice failed her. How pitifully simple Deoris was, as if by denying a fact she could wish it out of existence!

Deoris twisted her hand free, staring at the floor, her face white and pinched. Guilt, embarrassment and fear seemed to mingle in her dark eyes, and Domaris took the younger girl in her arms.

"Deoris, Deoris, don't look like that! I'm not blaming *you!*"

Deoris was rigid in her sister's kind arms. "Domaris, believe me, I didn't."

Domaris tipped back the little face until her sister's eyes, dark as crushed violets, met her own. "The father is Riveda," she said quietly; and this time, Deoris did not contradict her. "I like this not even a little. Something is very wrong, Deoris, or you would not be acting this way. You are not a child, you are not ignorant, you have had the same teaching as I, and more in this particular matter . . . you *know*—listen to me, Deoris! You know you need not have conceived a child save at your own and Riveda's wish," she finished inexorably, although Deoris sobbed and squirmed to get free of her hands and her condemning eyes. "Deoris—no, look at me, tell me the truth—did he force you, Deoris?"

"*No!*" And now the denial had the strength of truth. "I gave myself to Riveda of my free will, and he is not by law celibate!"

"This is so; but why then does he not take you to wife, or at the very least acknowledge your child?" Domaris demanded, stern-faced. "There is no need of this, Deoris. You bear the child of óne of the great Adepts—no matter what I may think of him. You should walk in honor before all, not skulk girdled with a triple cord, forced to lie even to me. Enslaved! Does he know?"

"I—I think. . . ."

"You *think!*" Domaris's voice was as brittle as ice. "Be assured, little sister, if he does *not* know, he very soon shall! Child, child—the man wrongs you!"

"You—you have no right to *interfere!*" With a sudden burst of strength, Deoris twisted free of her sister, glaring angrily though she made no move to go.

"I do have the right to protect you, little sister."

"If I choose to bear Riveda's child. . . ."

"Then Riveda must assume his responsibility," said Domaris sharply. Her hands went out to the girdle at her sister's waist again. "As for this foul thing . . ." Her fingers shrank from the emblems even as they plucked at the knotted cords. "I am going to burn it! My sister is no man's slave!"

Deoris sprang up, Clutching at the links. "Now you go too far!" she raged, and seized the woman's wrist in strong hands, holding Domaris away from her. "You shall not touch it!"

"Deoris, I *insist!*"

"No, I say!" Though she looked frail, Deoris was a strong girl, and too angry to care what she did. She flung Domaris away from her with a furious blow that made the older woman cry out with pain. "Let me alone!"

Domaris dropped her hands—then gasped as her knees gave way.

Deoris quickly caught her sister in her arms, just in time to save her from falling heavily. "Domaris," she begged, in swift repentance, "Domaris, forgive me. Did I hurt you?"

Domaris, with repressed anger, freed herself from her sister's supporting arm and lowered herself slowly onto the divan.

Deoris began to sob. "I didn't mean to hurt you, you know I'd never. . . ."

"How can I know that!" Domaris flung at her, almost despairingly. "I have never forgotten what you . . ." She stopped, breathing hard. Micon had made her swear never to speak of that, impressing it on her repeatedly that Deoris had not had, would never have, the slightest memory of what she had almost done. At the stricken misery in Deoris's eyes, Domaris said, more gently, "I know you would never harm me willingly. But if you hurt my child I could not forgive you again: Now—*give me that damned thing!*" And she advanced on Deoris purposefully, her face one of disgust as she unfastened the cords, as if she touched something unclean.

The thin nightdress fell away as the girdle was loosened, and Domaris, putting out a hand to draw the folds together, stopped—jerked her hand back involuntarily from the bared breast. The girdle fell unheeded to the floor.

"Deoris!" she cried out in horror. "Let me see—no, I said *let me see!*" Her voice tightened commandingly as Deoris tried to pull the loosened robe over the betrayal of those naked scars. Domaris drew the folds aside; gently touched the raised sigil that gaped raggedly red across both rounded breasts, running swollen and raw like a jagged parody of a lightning-flash down the tender sides. "Oh, Deoris!" Domaris gasped in dismay. "Oh, little sister!"

"No, please, Domaris!" The girl pulled feverishly at her loosened clothing. "It's nothing . . ." But her frantic efforts at concealment only confirmed Domaris's worst suspicions.

"Nothing, indeed!" said Domaris wrathfully. "I suppose you will try to tell me that those are ordinary burns? More of Riveda's work, I suppose!" She loosed her grip on the girl's arm, staring somberly at her. "Riveda's work. Always Riveda," the whispered, looking down at the cowering girl . . . Then, slowly, deliberately, she raised her arms in invocation, and her voice, low and quiveringly clear, rang through the silent room: "*Be he accurst!*"

Deoris started back, raising her hands to her mouth as she stared in horror.

"Be he accurst!" Domaris repeated. "Accurst in the lightning that reveals his work, accurst in thunder that will lay it low! Be he accurst in the waters of the flood that shall sweep his life sterile! Be he cursed by sun and moon and earth, rising and setting, waking and sleeping, living and dying, here and hereafter! Be he accurst beyond life and beyond death and beyond redemption—forever!"

Deoris choked on harsh sobs, staggering away from her sister as if she were herself the target of Domaris's curses. "No!" she whimpered, "no!"

Domaris paid her no heed, but went on, "Accurst be he sevenfold, a hundredfold, until his sin be wiped out, his karma undone! Be he cursed, he and his seed, unto the sons and the son's sons and their sons unto eternity! Be he accurst in his last hour— and my life ransom for his, lest I see this undone!"

With a shriek, Deoris crumped to the floor and lay as if dead; but Micail only twisted slightly beneath his blanket as he slept.

II

When Deoris drifted up out of her brief spell of unconsciousness, she found Domaris kneeling beside her, gently examining the *dorje* scars on her breasts. Deoris closed her eyes, her mind still half blank, poised between relief, terror, and nothingness.

"Another experiment which he could not control?" asked Domaris, not unkindly.

Deoris looked up at her older sister and murmured, "It was not all his fault—he himself was hurt far worse. . . ." Her words had pronounced a final indictment, but Deoris did not realize the fact.

Domaris's horror was evident, however. "The man has you bewitched! Will you always defend . . . ?" She broke off, begging almost desperately, "Listen, you must—a stop must and shall be put to this, lest others suffer! If you cannot—then you are incapable of acting like an adult, and others must intervene to protect you! Gods, Deoris, are you insane, that you would have allowed—this?"

"What right have you—" Deoris faltered as her sister drew away.

"My sworn duty," Deoris rebuked sternly, in a very low voice. "Even if you were not my sister— did you not *know?* I am Guardian here."

Deoris, speechless, could only stare at Domaris; and it was looking at a complete stranger who only resembled her sister. An icy rage showed in Domaris's forced stillness, in her brittle voice and the smoldering sparks behind her eyes—a cold wrath all the more dreadful for its composure.

"Yet I must consider you in this, Deoris," Domaris went on, tight-lipped.

"You—and your child."

"Riveda's," said Deoris dully. "What—what are you going to do?" she whispered.

Domaris looked down somberly, and her hands trembled as she fastened the robes about her little sister once more. She hoped she would not have to use what she knew against the sister she still loved more than anyone or anything, except her own children, Micail and the unborn. . . . But Domaris felt weak. The treble cord, and the awful control it implied; the fearful form of the scars on Deoris's body; she bent, awkwardly, and picked up the girdle from the floor where it lay almost forgotten.

"I will do what I must," Domaris said. "I do not want to take from you something you seem to prize, but . . ." Her face was white and her knuckles white as she gripped the carven links, hating the symbols and what she considered the vile use to which they had been put. "Unless you swear not to wear it again, I will burn the damned thing!"

"No!" Deoris sprang to her feet, a feverish sparkle in her eyes. "I won't let you! Domaris, give it to me!"

"I would rather see you dead than made a tool—and to such use!" Domaris's face might have been chiselled in stone, and her voice, too, had a rock-like quality as the words clanged harshly in the air. The skin of her face had stretched taut over her cheekbones, and even her lips were colorless.

Deoris stretched imploring hands—then shrank from the clear, contemptuous judgment in Domaris's eyes.

"You have been taught as I have," the older woman said. "How could you permit it, Deoris? You that Micon loved—you that he treated almost as a disciple! You, who could have . . ." With a despairing gesture, Domaris broke off and turned away, moving clumsily toward the brazier in the near corner. Deoris, belatedly realizing her intention, sprang after her—but Domaris had already thrust the girdle deep into the live coals. The tinder-dry wood blazed up with a flickering and a roar as the cord writhed like a white-hot snake. In seconds the thing was only ashes.

Domaris turned around again and saw her sister gazing helplessly into the flames, weeping as if she saw Riveda himself burning there—and at the sight, much of her hard, icy anger melted away. "Deoris," she said, "Deoris, tell me—you have been to the Dark Shrine? To the Sleeping God?"

"Yes," Deoris whispered.

Domaris needed to know no more; the pattern of

the girdle had told her the rest. *Well for Deoris that I have acted in time! Fire cleanses!*

"Domaris!" It was a pathetic, horrified plea.

"Oh, my little sister, little cat . . ." Domaris was all protective love now, and crooning, she took the trembling girl into her arms again.

Deoris hid her face on her sister's shoulder. With the burning of the girdle, she had begun to dimly see certain implications, as if a fog had lifted from her mind; she could not cease from thinking of the things that had taken place in the Crypt—and now she knew that none of it had been dream.

"I'm afraid, Domaris! I'm so afraid—I wish I were dead! Will they—will they burn me, too?"

Domaris's teeth gritted with sudden, sick fear. For Riveda there could be no hope for clemency; and Deoris, even if innocent—and of that, Domaris had grave doubts—bore the seed of blasphemy, begotten in sacrilege and fostered beneath that hideous treble symbol—*A child I myself have cursed!* And with this realization, an idea came to her; and Domaris did not stop to count the cost, but acted to comfort and protect this child who was her sister—even to protect that other child, whose black beginnings need not, perhaps, end in utter darkness. . . .

"Deoris," she said quietly, taking her sister's hand, "ask me no questions. I can protect you, and I will, but do not ask me to explain what I must do!"

Deoris swallowed hard, and somehow forced herself to murmur her promise.

Domaris, in a last hesitation, glanced at Micail. But the child still sprawled in untidy, baby sleep:

Domaris discarded her misgivings and turned her attention once more to Deoris.

A low, half-sung note banished the brilliance from the room, which gave way to a golden twilight; in this soft radiance the sisters faced one another, Deoris slim and young, the fearful scars angry across her breasts, her coming motherhood only a shadow in the fall of her light robes—and Domaris, her beautiful body distorted and big, but still somehow holding something of the ageless calm of what she invoked. Clasping her hands, she lifted them slowly before her; parted and lowered them in an odd, ceremonious manner. Something in the gesture and movement, some instinctive memory, perhaps, or intuition, struck the half-formed question from Deoris's parted lips.

"Be far from us, all profane," Domaris murmured in her clear soprano. "Be far from us, all that lives in evil. Be far from where we stand, for here has Eternity cast its shadow. Depart, ye mists and vapors, ye stars of darkness, begone; stand ye afar from the print of Her footsteps and the shadow of Her veil. Here have we taken shelter, under the curtain of the night and within the circle of Her own white stars."

She let her arms drop to her sides; then they moved together to the shrine to be found in every sleeping-room within the Temple precincts. With difficulty, Domaris knelt—and divining her intention, Deoris knelt quickly at her side and, taking the taper from her sister's hand, lighted the perfumed oil of devotion. Although she meant to honor her promise not to question, Deoris was beginning to guess what Domaris was doing. Years ago she had fled from a suggestion of this rite;

now, facing unthinkable fear, her child's immi-
nence a faint presence in her womb, Deoris could
still find a moment to be grateful that it was with
Domaris that she faced this, and not some woman
or priestess whom she must fear. By taking up her
own part, by touching the light to the incense
which opened the gates to ritual, she accepted it;
and the brief, delicate pressure of Domaris's long
narrow fingers on hers showed that the older
woman was aware of the acceptance, and of what
it meant ... It was only a fleeting touch; then
Domaris signalled to her to rise.

Standing, Domaris stretched a hand to her sister
yet again, to touch her brow, lips, breasts, and—
quided by Domaris—Deoris repeated the sign. Then
Domaris took her sister in her arms and held her
close for a moment.

"Deoris, repeat my words," she commanded
softly—and Deoris, awed, but in some secret part
of her being feeling the urge to break away, to
laugh, to scream aloud and shatter the gathering
mood, only closed her eyes for a moment.

Domaris's low voice intoned quiet words; Deoris's
voice was a thin echo, without the assurance that
was in her sister's.

"Here we two, women and sisters, pledge thee,
Mother of Life—
Woman—and more than woman . . .
Sister—and more than sister . . .
Here where we stand in darkness . . .
And under the shadow of death . . .
We call on thee, O Mother . . .
By thine own sorrows, O woman . . .
By the life we bear . . .

Together before thee, O Mother, O Woman Eternal . . .
And this be our plea. . . ."

Now even the golden light within the room was gone, extinguished without any signal from them. The streaming moonlight itself seemed to vanish, and it seemed to the half-terrified, half-fascinated Deoris that they stood in the center of a vast and empty space, upon nothingness. All the universe had been extinguished, save for a single, flickering flame which glowed like a tiny, pulsating eye. Was it the brazier fire? The reflection of a vaster light which she sensed but could not see? Domaris's arms, still close about her, were the only reality anywhere, the only real and living thing in the great spaces, and the words Domaris intoned softly, like spun fibers of silken sound, mantras which wove a silvery net of magic within the mystical darkness. . . .

The flame, whatever it was, glowed and darkened, glowed and darkened, with the hypnotic intensity of some vast heart's beating, in time to the murmured invocation:

"May the fruit of our lives be bound and sealed
To thee, O Mother, O Woman Eternal,
Who holdest the inmost life of each of thy
*   daughters*
Between the hands upon her heart. . . ."

And there was more, which Deoris, frightened and exalted, could scarce believe she heard. This was the most sacred of rituals; they vowed themselves to the Mother-Goddess from incarnation to incarnation, from age to age, throughout eternity, with the lesser vow that bound them and their children inextricably to one another—a karmic knot, life to life, forever.

Carried away by her emotion, Domaris went much further into the ritual than she had realized, far further than she had intended—and at last an invisible Hand signed them both with an ancient seal. Full Initiates of the most ancient and holy of all the rites in the Temple or in the world, they were protected by and sealed to the Mother—not Caratra, but the Greater Mother, the Dark Mother behind all men and all rites and all created things. The faint flickerings deepened, swelled, became great wings of flame which lapped out to surround them with radiance.

The two women sank to their knees, then lay prostrate, side by side. Deoris felt her sister's child move against her body, and the faint, dreamlike stirring of her own unborn child, and in a flutter of insensate, magical prescience, she guessed some deeper involvement beyond this life and beyond this time, a ripple moving out into the turbulent sea which must involve more than these two . . . and the effulgent glory about them became a voice; not a voice that they could hear, but something more direct, something they felt with every nerve, every atom of their bodies.

"Thou art mine, then, from age to age, while Time endures . . . while Life brings forth Life. Sisters, and more than sisters . . . women, and more than women . . . know this, together, by the Sign I give you. . . ."

III

The fire had burned out, and the room was very dark and still. Deoris, recovering a little, raised herself and looked at Domaris, and saw that a curious radiance still shone from the swollen breasts and burdened body. Awe and reverence dawned in her anew and she bent her head, turning her eyes on herself—and yes, there too, softly glowing, the Sign of the Goddess. . . .

She got to her knees and remained there, silent, absorbed in prayer and wonder. The visible glow soon was gone; indeed, Deoris could not be certain that she had ever seen it. Perhaps, her consciousness exalted and steeped in ritual, she had merely caught a glimpse of some normally invisible reality beyond her nowness and her present self.

The night was waning when Domaris stirred at last, coming slowly back to consciousness from the trance of ecstasy, dragging herself upright with a little moan of pain. Labor was close on her, she knew it—knew also that she had brought it closer by what she had done. Not even Deoris knew so well the effects of ceremonial magic upon the complex nervous currents of a woman's body. Lingering awe and reverence helped her ignore the warning pains as Deoris's arms helped her upright—but for an instant Domaris pressed her forehead against her sister's shoulder, weak and not caring if it showed.

"May my son never hurt anyone else," she whispered, "as he hurts me. . . ."

"He'll never again have the opportunity," Deoris said, but her lightness was false. She was acutely conscious that she had been careless and added to her sister's pain; knew that words of contrition could not help. Her abnormal sensitivity to Domaris was almost physical, and she helped her sister with a comprehending tenderness in her young hands.

There was no reproach in Domaris's weary glance as she closed her hand around her sister's wrist. "Don't cry, kitten." Once seated on the divan, she stared into the dead embers of the brazier for several minutes before saying, quietly, "Deoris, later you shall know what I have done—and why. Are you afraid now?"

"Only—a little—for you." Again, it was not entirely a true statement, for Domaris's words warned Deoris that there was more to come. Domaris was bound to action by some rigid code of her own, and nothing Deoris could say or do would alter that; Domaris was in quiet, deadly earnest.

"I must leave you now, Deoris. Stay here until I return—promise me! You will do that for me, my little sister?" She drew Deoris to her with an almost savage possessiveness, held her and kissed her fiercely. "More than my sister, now! Be at peace," she said, and went from the room, moving swiftly despite her heaviness.

Deoris knelt, immobile, watching the closed door. She knew better than Domaris imagined what was encompassed by the rite into which she had been admitted; she had heard of it, guessed at its power—but had never dared dream that one day she herself might be a part of it!

Can this, she asked herself, *be what gave Maleina entry where none could deny her? What permitted Karahama—a saji, one of the no-people—to serve the Temple of Caratra? A power that redeems the damned?*

Knowing the answer, Deoris was no longer afraid. The radiance was gone, but the comfort remained, and she fell asleep there, kneeling, her head in her arms.

IV

Outside, clutched again with the warning fingers of her imminent travail, Domaris leaned against the wall. The fit passed quickly, and she straightened, to hurry along the corridor, silent and unobserved. Yet again she was forced to halt, bending double to the relentless pain that clawed at her loins; moaning softly, she waited for the spasm to pass. It took her some time to reach the seldom-used passage that gave on a hidden doorway.

She paused, forcing her breath to come evenly. She was about to violate an ancient sanctuary—to risk defilement beyond death. Every tenet of the hereditary priesthood of which she was product and participant screamed at her to turn back.

The legend of the Sleeping God was a thing of horror. Long ago—so ran the story—the Dark One had been chained and prisoned, until the day he should waken and ravage time and space alike with unending darkness and devastation, unto the total destruction of all that was or could ever be. . . .

Domaris knew better. It was power that had been sealed there, though—and she suspected that the power had been invoked and unleashed, and this made her afraid as she had never dreamed of being afraid; frightened for herself and the child she carried, for Deoris and the child conceived in that dark shrine, and for her people and everything that they stood for. . . .

She set her teeth, and sweat ran cold from her armpits. "*I must!*" she whispered aloud; and giv-

ing herself no more time to think, she opened the
door and slipped through, shutting it quickly behind her.

She stood at the top of an immense stairwell
leading down ... and down ... and down, grey
steps going down between grey walls in a grey
haze beneath her, to which there seemed no end.
She set her foot on the first step; holding to the
rail, she began the journey ... down.

It was slow, chill creeping. Her heaviness dragged
at her. Pain twisted her at intervals. The thud of
her sandalled feet jerked at her burdened belly
with wrenching pulls. She moaned aloud at each
brief torture—but went on, step down, thud, step
down, thud, in senseless, dull repetition. She tried
to count the steps, in an effort to prevent her mind
from dredging up all the half-forgotten, awful stories she had heard of this place, to keep herself
from wondering if she did, indeed, know better
than to believe old fairy-tales. She gave it up after
the hundred and eighty-first step.

Now she was no longer holding the rail, but
reeling and scraping against the wall; again pain
seized her, doubled and twisted her, forcing her to
her knees. The greyness was shot through with
crimson as she straightened, bewildered and en-
raged, almost forgetting what grim purpose had
brought her to this immemorial mausoleum. . . .

She caught at the rain with both hands, fighting
for balance as her face twisted terribly and she
sobbed aloud, hating the sanity that drove her on
and down.

"Oh Gods! No, no, take me instead!" she whispered, and clung there desperately for a moment;

then, her face impassive again, holding herself
grimly upright, she let the desperate need to do
what must be done carry her down, into the pallid
greyness.

Chapter Three

DARK DAWN

I

The sudden, brief jar of falling brought Deoris sharply upright, staring into the darkness in sudden fear. Micail still slept in a chubby heap, and in the shadowy room, now lighted with the pale pink of dawn, there was no sound but the little boy's soft breathing; but like a distant echo Deoris seemed to hear a cry and a palpable silence, the silence of the tomb, of the Crypt.

Domaris! Where was Domaris? She had not returned. With sudden and terrible awareness, Deoris *knew* where Domaris was! She did not pause even to throw a garment over her nightclothes; yet she glanced unsurely at Micail. Surely Domaris's slaves would hear if he woke and cried—and there was no time to waste! She ran out of the room and fled downward, through the deserted garden.

Blindly, dizzily, she ran as if sheer motion could ward off her fear. Her heart pounded frantically, and her sides sent piercing ribbons of pain through her whole body—but she did not stop until she stood in the shadow of the great pyramid. Holding her hands hard against the hurt in her sides, she was shocked at last into a wide-awake sanity by the cold winds of dawn.

A lesser priest, only a dim figure in luminous robes, paced slowly toward her. "Woman," he said severely, "it is forbidden to walk here. Go your way in peace."

Deoris raised her face to him, unafraid. "I am Talkannon's daughter," she said in a clear and ringing voice. "Is the Guardian Rajasta within?"

The priest's tone and expression changed as he recognized her. "He is there, young sister," he said courteously, "but it is forbidden to interrupt the vigil—" He fell silent in amazement; the sun, as they talked, had crept around the pyramid's edge, to fall upon them, revealing Deoris's unbound hair, her disarranged and insufficient clothing.

"It is life or death!" Deoris pleaded, desperately. *"I must see him!"*

"My child—I do not have the authority. . . ."

"Oh, you fool!" Deoris raged, and with a catlike movement, she dodged under his startled arm and fled up the gleaming stone steps. She struggled a moment with the unfamiliar workings of the great brazen door; twitched aside the shielding curtain, and stepped into brilliant light.

At the faint whisper of her bare feet—for the door moved silently despite its weight—Rajasta turned from the altar. Disregarding his warning gesture, Deoris ran to fling herself on her knees before him.

"Rajasta, Rajasta!"

With cold distaste, the Priest of Light bent and raised her, eyeing the wild disarray of her clothing and hair sternly. "Deoris," he said, "what are you doing here, you know the law—and why like this! You're only half dressed, have you gone completely mad?"

Indeed, there was some justification for his question, for Deoris met his gaze with a feverish face, and her voice was practically a babble as her last scraps of composure deserted her. "Domaris! Domaris! She must have gone to the Crypt—to the Dark Shrine."

"You *have* taken leave of your senses!" Unceremoniously, Rajasta half thrust her to a further distance from the altar. "*You know* you may not stand here like this!"

"I know, yes, I know, but listen to me! I feel it, I know it! She burned the girdle and made me tell her . . ." Deoris stopped, her face drawn with conflict and guilt, for she had suddenly realized that she was now of her own volition betraying her sworn oath to Riveda! And yet—she was bound to Domaris by an oath stronger still.

Rajasta gripped her shoulder, demanding, "What sort of gibberish is this!" Then, seeing that the girl was trembling so violently that she could hardly stand upright, he put an arm gingerly about her and helped her to a seat. "Now tell me sensibly, if you can, what you are talking about," he said, in a voice that held almost equal measures of compassion and contempt, "if you are talking about anything at all! I suppose Domaris has discovered that you were Riveda's *saji*."

"I wasn't! I never was!" Deoris flared; then said, wearily, "Oh, that doesn't matter, you don't understand, you wouldn't believe me anyhow! What matters is this: Domaris has gone to the Dark Shrine."

Rajasta's face was perceptibly altering as he began to guess what she was trying to say. "What—but why?"

"She saw—a girdle I was wearing, that Riveda gave me—and the scars of the *dorje.*"

Almost before she had spoken the word, Rajasta moved like lightning to clamp his hand across her lips. "Say that not here!" he commanded, white-faced. Deoris collapsed, crying, her head in her arms, and Rajasta seized her shoulders and forced her to look at him. "Listen to me, girl! For Domaris's sake—for your own—yes, even for Riveda's! *A girdle?* And the—that word you spoke; what of that? *What is this all about?*"

Deoris dared not keep silent, dared not lie—and under his deep-boring eyes, she stammered, "A treble cord—knotted—wooden links carved with . . ." She gestured.

Rajasta caught her wrist and held it immobile. "Keep your disgusting Grey-robe signs for the Grey Temple! But even there that would not have been allowed! You must deliver it to me!"

"Domaris burned it."

"Thank the Gods for that," said Rajasta bleakly. "Riveda has gone among the Black-robes?" But it was a statement, not a question. "Who else?"

"Reio-ta—I mean, the chela." Deoris was crying and stammering; there was a powerful block in her mind, inhibiting speech—but the concentrated power of Rajasta's will forced her. The Priest of Light was well aware that this use of his powers had only the most dubious ethical justification, and regretted the necessity; but he knew that all of

Riveda's spells would be pitted against him, and if he was to safeguard others as his Guardian's vows commanded, he dared not spare the girl. Deoris was almost fainting from the hypnotic pressure Rajasta exerted against the bond of silence Riveda had forced on her will. Slowly, syllable by syllable at times, at best sentence by reluctant sentence, she told Rajasta enough to damn Riveda tenfold.

The Priest of Light was merciless; he had to be. He was hardly more than a pair of bleak eyes and toneless, pitiless voice, commanding, "Go on. What—and how—and who . . ."

"I was sent over the Closed Places—as a channel of power—and when I could no longer serve, then Larmin—Riveda's son—took my place as scryer. . . ."

"Wait!" Rajasta leaped to his feet, pulling the girl upright with him. "By the Central Sun! You are lying, or out of your senses! A boy cannot serve in the Closed Places, only a virgin girl, or a woman prepared by ritual, or—or—a boy cannot, unless he is . . ." Rajasta was pasty-faced now, stammering himself, almost incoherent. "Deoris. *What was done to Larmin?*"

Deoris trembled before Rajasta's awful eyes, cowering before the surge of violent, seemingly uncontrollable wrath and disgust that surged across the Guardian's face. He shook her, roughly.

"Answer, me, girl! *Did he castrate the child?*"

She did not have to answer. Rajasta abruptly took his hands from her as if contaminated by her presence, and when she collapsed he let her fall heavily to the floor. He was physically sick with the knowledge.

Weeping, whimpering, Deoris moved a little toward him, and he spat, pushing her away with his sandalled foot. "Gods, Deoris—you of all people! Look at me if you dare—you that Micon called sister!"

The girl cringed at his feet, but there was no mercy in the Guardian's voice: "On your knees! On your knees before the shrine you have defiled— the Light you have darkened—the fathers you have shamed—the Gods you have forgotten!"

Rocking to and fro in anguished dread, Deoris could not see the compassion that suddenly blotted out the awful fury on Rajasta's face. He was not blind to the fact that Deoris had willingly risked all hope of clemency for herself in order to save Domaris—but it would take much penance to wipe out her crime. With a last, pitying look at the bent head, he turned and left the Temple. He was more shocked than angry; more sickened even than shocked. His maturity and experience foresaw what even Domaris had not seen.

He hastened down the steps of the pyramid, and the priest on guard sprang to attend him—then stopped, his mouth wide.

"Lord Guardian!"

"Go you," said Rajasta curtly, "with ten others, to take the Adept Riveda into custody, in my name. Put him in chains if need be."

"The Healer-priest, Lord? Riveda?" The guard was bug-eyed with disbelief. "The Adept of the Magicians—*in chains?*"

"The damned filthy sorcerer Riveda—Adept and *former* Healer!" With an effort, Rajasta lowered his hoarse voice to a normal volume. "Then go and find a boy, about eleven years old, called Larmin— Karahama's son."

Stiffly, the priest said, "Lord, with your pardon, the woman Karahama has no child."

Rajasta, impatient with this reminder of Temple etiquette which refused the *no-people* even a legal existence, said angrily, "You will find a boy of the Grey Temple who is called Larmin—and don't bother with that nonsense of pretending not to know who he is! Don't harm or frighten the boy, just keep him safely where he can be produced at a moment's notice—and where he can't be conveniently murdered to destroy evidence! Then find . . ." He paused. "Swear you will not reveal the names I speak!"

The priest made the holy sign. "I swear, Lord!"

"Find Ragamon the Elder and Cadamiri, and bid them summon the Guardians to meet here at high noon. Then seek the Arch-priest Talkannon, and say to him quietly that we have at last found evidence. No more—he will understand."

The priest hurried away, leaving for the first time in easily three centuries—the Temple of Light unattended. Rajasta, his face grim, broke into a run.

II

Just as Domaris had, he hesitated, uncertain, at the entrance to the concealed stairs. Was it wise, he wondered, to go alone? Should he not summon aid?

A rush of cool air stirred up from the long shaft beneath him; borne out of unfathomable spaces came a sound, almost a cry. Indredibly far down, dimmed and distorted by echo, it might have been the shriek of a bat, or the echoes of his own sighing breath—but Rajasta's hesitation was gone.

Down the long stairway he hurried, taking the steps two and three at a time, steadying himself now against one sheer wall, now against the shuddering railing. His steps clattered with desperate haste, waking hurried, clanging echoes—and he knew he warned away anyone below, but the time was past for stealth and silence. His throat was dry and his breath came in choking gasps, for he was not a young man and ever at his back loomed the nightmare need for haste that pushed him down and down the lightless stairs, down that grey and immemorial shaft through reverberating eternities that clutched at him with tattered cobweb fingers, his heels throwing up dust long, long undisturbed, to begrime the luminous white of his robes ... Down and down and down he went, until distance became a mockery.

He stumbled, nearly falling as the stairs abruptly ended. Staring dizzily about, trying to orient himself, Rajasta again felt the hopeless futility of his plight. He knew this place only from maps and the tales and writings of others. Yet, at last, he located the entrance to the great arched vault, though he was not sure of himself until he saw the monstrous sarcophagus, the eon-blackened altar, the shadowy Form swathed in veils of stone. But he saw no human being within the shrine, and for a moment Rajasta knew fear beyond comprehension, for not for Domaris but for himself ...

A moan rose to his ear, faint and directionless, magnified by the echoing darkness. Rajasta whirled, staring about him wildly, half mad from fear of what he might see. Again the moaning sounded, and this time Rajasta saw, dimly, a woman who lay crumpled, writhing, in the fiery shroud of her long hair, before the sarcophagus. . . .

"Domaris!" On his lips the name was a sob. "Domaris! Child of my soul!" In a single stride he was beside the inert, convulsed body. He shut his eyes a moment as his world reeled: the depth of his love for Domaris had never been truly measured until this moment when she lay apparently dying in his frightened arms.

Grimly he raised his head, glancing about with a steady wrath. *No, she has not failed!* he thought, with some exultation. *The power was unchained, but it has again been sealed, if barely. The sacrilege is undone—but at what cost to Domaris? And I dare not leave her, not even to bring aid. Better, in any case, she die than deliver her child here!*

After a moment of disordered thought, he bent and raised her in his arms. She was no light burden—but Rajasta, in his righteous anger, barely noticed the weight. He spoke to her, soothingly, and although she was long past hearing, the tone of his voice penetrated to her darkened brain and she did not struggle when he lifted her and, with a dogged desperation, started back toward the long stairway. His breath came laboringly, and his strained face had a look no one would ever see as he turned toward that incredibly distant summit. His lips moved; he breathed deeply once—and began climbing.

Chapter Four

THE LAWS OF THE TEMPLE

I

Elara, moving around the court and singing serenely at her work, dropped the half-filled vase of flowers and scurried toward the Guardian as he crossed the garden with his lifeless burden. Alarmed anxiety widened her dark eyes as she held the door, then ran around him to clear cushions from a divan and assist Rajasta to lay the inert body of Domaris upon it.

His face grey with exhaustion, the Guardian straightened and stood a moment, catching his breath. Elara, quickly taking in his condition, guided him toward a seat, but he shook her off irritably. "See to your mistress."

"She lives," the slave-woman said quickly, but in anticipation of Rajasta's command, she hurried back to Domaris's side and bent, searching for a pulse-beat. Satisfied, she jumped up and spent a moment seeking in a cabinet; then returned to hold a strong aromatic to her mistress's pinched nostrils. After a long, heart-wrenching moment, Domaris moaned and her eyelids quivered.

"Domaris—" Rajasta breathed out the word. Her wide eyes were staring, the distended pupils seeing neither priest nor anxious attendant. Domaris moaned again, spasmodically gripping nothing with taloning hands, and Elara caught them gently, bending over her mistress, her shocked stare belatedly taking in the torn dress, the bruised arms and cheeks, the great livid mark across her temples.

Suddenly Domaris screamed, "No, no! No—not for myself, but can you—no, no, they will tear me apart—let me go! Loose your hands from me—Arvath! Rajasta! Father, father . . ." Her voice trailed again into moaning sobs.

Holding the woman's head on her arm, Elara whispered gently, "My dear Lady, you are safe here with me, no one will touch you."

"She is delirious, Elara," Rajasta said wearily.

Tenderly, Elara fetched a wet cloth and blotted away the clotted blood at her mistress's hairline. Several slave-women crowded at the door, eyes wide with dread. Only the presence of the Priest stilled their questions. Elara drove them out with a gesture and low utterances, then turned to the Priest, her eyes wide with horror.

"Lord Rajasta, what in the name of all the Gods has come to her?" Without waiting for an answer, perhaps not even expecting one, she bent over Domaris again, drawing aside the folds of the shredded robe. Rajasta saw her shiver with dismay; then she straightened, covering the woman decently and saying in a low voice, "Lord Guardian, you must leave us. And she must be carried at

once to the House of Birth. There is no time to
lose—and you know there is danger."

Rajasta shook his head sadly. "You are a good
girl, Elara, and you love Domaris, I know. You
must bear what I have to tell you. Domaris must
not—she *cannot*—be taken to the House of Birth,
nor—"

"My Lord, she could be carried there easily in a
litter, there is not so much need for haste as that."

Rajasta signed her impatiently to silence. "Nor
may she be attended by any consecrated priestess.
She is ceremonially unclean."

Elara exploded with outrage at this. "A priestess?
How!"

Rajasta sighed, miserably. "Daughter, please, hear
me out. Cruel sacrilege has been done, and penalties even more terrible may be to come. And Elara—
you too are awaiting a child, is that not so?"

Timidly, Elara bowed her head. "The Guardian
has seen."

"Then, my daughter, I must bid you leave her,
as well; or your child's life too may be forfeit."
The Priest looked down at the troubled round face
of the little woman and said quietly, "She has
been found in the Crypt of the Sleeping God."

Elara's mouth fell open in shock and involun-
tary dread, and she now started back a pace from
Domaris, who continued to lie as if lifeless. Then,
resolutely, Elara armed herself with calm and met
the Guardian's eyes levelly, saying, "Lord Guardian,
I cannot leave her to these ignorant ones. If no
Temple woman may come near her—I was fostered with the Lady Domaris, Lord Guardian, and
she has treated me not as a servant but as a friend
all my life! Whatever the risk, I will bear it."

Rajasta's eyes lighted with a momentary relief, which faded at once. "You have a generous heart, Elara, but I cannot allow that," he said sternly. "If it were only your own danger—but you have no right to endanger the life of your child. Enough causes have been set already in motion; each person must bear the penalties which have been invoked. Place not another life on your mistress's head! Let her not be guilty of your child's life, too!"

Elara bowed her head, not understanding. She pleaded, "Lord Guardian, in the Temple of Caratra there are priestesses who might be willing to bear the risk, and who have the right and the power to make it safe! The Healer woman, Karahama—she is skilled in the magical arts. . . ."

"You may ask," conceded Rajasta, without much hope, and straightened his bent shoulders with an effort. "Nor may I remain, Elara; the Law must be observed."

"Her sister—the Priestess Deoris . . ."

Rajasta exploded in blind fury. "Woman! Hold your foolish tongue! Hearken—*least of all* may Deoris come near her!"

"You cruel, heartless, wicked old man!" Elara flared, beginning to sob; then cringed in fright.

Rajasta had hardly heard the outburst. He said, more gently, "Hush, daughter, you do not know what you are saying. You are fortunate in your ignorance of Temple affairs, but do not try to meddle in them! Now heed my words, Elara, lest worse come to pass."

II

In his own rooms, Rajasta cleansed himself ceremonially, and put aside to be burnt the cloth-

ing he had worn into the Dark Shrine. He was
exhausted from that terrible descent and the more
terrible return, but he had learned long ago to
control his body. Clothing himself anew in full
Guardian's regalia, he finally ascended the pyramid,
where Ragamon and Cadamiri awaited him; and a
dozen white-clad priests, impassive, ranged in a
ghostly procession behind the Guardians.

Deoris still lay prostrate, in a stupor of numbed
misery, before the altar. Rajasta went to her, raised
the girl up and looked long into her desperate face.

"Domaris?" she said, waveringly.

"She is alive—but she may die soon." He frowned
and gave Deoris a shake. "It is too late to cry! You,
and you!" He singled out two Priests. "Take Deoris
to the house of Talkannon, and bring her women
to her there. Let her be clothed and tended and
cared for. Then go with her to find Karahama's
other brat—a girl of the Grey Temple called Demira.
Harm her not, but let her be carefully confined."
Turning to the apathetic Deoris once again, Rajasta
said, "My daughter, you will speak to no one but
these Priests."

Nodding dumbly, Deoris went between her
guards.

Rajasta turned to the others. "Has Riveda been
apprehended?"

One man replied, "We came on him while he
slept. Although he wakened and raved and struggled like a madman, we finally subdued him.
He—he has been chained, as you said."

Rajasta nodded wearily. "Let search be made
through his house and in the Grey Temple, for the
things of magic."

At that moment, the Arch-priest Talkannon entered the chamber, glancing around him with that swift searching look that took in everyone and everything.

Rajasta strode to him and, his lips pressed tight together, confronted him with formal signs of greeting. "We have concrete evidence at last," he said, "and we can arrest the guilty—for we *know!*"

Talkannon paled slightly. "You know—what?"

Rajasta mistook his distressed disquiet. "Aye, we know the guilty, Talkannon. I fear the evil has touched even your house; Domaris still lives, but for how long, no one can tell. Deoris has turned from this evil, and will help us to apprehend these— these demons in human form!"

"Deoris?" Talkannon stared in disbelief and shock at the Priest of Light. "What?" Absently, he wiped at his forehead; then, with a mighty effort, he recovered his composure. When he spoke, his voice was steady again. "My daughters have long been of an age to manage their own affairs," he murmured. "I knew nothing of this, Rajasta. But of course I, and all those under my orders, are at your service in this, Lord Guardian."

"It is well said." Rajasta began to outline what he wanted Talkannon to do . . .

But behind the Arch-priest's back, Ragamon and Cadamiri exchanged troubled glances.

III

"Good Mother Ysouda!"

The old Priestess looked down at Elara with a kindly smile. Seeing the trembling terror in the little dark face, she spoke with gentle condescension.

"Have no fear, my daughter, the Mother will guard and be near you. Is it time for you, Elara?"

"No, no, I am all right," said Elara distractedly, "it is my lady, the Priestess Domaris—"

The old lady drew in her breath. "May the gods have pity!" she whispered. "What has befallen her, Elara?"

"I may not tell thee here, Mother," Elara whispered. "Take me, I beg you, to the Priestess Karahama—"

"To the High Priestess?" At Elara's look of misery, however, Mother Ysouda wasted no more time on questions, but drew Elara along the walk until they reached a bench in the shade. "Rest here, daughter, or your own child may suffer; the sun is fierce today. I will myself seek Karahama; she will come more quickly for me than if I sent a servant or novice to summon her."

She did not wait for Elara's grateful thanks, but went quickly toward the building. Elara sat on the indicated bench, but she was too impatient, too fearful to rest as Mother Ysouda had bidden. Clasping and unclasping her hands, she rose restlessly and walked up and down the path.

Elara knew Domaris was in grave danger. She had done a little service in the Temple of Caratra, and had only the most elementary knowledge—but this much she knew perfectly well: Domaris had been in labor for many hours, and if all had been well, her child would have been born without need of assistance.

Rajasta's warning was like a terrible echo in her ears. Elara was a free city woman, whose mother had been milk nurse to Domaris; they had been fostered together and Elara served Domaris freely, as a privilege rather than a duty. She would have risked death without a second thought for the Priestess she loved, almost worshipped—but Rajasta's words, remembered, made a deafening thunder in her mind.

She is contaminated . . . you are generous, but this I cannot allow! You have no right to endanger the life of your child-to-be . . . place not another crime on Domaris's head! Let her not be guilty of your unborn child's life too!

She turned suddenly, hearing steps on the path behind her. A very young priestess stood there; glancing at Elara's plain robe with indifferent contempt, she said, "The Mother Karahama will receive you."

In trembling haste, Elara followed the woman's measured steps, into the presence of Karahama. She knelt.

Not unkindly, Karahama signalled her to rise. "You come on behalf of—Talkannon's daughters?"

"Oh, my Lady," Elara begged, "sacrilege has been done, and Domaris may not be brought to the House of Birth—nor is Deoris permitted to attend her! Rajasta has said—that she is ceremonially unclean. She was found in the Crypt, in the Dark Shrine. . . ." Her voice broke into a sob; she did not hear Mother Ysouda's agonized cry, nor the scandalized gasp of the young novice. "Oh, my Lady, you are Priestess! If you permit—I beg you, I beg you!"

"If I permit," Karahama repeated, remembering the birth of Micon's son.

Four years before, with a few considered words, Domaris had humiliated Karahama before her pupils, sending the "nameless woman"—her unacknowledged half-sister—from her side. *"You have said I must be tended only by my equals,"* Karahama could hear the words as if they had been spoken that very morning, *"Therefore—leave me."* How clearly Karahama remembered!

Slowly, Karahama smiled, and the smile froze Elara's blood. Karahama said in a her melodious voice, "I am High Priestess of Caratra. These women under my care must be safeguarded. I cannot permit any Priestess to attend her, nor may I myself approach one so contaminated. Bear greetings to my sister, Elara, and say to her—" Karahama's lips curved—"say that I could not so presume; that the Lady Domaris should be tended only by her equals."

"Oh, Lady!" Elara cried in horror. "Be not cruel—"

"Silence!" said Karahama sternly. "You forget yourself. But I forgive you. Go from me, Elara. And mark you—stay not near your mistress, lest your own child suffer!"

"Karahama—" Mother Ysouda quavered. Her face was as white as her faded hair, and she moved her lips, but for a moment no sound came forth. Then she begged, "Let me go to her, Karahama! I am long past my own womanhood, I cannot be harmed. If there is risk, let it fall on me, I will suffer it gladly, gladly, she is my little girl—she is like my own child, Karahama, let me go to my little one—"

"Good Mother, you may not go," said the High Priestess, with sharp sternness. "Our Goddess shall not be so offended! What—shall Her Priestesses tend the unclean? Such a thing would defile our Temple. Elara, leave us! Seek aid for your lady, if there is need, among the Healers—but seek no woman to aid her! And—heed me, Elara—stay you afar from her! If harm comes to your child, I shall know you disobedient, and you will suffer full penalty for the crime of abortion!" Karahama gestured contemptuous dismissal, and as the woman, sobbing aloud, rushed from their presence, Mother Ysouda opened her mouth to make angry protest—and checked it, despairing. Karahama had only invoked the literal laws of the Temple of Caratra.

Again—very slightly—Karahama smiled.

Chapter Five

THE NAMING OF THE NAME

I

Toward sunset, Rajasta, gravely troubled, went to Cadamiri's rooms.

"My brother, you are a Healer—priest—the only one I know who is not a Grey-robe." He did not add, *The only one I dare to trust*, but it was understood between them. "Do you fear—contamination?"

Cadamiri grasped this also without explanation. "Domaris? No, I fear it not." He looked into Rajasta's haggard face and asked, "But could no priestess be found to bear the risk?"

"No." Rajasta did not elaborate.

Cadamiri's eyes narrowed, and his austere features, usually formidable, hardened even more. "If Domaris should die for lack of skilled tending, the shame to our Temple will live long past the karma which might be engendered by a fracture of the Law!"

Rajasta regarded his fellow-Guardian thoughtfully for a silent moment, then said, "The slavewoman brought two of Riveda's Healers to her—but . . ." Rajasta let the appeal drop.

Cadamiri nodded, already seeking the small case which contained the appurtenances of his art. "I will go to her," he said with humility; then added, slowly, as if against his will, "Expect not too much of me, Rajasta! Men are not—instructed in these arts, as you know. I have only the barest gleaming of the secrets which the Priestesses guard for such emergencies. However, I will do what I may." His face was sorrowful, for he loved his young kinswoman with that passionate love which a sworn ascetic may sometimes feel for a woman of pure beauty.

Swiftly they passed through the halls of the building, pausing only to pick three strong lesser priests in the event of trouble. They did not speak to one another as they hurried along the paths to Domaris's home, and parted at the door; but although Rajasta was already late for an appointment, he stood a moment watching as Cadamiri disappeared from his view.

In her room, Domaris lay as one lifeless, too weak even to struggle. Garments and bed-linen alike were stained with blood. Two Grey-robes stood, one on either side of the bed; there was no one else in the room, not even the saving presence of a slave-woman. Later, Cadamiri was to learn that Elis had stubbornly remained with her cousin most of the day, defying Karahama's reported threats and doing her ineffectual best—but the air of authority with which the Grey-robes had presented themselves had misled her; she had been persuaded, at last, to leave Domaris to them.

One of the Grey-robes turned as the Guardian entered. "Ah, Cadamiri," he said, "I fear you come too late."

Cadamiri's blood turned to icy water. These men were not Healers and never had been, but Magicians —Nadastor and his disciple Har-Maen. Clenching his teeth on angry words, Cadamiri walked to the bed. After a brief examination he straightened, appalled. "Clumsy butchers!" he shouted. "If this woman dies, I will have you strangled for murder— and if she lives, for torture!"

Nadastor bowed smoothly. "She will not die— yet," he murmured. "And as for your threats . . ."

Cadamiri wrenched open the door and summoned the escort of Priests. "Take these—these filthy *sorcerers!*" he commanded, in a voice hardly recognizable as his own. The two Magicians allowed themselves to be led from the room without protest, and Cadamiri, through half-clenched teeth, called after them, "Do not think you will escape justice! I will have your hands struck off at the wrists and you will be scourged naked from the Temple like the dogs you are! May you rot in leprosy!"

Abruptly Har-Maen swayed and crumpled. Then Nadastor too reeled and fell into the arms of his captor. The white-robed Priests jumped away from them and made the Holy Sign frantically, while Cadamiri could only stare, wondering if he were going mad.

The two Grey-robed figures rising from the floor, meek and blank-eyed in oddly-shrunken robes, were—not Har-Maen and Nadastor, but two young Healers whom Cadamiri himself had trained. They stared about them, dumb and smitten with terror, and quite obviously oblivious to everything that had happened.

Illusion! Cadamiri clenched his fists against a flood of dread. *Great Gods, help us all!* He gazed helplessly at the quivering, confused young novice-Healers, controlling himself with the greatest effort of his life. At last he said hoarsely, "I have no time to deal with—with this, now. Take them and guard them carefully until I . . ." His voice faltered and failed. "Go! Go!" he managed to say, "Take them out of my sight!"

Almost slamming the door shut, Cadamiri went again to bend over Domaris, baffled and desolate. His sister Guardian had indeed been cruelly treated by—by devils of Illusion! With a further effort, he put rage and sadness both aside, concentrating on the abused woman who lay before him. It was certainly too late to save the baby—and Domaris herself was in the final stage of exhaustion: the convulsive spasms tearing at her were so weak it seemed her body no longer had the strength even to reject the burden of death.

Her eyes fluttered open. "Cadamiri?"

"Hush, my sister," he said in a rough, kindly voice. "Do not try to talk."

"I must—Deoris—the Crypt . . ." Twisting spasmodically, she dragged her hands free of the Guardian's; but so exhausted was she that her eyes dropped shut again on the tears that welled from them, and she slept for a moment. Cadamiri's expression was soft with pity; he could understand, as not even Rajasta would have. This, from infancy, was every Temple woman's ultimate nightmare of obscene humiliation—that a man might approach

a woman in labor. When Elis had been bullied
into leaving her, her mind—sick and tormented—
had receded into some depth of shame and hurt
where no one could reach or follow her. Cadamiri's
kindness was little better than the obscene brutality of the sorcerers.

When it was clear that there was no more that
he could do, Cadamiri went to the inner door and
quietly beckoned Arvath to approach. "Speak to
her," he suggested gently. It was a desperate
measure—if her husband could not reach her, probably no one could.

Arvath's face was pinched and pallid. He had
waited, wracked by fear and trembling, most of
the day, seeing no one save Mother Ysouda, who
hovered about him for a time, weeping. From her
he had learned for the first time of the dangers
Domaris had deliberately faced; it had made him
feel guilty and confused, but he forgot it all as he
bent over his wife.

"Domaris—beloved—"

The familiar, loving voice brought Domaris back
for a moment—but not to recognition. Agony and
shame had loosed her hold on reason. Her eyes
opened, the pupils so widely distended that they
looked black and blind, and her bitten-bloody lips
curved in the old, sweet smile.

"*Micon!*" she breathed. "Micon!" Her eyelids fluttered shut again and she slept, smiling.

Arvath leaped away with a curse. In that instant,
the last remnant of his love died, and something
cruel and terrible took its place.

Cadamiri, sensing some of this, caught restrain-
ingly at his sleeve. "Peace, my brother," he implored. "The girl is delirious—she is not here at all."

"Observant, aren't you?" Arvath snarled. "Damn you, *let me go!*" Savagely, he shook off Cadamiri's hands and, with another frightful curse, went from the room.

Rajasta, still standing in the courtyard, unable to force himself to go, whirled around with instant alertness as Arvath reeled staggering out of the building.

"Arvath! Is Domaris . . . ?"

"Domaris be damned forever," the young priest said between his teeth, "and you too!" He tried to thrust his way past Rajasta, too, as he had Cadamiri; but the old man was strong, and determined.

"You are overwrought or drunken, my son!" said Rajasta sorrowfully. "Speak not so bitterly! Domaris has done a brave thing, and paid with her child's life—and her own may be demanded before this is over!"

"And glad she was," said Arvath, very low, "to be free of *my* child!"

"Arvath!" Rajasta's grip loosed on the younger Priest as shock whitened his face. "Arvath! She is your wife!"

With a furious laugh, he pulled free of Rajasta. "My wife? Never! Only harlot to that Atlantean bastard who has been held up all my life as a model for my virtue! Damn them both and you too! I swear—but that you are just a stupid old man . . ." Arvath let his menacing fist fall to his side, turned, and in an uncontrollable spasm of retching, was violently sick on the pavement.

Rajasta sprang to him, murmuring, "My son!"

Arvath, fighting to master himself, thrust the Guardian away. "Always forgiving!" he shouted, "Ever compassionate!" He stumbled to his feet and shook his fist at Rajasta. "I spit on thee—on Domaris—and on the Temple!" he cried out in a breaking falsetto—and, elbowing Rajasta savagely aside, rushed away, into the gathering darkness.

II

Cadamiri turned to see a tall and emaciated form in a grey, shroud-like garment, standing a little distance from him. The door was still quivering in its frame from Arvath's departure; nothing had stirred.

Cadamiri's composure, for the second time that day, deserted him. "What—how did you get in here?" he demanded.

The grey figure raised a narrow hand to push aside the veil, revealing the haggard face and blazing eyes of the woman Adept Maleina. In her deep, vibrant voice she murmured, "I have come to aid you."

"You Grey-robe butchers have done enough already!" Cadamiri shouted. "Now leave this poor girl to die in peace!"

Maleina's eyes looked shrunken and sad then. "I have no right to resent that," she said. "But thou art Guardian, Cadamiri. Judge by what you know of good and of evil. I am no sorceress; I am Magician and Adept!" She stretched her empty, gaunt hand toward him, palm upward—and as Cadamiri stared, the words died in his throat; within her palm shone the sign he could not mistake, and Cadamiri bent in reverence.

Scornfully, Maleina gestured him to rise. "I have not forgotten that Deoris was punished because she aided one no priestess might dare to touch! I am—hardly a woman, now; but I have served Caratra, and my skill is not small. More, I hate Riveda! He, and worse, what he has done! Now stand aside."

Domaris lay as if life had already left her—but as Maleina's gaunt, bony hands moved on her body, a little voiceless cry escaped her exhausted lips. The woman Adept paid no more heed to Cadamiri, but murmured, musingly, "I like not what I must do." Her shoulders straightened, and she raised both hands high; her low, resonant voice shook the room.

"Isarma!"

Not for nothing were true names kept sacred and secret; the intonation and vibration of her Temple name penetrated even to Domaris's withdrawn senses, and she heard, though reluctanlty.

"Who?" she whispered.

"I am a woman and thy sister," Maleina said, with gentle authority, calming her with a hand on the sensitive centre of the brow chakra. Abruptly she turned to Cadamiri.

"The soul lives in her again," she said. "Believe me, I do no more than I must, but now she will fight me—you must help me, even if it seems fearful to you."

Domaris, all restraint gone, roused up screaming, in the pure animal instinct for survival, as Maleina touched her; Maleina gestured, and Cadamiri flung his full weight to hold the struggling woman motionless. Then there was a convulsive cry from Domaris; Cadamiri felt her go limp and mercifully unconscious under his hands.

With an expression of horror, Maleina caught up a linen cloth and wrapped it around the terribly

torn thing she held. Cadamiri shuddered; and
Maleina turned to him a sombre gaze.

"Believe me, I did not kill," she said. "I only
freed her of . . ."

"Of certain death," Cadamiri said weakly. "I
know. I would not have —dared."

"I learned that for a cause less worthy," said
Maleina, and the old woman's eyes were wet as
she looked down at the unconscious form of
Domaris.

Gently she bent and straightened the younger
woman's limbs, laid a fresh coverlet over her.

"She will live," said Maleina. "This—" she covered the body of the dead, mutilated child. "Say
no word about who has done this."

Cadamiri shivered and said "So be it."

Without moving, she was gone; and only a shaft
of sunlight moved where the Adept had stood a
moment before. Cadamiri clutched at the foot of
the bed, afraid that for all his training he would
fall in a faint. After a moment he steadied himself
and made ready to bear the news to Rajasta; that
Domaris was alive and that Arvath's child was
dead.

Chapter Six

THE PRICE

They had allowed Demira to listen to the testimony of Deoris, wrung from her partially under hypnosis, partially under the knowledge that her sworn word could not be violated without karmic effect that would spread over centuries. Riveda, too, had answered all questions truthfully—and with contempt. The others had taken refuge in useless lies.

All this Demira endured calmly enough—but when she heard who had fathered her child, she screamed out between the words, "No! No, no, no . . ."

"Silence!" Ragamon commanded, and his gaze transfixed the shrieking child as he adjured solemnly. "This testimony shall bear no weight. I find no record of this child's parentage, nor any grounds save hearsay for believing that she is daughter to any man. We need no charges of incest!"

Maleina caught Demira in her arms, pressing the golden head to her shoulder, holding the girl close, with an agonized, protective love. The look on the woman's face might have belonged to a sorrowing angel—or an avenging demon.

Her eyes rested on Riveda, seeming to burn out of her dark, gaunt face, and she spoke as if her voice came from a tomb. "Riveda! If the Gods meted justice, you would lie in this child's place!"

But Demira pulled madly away from her restraining hands and ran screaming from the Hall of Judgment.

All that day they sought her. It was Karahama who, toward nightfall, found the girl in the innermost sanctuary of the Temple of the Mother. Demira had hanged herself from one of the crossbeams, a blue bridal girdle knotted about her neck, her slight distorted body swaying horribly as if to reprove the Goddess who had denied her, the mother who had forsworn her, the Temple that had never allowed her to know life. . . .

Chapter Seven

THE DEATH CUP

I

Silence ... and the beating of her heart ... and the dripping of water as it trickled, drop by slow drop, out of the stone onto the damp rock floor. Deoris stole through the black stillness, calling almost in a whisper, "*Riveda!*" The vaulted roof cast the name back, hollow and gutteral echoes: "*Riveda ... veda ... veda ... eda ... da....*"

Deoris shivered, her wide eyes searching the darkness fearfully. Where have they taken him?

As her sight gradually became accustomed to the gloom, she discerned a pale and narrow chink of light—and, almst at her feet, the heavy sprawled form of a man.

Riveda! Deoris fell to her knees.

He lay so desperately still, breathing as if drugged. The heavy chains about his body forced him backward, strained and unnaturally cramped ...

Abruptly the prisoner came awake, his hands grop-
ing in the darkness.

"Deoris," he said, almost wonderingly, and stirred
with a metallic rasp of chains. She took his seeking hands in hers, pressing her lips to the wrists
chafed raw by the cold iron. Riveda fumbled to
touch her face. "Have they—they have not impris-
oned you too, child?"

"No," she whispered.

Riveda struggled to sit up, then sighed and gave
it up. "I cannot," he acknowledged wearily. "These
chains are heavy—and cold!"

In horror, Deoris realized that he was literally
weighed down with bronze chains that enlaced his
body, fettering hands and feet close to the floor so
that he could not even sit upright—his giant
strength oppressed so easily! *But how they must
fear him!*

He smiled, a gaunt, hollow-eyed grimace in the
darkness. "They have even bound my hands lest I
weave a spell to free myself! The half-witted, superstitious cowards," he muttered, "knowing nothing
of magic—they are afraid of what no living man
could accomplish!" He chuckled. "I suppose I *could*,
possibly, bespeak the fetters off my wrists—if I
wanted to bring the dungeon down on top of me!"

Awkwardly, because of the weight of the chains
and the clumsiness of her own swelling body, Deoris
got her arms half-way around him and held him,
as closely as she could, his head softly pillowed on
her thighs.

"How long have I been here, Deoris?"

"Seven days," she whispered.

He stirred with irritation at the realization that
she was crying softly. "Oh, stop it!" he commanded.

"I suppose I am to die—and I can stand that—but I will *not* have you snivelling over me!" Yet his hand, gently resting upon hers, belied the anger in his voice.

"Somehow," he mused, after a little time had passed, "I have always thought my home was— out there in the dark, somewhere." The words dropped, quiet and calm, through the intermittent drip-dripping of the subterranean waters. "Many years ago, when I was young, I saw a fire, and what looked like death—and beyond that, in the dark places, something . . . or some One, who knew me. Shall I at last find my way back to that wonder-world of Night?" He lay quiet in her arms for many minutes, smiling. "Strange," he said at last, "that after all I have done, my one act of mercy condemns me to death—that I made certain Larmin, with his tainted blood, grew not to manhood —complete."

Suddenly Deoris was angry. "Who were you to judge?" she flared at him.

"I judged—because I had the power to decide."

"Is there no right beyond power?" Deoris asked bitterly.

Riveda's smile was wry now. "None, Deoris. None."

Hot rebellion overflowed in Deoris, and the right of her own unborn child stirred in her. "You yourself fathered Larmin, and insured that taint its further right! And what of Demira? What of the child you, of your own free will, begot on me? Would you show that child the same mercy?"

"There were—things I did not know, when I begot Larmin." In the darkness she could not see the full grimness of the smile lurking behind

Riveda's words. "To your child, I fear I show only the mercy of leaving it fatherless!" And suddenly he raised up in another fit of raving, heretical blasphemies, straining like a mad beast at his chains; battering Deoris away from him, he shouted violently until his voice failed and, gasping hoarsely, he fell with a metallic clamor of chains.

Deoris pulled the spent man into her arms, and he did not move. Silence stole toward them on dim feet, while the crack of light crept slowly across her face and lent its glow at last to Riveda's rough-hewn, sleeping face. Heavy, abandoned sleep enfolded him, a sleep that seemed to clasp fingers with death. Time had run down; Deoris, kneeling in the darkness, could feel the sluggish beating of its pulse in the water that dripped crisply, drearily, eroding a deep channel through her heart, that flowed with brooding silence . . .

Riveda moved finally, as if with pain. The single ray of light outlined his face, harshly unrelenting, before her longing eyes. "Deoris," he whispered, and the manacled hand groped at her waist . . . then he sighed. "Of course. They have burned it!" He stopped, his voice still hoarse and rasping. "Forgive me," he said. "It was best—you never knew—*our* child!" He made a strange blurred sound like a sob, then turned his face into her hand and with a reverence as great as it was unexpected, pressed his lips into the palm. His manacled hand fell, with a clashing of chains.

For the first time in his long and impersonally concentrated life, Riveda felt a deep and personal despair. He did not fear death for himself; he had cast the lots and they had turned against him. *But what lot have I cast for Deoris? She must live—and after me her child will live—that child!* Suddenly Riveda knew the full effect of his actions, faced responsibility and found it a bitter, self-poisoned brew. In the darkness, he held Deoris as close and as tenderly as he could in the circumstances, as if straining to give the protection he had too long neglected . . . and his thoughts ran a black torrent.

But for Deoris the greyness was gone. In despair and pain she had finally found the man she had always seen and known and loved behind the fearful outer mask he wore to the world. In that hour, she was no longer a frightened child, but a woman, stronger than life or death in the soft violence of her love for this man she could never manage to hate. Her strength would not last—but as she knelt beside him, she forgot everything but her love of Riveda. She held his chained body in her arms, and time stopped for them both.

She was still holding him like that when the Priests came to take them away.

II

The great hall was crowded with the robes of priests: white, blue, flaxen and grey-robed, the men and women of the Temple precincts mingled before the raised däis of judgment. They parted with hushed murmurings as Domaris walked slowly forward, her burning hair the only fleck of color about her, and her face whiter than the pallid glimmer of her mantle. She was flanked by two white-robed priests who paced with silent gravity one step behind her, alert lest she fall—but she moved steadily, though slowly, and her impassive eyes betrayed nothing of her thoughts.

Inexorably they came to the däis; here the priests halted, but Domaris went on, slow-paced as fate, and mounted the steps. She spared no glance at the gaunt, manacled scarecrow at the foot of the däis, nor for the girl who crouched with her face hidden in Riveda's lap, her long hair scattered in a dark tangle about them both. Domaris forced herself to climb regally upward, and take her place between Rajasta and Ragamon. Behind them, Cadamiri and the other Guardians were shadowy faces hidden within their golden hoods.

Rajasta stepped forward, looking out over the assembled Priests and Priestesses; his eyes seemed to seek out each and every face in the room. Finally he sighed, and spoke with ceremonious formality: "Ye have heard the accusations. Do you believe? Have they been proven?"

A deep, threatening, ragged thunder rolled the answer: *"We believe! It is proven!"*

"Do you accept the guilt of this man?"

"We accept!"

"And what is your will?" Rajasta questioned gravely. "Do ye pardon?"

Again the thunder of massed voices, like the long roll of breakers on the seashore: *"We pardon not!"*

Riveda's face was impassive, though Deoris flinched.

"What is your will?" Rajasta challenged. "Do ye then condemn?"

"We condemn!"

"What is your will?" said Rajasta again—but his voice was breaking. He knew what the answer would be.

Cadamiri's voice came, firm and strong, from

the left: "Death to him who has misused his power!"

"*Death!*" The word rolled and reverberated around the room, dying into frail, whispering echoes.

Rajasta turned and faced the judgment seat. "Do ye concur?"

"We concur!" Cadamiri's strong voice drowned other sounds: Ragamon's was a harsh tremolo, the others mere murmurs in their wake. Domaris spoke so faintly that Rajasta had to bend to hear her, "We—concur."

"It is your will. I concur." Rajasta turned again, to face the chained Riveda. "You have heard your sentence," he charged gravely. "Have you anything to say?"

The blue, frigid eyes met Rajasta's, in a long look, as if the Adept were pondering a number of answers, any one of which would have shaken the ground from under Rajasta's feet—but the rough-cut jaw, covered now by a faint shadow of reddish-gold beard, only turned up a little in something that was neither smile nor grimace. "Nothing, nothing at all," he said, in a low and curiously gentle voice.

Rajasta gestured ritually. "The decree stands! Fire cleanses—and to the fire we send you!" He paused, and added sternly, "Be ye purified!"

"What of the *saji?*" shouted someone at the back of the hall.

"Drive her from the Temple!" another voice cried shrilly.

"Burn her! Stone her! Burn her too! Sorceress! Harlot!" It was a storm of hissing voices, and not for several minutes did Rajasta's upraised hand command silence. Riveda's hand had tightened on Deoris's shoulder, and his jaw was set, his teeth clenched in his lip. Deoris did not move. She might have been lying dead at his knees already.

"She shall be punished," said Rajasta severely, "but she is woman—and with child!"

"Shall the seed of a sorcerer live?" an anonymous voice demanded; and the storm of voices rose again, drowning Rajasta's admonitions with the clamor and chaos.

Domaris rose and stood, swaying a little, then advanced a step. The riot slowly died away as the Guardian stood motionless, her hair a burning in the shadowy spaces. Her voice was even and low: "My Lords, this cannot be. I pledge my life for her."

Sternly, Ragamon put the question: "By what right?"

"She has been sealed to the Mother," said Domaris; and her great eyes looked haunted as she went on, "She is Initiate, and beyond the vengeance of man. Ask of the Priestesses—she is sacrosanct, under the Law. Mine be her guilt; I have failed as Guardian, and as sister. I am guilty further: with the ancient power of the Guardians, invested in me, I have cursed this man who stands condemned before you." Domaris's eyes rested, gently almost, on Riveda's arrogant head. "I cursed him life to life, on the circles of karma ... by Ritual and Power, I cursed him. Let my guilt be punished." She dropped her hands and stood staring at Rajasta, self-accused, waiting.

He gazed back at her in consternation. The future had suddenly turned black before his eyes. *Will Domaris never learn caution? She leaves me no choice....* Wearily, Rajasta said, "The Guardian has claimed responsibility! Deoris I leave to her sister, that she may bring forth, and her fate shall be decided later—but I strip her of honor. No more may she be called Priestess or Scribe." He paused, and addressed the assembly again. "The Guardian claims that she has cursed—by the ancient Ritual, and the ancient Power. Is that misuse?"

The hall hissed with the sibilance of vague replies; unanimity was gone, the voices few and doubtful, half lost in the vaulted spaces. Riveda's guilt had been proved in open trial, and it was a tangible guilt; this was a priestly secret known but to a few, and when it was forced out like this, the common priesthood was more bewildered than indignant, for they had little idea what was meant.

One voice, bolder than the rest, called through the uneasy looks and vague shiftings and whispers: "Let Rajasta deal with his acolyte!" A storm of voices took up the cry: "On Rajasta's head! Let Rajasta deal with his acolyte!"

"Acolyte no longer!" Rajasta's voice was a whiplash, and Domaris winced with pain. "Yet I accept the responsibility. So be it!"

"*So be it!*" the thronged Priests thundered, again with a single voice.

Rajasta bowed ceremoniously. "The decrees stand," he announced, and seated himself, watching Domaris, who was still standing, and none too steadily. In anger and sorrow, Rajasta wondered if she had the faintest idea what might be made of her confession. He was appalled at the chain of events which she—Initiate and Adept—had set in motion. The power vested in her was a very real thing, and in cursing Riveda as she had, she had

used it to a base end. He knew she would pay—
and the knowledge put his own courage at a low
ebb. She had generated endless karma for which
she, and who knew how many others, must pay . . .
It was a fault in him, also, that Domaris should
have let this happen, and Rajasta did not deny the
responsibility, even within himself.

And Deoris. . . .

Domaris had spoken of the Mystery of Caratra,
which no man might penetrate; in that single
phrase, she had effectively cut herself off from
him. Her fate was now in the hands of the Goddess;
Rajasta could not intervene, even to show mercy.
Deoris, too, was beyond the Temple's touch. It
could only be decided whether or no this Temple
might continue to harbor the sisters. . . .

Domaris slowly descended the steps, moving with
a sort of concentrated effort, as if force of will
would overcome her body's frailty. She went to
Deoris and, bending, tried to draw her away. The
younger girl resisted frantically, and finally, in
despair, Domaris signalled to one of her attendant
Priests to carry her away—but as the Priest laid
hands on the girl, Deoris shrieked and clung to
Riveda in a frenzy.

"No! Never, never! Let me die too! I won't go!"

The Adept raised his head once more, and looked
into Deoris's eyes. "Go, child," he said softly. "This
is the last command I shall ever lay upon you."
With his manacled hands, he touched her dark
curls. "You swore to obey me to the last," he
murmured. "Now the last is come. Go, Deoris."

The girl collapsed in terrible sobbing, but allowed herself to be led away. Riveda's eyes followed her, naked emotion betrayed there, and his

lips moved as he whispered, for the first and last time, "Oh, my beloved!"

After a long pause, he looked up again, and his eyes, hard and controlled once more, met those of the woman who stood before him robed in white.

"Your triumph, Domaris," he said bitterly.

On a strange impulse, she exclaimed, "*Our* defeat!"

Riveda's frigid blue eyes glinted oddly, and he laughed aloud. "You are—a worthy antagonist," he said.

Domaris smiled fleetingly; never before had Riveda acknowledged her as an equal.

Rajasta had risen to put the final challenge to the Priests. "Who speaks for mercy?"

Silence.

Riveda turned his head and looked out at his accusers, facing them squarely, without appeal.

And Domaris said quietly, "I speak for mercy, my lords. *He could have let her die!* He saved Deoris, he risked his own life—when he could have let her die! He let her live, to bear the scars that would forever accuse him. It is but a feather against the weight of his sin—but on the scales of the Gods, a feather may balance against a whole human soul. I speak for mercy!"

"It is your privilege," Rajasta conceded, hoarsely.

Domaris drew from her robe the beaten-gold dagger, symbolic of her office. "To your use, this," she said, and thrust it into Riveda's hand. "I too have need of mercy," she added, and was gone, her white and golden robes retreating slowly between the ranks of Priests.

Riveda studied the weapon in his hands for a long moment. By some strange fatality, Domaris's one gift to him was death, and it was the supreme gift. In a single, fleeting instant, he wondered if Micon had been right; had he, Domaris, Deoris, sowed events that would draw them all together yet again, beyond this parting, life to life . . . ?

He smiled—a weary, scholarly smile. He sincerely hoped not.

Rising to his feet, he surrendered the symbol of mercy to Rajasta—long centuries had passed since the mercy-dagger was put to its original use—and in turn accepted the jewelled cup. The Adept held it, as he had the dagger, in his hands for a long, considering minute, thinking—with an almost sensuous pleasure, the curious sensuality of the ascetic —of the darkness beyond; that darkness which he had, all his life, loved and sought. His entire life had led to this moment, and in a swift, half-conscious thought, it occurred to him that it was precisely this he had desired—and that he could have accomplished it far more easily.

Again he smiled. "The wonder-world of Night," he said aloud, and drained the death-cup in a single draught; then, with his last strength, raised it—and with a laugh, hurled it straight and unerring toward the däis. It struck Rajasta on the temple, and the old man fell senseless, struck unconscious at the same instant that Riveda, with a clamor of brazen chains, fell lifeless on the stone floor.

Chapter Eight

LEGACY

I

The small affairs of everyday went on with such sameness that Deoris was confused. She lived almost in a shell of glass; her mind seemed to have slid back somehow to the old days when she and Domaris had been children together. Deliberately she clung to these daydreams and fancies, encouraging them, and if a thought from the present slipped through, she banished it at once.

Although her body was heavy, quickened with that strange, strong other life, she refused to think of her unborn child. Her mind remained slammed shut on that night in the Crypt—except for the nightmares that woke her screaming. *What monster demon did she bear, what lay in wait for birth . . . ?*

On a deeper level, where her thoughts were not clear, she was fascinated, afraid, outraged. Her body—the invincible citadel of her very being—was no longer her own, but invaded, defiled. *By what night-haunted thing of darkness, working in Riveda, has she been made mother—and to what hell-spawn?*

She had begun to hate her rebel body as a thing violated, an ugliness to be hidden and despised. Of late she had taken to binding herself tightly with a wide girdle, forcing the rebellious contours into some semblance of her old slenderness, although she was careful to arrange her clothing so that this would not be too apparent, and to conceal it from Domaris.

Domaris was not ignorant of Deoris's feelings—she could even understand them to some faint extent: the dread, the reluctance to remember and to face the future, the despairing horror. She gave the younger girl a few days of dreams and silence, hoping Deoris would come out of it by herself . . . but finally she forced the issue, unwillingly, but driven by real necessity. This latest development was no daydream, but painfully real.

"Deoris, your child will almost certainly be born crippled if you bind the life from him that way," she said. She spoke gently, pityingly, as if to a child. "You know better than that!"

Deoris flung rebelliously away from her hand. "I won't go about shamed so that every slut in the Temple can point her finger at me and reckon up when I am to give birth!"

Domaris covered her face with her hands for a moment, sick with pity. Deoris had, indeed, been mocked and tormented in the days following Riveda's death. *But this—this violence to nature! And Deoris, who had been Priestess of Caratra!*

"Listen, Deoris," she said, more severely than she had spoken since the disasters, "if you are so sensitive, then stay within our own courts where no one will see you. But you must not injure yourself and your child this way!" She took the tight binding in her hands, gently loosening the fastenings; on the reddened skin beneath were white lateral marks where the bandages had cut deep. "My child, my poor little girl! What drove you to this? How could you?"

Deoris averted her face in bitter silence, and Domaris sighed. *The girl must stop this—this idiotic refusal to face the plain facts!*

"You must be properly cared for," said Domaris. "If not by me, then by another."

Deoris said a swift, frightened, "No! No, Domaris, you—you won't leave me!"

"I cannot if I would," Domaris answered; then, with one of her rare attempts at humor, she teased, "Your dresses will not fit you now! But are you so fond of these dresses that you come to this?"

Deoris gave the usual listless, apathetic smile.

Domaris, smiling, set about looking through her sister's things. After a few minutes, she straightened in astonishment. "But you have no others that are suitable! You should have provided yourself . . ."

Deoris turned away in a hostile silence; and it was evident to the stunned Domaris that the oversight had been deliberate. Without further speech, but feeling as if she had been attacked by a beast that leaped from a dark place, Domaris went and searched here and there among her own possessions, until she found some lengths of cloth, gossamer-fine, gaily colored, from which the loose conventional robes could be draped. *I wore these before Micail's birth*, she mused, reminiscent. She had been more slender then—they could be made to fit Deoris's smaller slighter body. . . .

"Come then," she said with laughter, putting aside thoughts of the time she had herself worn this cloth, "I will show you one thing, at least, I know better than you!" As if she were dressing a doll, she drew Deoris to her feet, and with a pantomime of assumed gaiety, attempted to show her sister how to arrange the conventional robe.

She was not prepared for her sister's reaction. Deoris almost at once caught the lengths of cloth from her sister's hands, and with a frantic, furious gesture, rent them across and flung them to the floor. Then, shuddering, Deoris threw herself upon the cold tiles too, and began to weep wildly.

"I won't, I won't, I won't!" Deoris sobbed, over and over again. "Let me alone! I don't want to, I didn't want this! Go away, *just go away!* Leave me alone!"

II

It was late evening. The room was filled with drifting shadows, and the watery light deepened the vague flames of Domaris's hair, picked out the single streak of white all along its length. Her face was thin and drawn, her body narrowed, with an odd, gaunt limpness that was new. Deoris's face was a white oval of misery. They waited, together, in a hushed dread.

Domaris wore the blue robe and golden fillet of an Initiate of Caratra, and had bidden Deoris robe herself likewise. It was their only hope.

"Domaris," Deoris said faintly, "what is going to happen?"

"I do not know, dear." The older woman clasped her sister's hand tightly between her own thin blue-veined ones. "But they cannot harm you, Deoris. You are—*we are*, what we are! That they cannot change or gainsay."

But Domaris sighed, for she was not so certain as she wanted to seem. She had taken that course to protect Deoris, and beyond doubt it had served them in that—else Deoris would have shared Riveda's fate! But there was a sacrilege involved that went deep into the heart of the religion, for Deoris's child had been conceived in a hideous rite. Could any child so conceived ever be received into the Priest's Caste?

Although she did not, even now, regret the steps she had taken, Domaris knew she had been rash; and the consequences dismayed her. Her own child was dead, and through the tide of her deep grief, she knew it was only what she should have expected. She accepted her own guilt but she resolved, with a fierce and quiet determination, that Deoris's child should be safe. She had accepted responsibility for Deoris and for the unborn, and would not evade that responsibility by so much as a fraction.

And yet—*to what night-haunted monster, working in Riveda, had Deoris been made mother? What hell-spawn awaited birth?*

She took Deoris by the hand and they rose, standing together as their judges entered the room: the Vested Five, in their regalia of office; Karahama and attendant Priestesses; Rajasta and Cadamiri, their golden mantles and sacred blazonings making a brilliance in the dim room; and behind Karahama, a grey-shrouded, fleshless form stood, motionless, with long narrow hands folded across meagre breasts. Beneath the grey folds a dim

color burned blue, and across the blazing hair the
starred fillet of sapphires proclaimed the Atlantean
rites of Caratra in Maleina's corpse-like presence—
and even the Vested Five gave deference to the
aged Priestess and Adept.

There was sorrow in Rajasta's eyes, and Domaris
thought she detected a glint of sympathy in the
impassive face of the woman Adept, but the other
faces were stern and expressionless; Karahama's
even held a faintly perceptible triumph. Domaris
had long regretted her moment of pique, those
long years ago; she had made a formidable enemy.
*This is what Micon would have called karma ...
Micon!* She tried to hold to his name and image
like a talisman, and failed. Would he have cen-
sured her actions? He had not acted to protect
Reio-ta, even under torture!

Cadamiri's gaze was relentless, and Domaris
shrank from it; from Cadamiri, at least, they could
expect no mercy, only justice. The ruthless light of
the fanatic dwelt in his eyes—something of the
same fervor Domaris has sensed and feared in
Riveda.

Briefly Ragamon the Elder rehearsed the situation: Adsartha, once apprentice Priestess of Caratra,
saji to the condemned and accursed Riveda, bore
a child conceived in unspeakable sacrilege. Knowing this, the Guardian Isarma had taken it upon
herself to bind the apostate Priestess Adsartha with
herself in the ancient and holy Mystery of the Dark
Mother, which put them both forever beyond man's
justice ... "Is this true?" he demanded.

"In the main," Domaris said wearily. "There are
a few minor distinctions—but you would not recognize them as important."

Rajasta met her eyes. "You may state the case in your own way, daughter, if you wish."

"Thank you." Domaris clasped and unclasped her hands. "Deoris was no *saji*. To that, I believe, Karahama will bear witness. Is it not true, my sister *and more than my sister.* . . ." Her use of the ritual phrase was deliberate, based on a wild guess that was hardly more than a random hope. "Is it not true that no maiden can be made *saji* after her body is mature?"

Karahama's face had gone white, and her eyes were sick with concealed rage that she, Karahama, should be forced into a position where she was bound by solemn oath to aid Domaris in all things! "That is true," Karahama acknowledged tautly. "Deoris was no *saji*, but *Sākti sidhāna* and, thus, holy even to the Priests of Light."

Domaris went on quietly, "I bound her to Caratra, not altogether to shield her from punishment nor to protect her from violence, but to guide her again toward the Light." Seeing Rajasta's eyes fixed on her in almost skeptical puzzlement, Domaris added, on impulse, "Deoris too is of the Light-born, as much as I am myself; and I—felt her child also deserved protection."

"You speak truth," Ragamon the Elder murmured, "yet can a child begotten in such foul blasphemy be so received by the Mother?"

Domaris faced him proudly. "The Rites of Caratra," she said with quiet emphasis, "are devoid of all distinctions. Her Priestesses may be of royal blood—of the race of slaves—or even of the *nopeople*." Her eyes dwelt for an instant upon Karahama. "Is that not so, my sister?"

"My sister, it is so," Karahama acknowledged,

stifled, "even had Deoris been *saji* in truth." Under Maleina's eyes she had not dared keep silence, for Maleina had taken pity on Karahama too, years before; it had not been entirely coincidence which had brought Demira to Maleina's teaching. The three daughters of Talkannon looked at one another, and only Deoris lowered her eyes; Domaris and Karahama stood for almost a full minute, grey eyes meeting amber ones. There was no love in that gaze—but they were bound by a bond only slightly less close than that binding Domaris to Deoris.

Cadamiri broke the tense silence with blunt words: "Enough of this! Isarma is not guiltless, but she is not important now. The fate of Deoris has yet to be decided—but the child of the Dark Shrine must never be born!"

"What mean you?" Maleina asked sternly.

"Riveda begot this child in blasphemy and sacrilege. The child cannot be acknowledged, nor received. It must never be born!" Cadamiri's voice was loud, and as inflexible as his posture.

Deoris caught at her sister's hand convulsively, and Domaris said, faltering, "You cannot mean . . ."

"Let us be realistic, my sister," said Cadamiri. "You know perfectly well what I mean, Karahama . . ."

Mother Ysouda, shocked, burst out, "That is against our strictest law!"

But Karahama's voice followed, in honeyed and melodious, almost caressing tones. "Cadamiri is correct, my sisters. The law against abortion applies only to the Light-born, received and acknowledged under the Law. No letter of the Law prevents snuffing out the spawn of black magic. Deoris herself would be better freed from that burden." She spoke with great sweetness, but beneath her levelled thick brows she sent Deoris such a look of naked hatred that the girl flinched. Karahama had been her friend, her mentor—and now this! In the past weeks Deoris had grown accustomed to cold glances and averted faces, superstitious avoidance and whispering silence . . . even Elis looked at her with a hesitant embarrassment and found excuses to call Lissa away from her side . . . yet the ferocious hatred in Karahama's eyes was something different, and smote Deoris anew.

And in a way she is right, Domaris thought in despair. *How could any Priestess—or Priest—endure the thought of a child brought so unspeakably to incarnation?*

"It would be better for all," Karahama repeated, "most of all for Deoris, if that child never drew breath."

Maleina stepped forward, motioning Karahama to silence. "Adsartha," said the woman Adept severely—and the use of her priest-name wakened response even in the frightened, apathetic Deoris. "Your child was truly conceived within the Dark Shrine?"

Domaris opened her lips, but Maleina said stiffly, "I beg you, Isarma, allow her to speak for herself. That was on the Night of Nadir, you say?"

Timidly, Deoris whispered assent.

"Records within the Temple of Caratra, to which Mother Ysouda may testify," Maleina said, with chilly deliberateness, "show that each month, at the dark of the moon—observe this, with *perfect* regularity—Deoris was excused her duties, because at this time she was sacramentally impure. I myself noted this in the Grey Temple." Maleina's mouth tightened briefly as if with pain, remembering in whose company Deoris had spent most of her time in the Grey Temple. "The Night of Nadir falls at moon-dark. . . ." She paused; but Domaris and the men only looked baffled, though from Karahama's heavy-lidded eyes, something like comprehension glinted. "Look you," Maleina said, a little impatiently. "Riveda was Grey-robe long before he was sorcerer. The habits of the Magicians are strict and unbreakable. He would not have allowed a woman in the days of her impurity even to come into his presence! As for taking her into such a ritual—it would have invalidated his purpose entirely. Must I explain the rudimentary facts of nature to you, my brothers? Riveda may have been evil—but believe me, he was not an utter fool!"

"Well, Deoris?" Rajasta spoke impersonally, but hope began to show upon his face.

"On the Nadir-night?" Maleina pressed.

Deoris felt herself turning white and rigid; she would not let herself think why. "No," she whispered, trembling, "no, I wasn't!"

"Riveda was a madman!" Cadamiri snorted. "So he violated his own ritual—what of it? Was this not just another blasphemy? I do not follow your reasoning."

Maleina faced him, standing very erect. "It means this," she said, with a thin, ironic smile. "Deoris was already pregnant-and Riveda's rite was a meaningless charade which he, himself, had thwarted!" The woman Adept paused to savor the thought. "What a joke on him!"

But Deoris had crumpled, senseless, to the floor.

Chapter Nine

THE JUDGMENT OF THE GODS

I

After lengthy consideration, sentence had been pronounced upon Domaris: exile forever from the Temple of Light. She would go in honor, as Priestess and Initiate; the merit she had earned could not be taken from her. But she would go alone. Not even Micail could accompany her, for he had been confided by his father to Rajasta's guardianship. But by curious instinct, choice in her place of exile had fallen on the New Temple, in Atlantis, near Ahtarrath.

Deoris had not been sentenced; her penance could not be determined until after her child's birth. And because of the oath which could not be violated, Domaris could claim the right to remain with her younger sister until the child was born. No further concession could be made.

One afternoon a few days later, Rajasta sat alone in the library, a birth-chart spread before him—

but his thoughts were of the bitter altercation which had broken out when Deoris had been carried away in a faint.

"They do *not* hide behind mysteries, Cadamiri," Maleina had said quietly, heavily. "I who am Initiate of Ni-Terat—whom you call Caratra here—I have seen the Sign, which cannot be counterfeited."

Cadamiri's wrath had burst all bonds. "So they are to go unpunished, then? One for sorcery—since even if her child is not child to the Dark Shrine, she concurred in the ritual which would have made it so—and the other for a vile misuse of the holy rites? Then let us make all our criminals, apostates and heretics Initiates of the Holy Orders and have done with it!"

"It was not misuse," Maleina insisted, her face grey with weariness. "Any woman may invoke the protection of the Dark Mother, and if their prayers are answered, no one can gainsay it. And say not they go unpunished, Priest! They have thrown themselves upon the judgment of the Gods, and we dare not add to what they have invoked! Know you not," her old voice shook with ill-hidden dread, "they have bound themselves and the unborn till the end of Time? Through all their lives—*all* their lives, not this life alone but from life to life! Never shall one have home, love, child, but the pain of the other, deprived, shall tear her soul to shreds! Never shall one find love without searing the soul of the other! Never shall they be free, until they have wholly atoned; the life of one shall bear on the hearts of both. We could punish them, yes—in this life. But they have willfully invoked the judgment of the Dark Mother, until such time as the curse of Domaris has worked itself out on the cycles of karma, and Riveda goes free." Maleina's words rolled to silence; fading echoes settled slowly. At last, the woman Adept murmured, "The curses of men are little things compared to that!"

And for this, even Cadamiri could find no answer, but sat with hands clasped before him for some time after all others had left the hall; and none could say whether it was in prayer, or anger, or shock.

II

Rajasta, having read the stars for Deoris's unborn child, finally called Domaris to him, and spread out the scroll before her. "Maleina was right," he said. "Deoris lied. Her child could not possibly have been conceived on the Nadir-night. Not possibly."

"Deoris would not lie under that oath, Rajasta."

Rajasta looked shrewdly at the girl he knew so well. "You trust her still?" He paused, and accepted. "Had Riveda but known that, many lives would have been saved. I can think of nothing more futile than taking a girl already pregnant into a—a rite of that kind." His voice had a cold irony that was quite new to him.

Domaris, unheeding of it, caught her hands to her throat, and whispered weakly, "Then—her child is not—not the horror she fears?"

"No." Rajasta's face softened. "Had Riveda but known!" he repeated. "He went to his death thinking he had begotten the child of a foul sorcery!"

"Such was his intent." Domaris's eyes were cold and unforgiving. "Men suffer for their intentions, not their actions."

"And for them he will pay," Rajasta retorted. "Your curses will not add to his fate!"

"Nor my forgiveness lighten it," Domaris returned inflexibly, but tears began to roll slowly down her cheeks. "Still, if the knowledge had eased his death . . ."

Gently, Rajasta placed the scroll in her hand. "Deoris lives," he reminded her. "Wherever Riveda may be now, Domaris, the cruellest of all hells to him—he who worshipped the forces of Life with all that was best in him, so that he even bent in reverence to you,—this would be cruellest to him, that Deoris should hate his child; that she, who had been Priestess of Caratra, should torture herself, binding her body until it is like enough that the child will be born crippled, or worse!"

Domaris could only stare at him, speechless.

"Do you think I did not know that?" Rajasta murmured softly. "Now go. Take this to her, Domaris—for there is now no reason for her to hate her child."

III

His white robes whispering, Rajasta paced soberly to the side of the man who lay on a low, hard pallet in a small, cold room as austere as a cell. "Peace, younger brother," he said—then, quickly preventing him: "No, do not try to rise!"

"He is stronger today," said Cadamiri from his seat by the narrow window. "And there is something which he will say only to you, it seems."

Rajasta nodded, and Cadamiri withdrew from the room. Taking the seat thus vacated, Rajasta sat looking down at the man who had been Riveda's chela. The long illness had wasted the Atlantean to emaciation again, but Rajasta hardly needed Cadamiri's assurances to tell him that Reio-ta of Ahtarrath was as sane as the Guardian himself.

Now that the madness and vacancy were gone from his face, he looked serious and determined; the amber eyes were darkly intelligent. His hair had been shaven from his scalp during his illness, and was now only a soft, smooth dark nap; he had been dressed in the clothing of a Priest of the second grade. Rajasta knew that the man was twenty-four, but he looked many years younger.

Suddenly impelled to kindness, Rajasta said gently, "My younger brother, no man may be called to account for what he does when the soul is reft from him."

"You are—kind," said Reio-ta hesitantly. His voice had lost its timbre from being so little used over the years, and he was never to speak again without stammering and faltering in his speech. "But I was—at fault be—before." More shakily still, he added, "A man who loses—loses his soul as if it were a toy!"

Rajasta saw the rising excitement in his eyes and said, with gentle sternness, "Hush, my son, you will make yourself ill again. Cadamiri tells me there is something you insist upon telling me; but unless you promise not to overexcite yourself . . ."

"That fa—face has never left my memory for—for an instant!" Reio-ta said huskily. His voice steadied, dropped. "He was not a big man—rather, gross and florid—heavy of build, with great long hands and a wide nose flat at the bridge over large jaws and great teeth—dark hair going grey at the temples, and such eyes! And his mouth—smiling and cruel, the smile of a big tiger! He—he looked almost too good-natured to be so ruthless—and heavy brows, almost sand-colored, and rough, curt speech. . . ."

Rajasta felt as if he were stifling. It was all he could do to mutter the words, "Go on!"

"Two special marks he had—a gap between his great front teeth—and such eyes! Have you seen the pr–Priestess, Karahama? Cat's eyes, tiger's eyes—the eyes in his face might have been her own. . . ."

Rajasta covered his face with his hand. A hundred memories rushed over him. *I have been blinder than Micon! Fool—fool that I was not to question Micon's tale of kind men who brought him to Talkannon's house!* Fool to trust . . . Rajasta gritted his teeth, uncovered his eyes, and asked, still in that stifled voice, "Know you whom you have described, my son?"

"Aye." Reio-ta dropped back on the pillow, his eyes closed, his face weary and resigned. He was sure Rajasta had not believed a single word. "Aye, I know. Talkannon."

And Rajasta repeated, in stunned and bitter belief, *"Talkannon!"*

Chapter Ten

BLACK SHADOWS

I

Domaris laid the scroll in her sister's lap.
"Can you read a birth-chart, Deoris?" she asked
gently. "I would read this to you, but I have never
learned."

Listlessly, Deoris said, "Karahama taught me,
years ago. Why?"

"Rajasta gave me this for you. No," she checked
her sister's protest, "you have refused to face this
thing until the time was past when I could have
forced action. Now we must make some arrange-
ment. Your child must be acknowledged. If your
own position means nothing to you, think of your
child's as one of the *no-people!*"

"Does it matter?" Deoris asked indifferently.

"To you, now, perhaps not," Domaris returned,
"but to your child—*who must live*—it is the difference between living humanly or as an outcaste."
Her eyes dwelt sternly on the rebellious young

face. "Rajasta tells me you will bear a daughter. Would you have her live as Demira?"

"Don't!" cried Deoris convulsively. She slumped, and defeat was in her face. "But who, now, would acknowledge me?"

"One has offered."

Deoris was young, and against her will a gleam of curiosity lightened her apathetic face. "Who?"

"Riveda's chela." Domaris made no attempt to soften it; Deoris had denied too many facts. Let her chew on this one!

"Ugh!" Deoris sprang up defiantly. "No! Never! He's mad!"

"He is no longer mad," Domaris said quietly, "and he offers this as partial reparation."

"Reparation!" Deoris cried in rage. "What right has he . . .? She broke off as she met Domaris's unwavering stare. "You really think I should allow—"

"I do advise it," said Domaris inflexibly.

"Oh, Domaris! I hate him! Please, don't make me. . . ." Deoris was crying piteously now, but the older woman stood unbending at her side.

"All that is required of you, Deoris, is that you be present at the acknowledgement," she said curtly. "He will ask . . ." She looked straight into her sister's eyes. "He will *allow* no more!"

Deoris straightened, and tottered back into her seat, white and miserable. "You are hard, Domaris . . . Be it as you will, then." She sighed. "I hope I die!"

"Dying is not that easy, Deoris."

"Oh, Domaris, *why?*" Deoris begged, "Why do you make me do this?"

"I cannot tell you that." Relenting somewhat, Domaris knelt and gathered her sister into her arms. "You know I love you, Deoris! Don't you trust me?"

"Well, yes, of course, but . . ."

"Then do this—because you trust me, darling."

Deoris clung to the older woman in exhaustion. "I can't fight you," she murmured, "I will do as you say. There is no one else."

"Child, child—you and Micail are all I love. And I shall love your baby, Deoris!"

"I—cannot!" It was a bewildered cry of torment, of shame.

The older woman's throat tightened and she felt tears gathering in her eyes; but she only patted the listless head and promised, "You will love her, when you see her."

Deoris only whimpered and stirred restlessly in her arms, and Domaris, letting her embrace loosen, bent to retrieve the scroll, wincing a little—for she was not altogether free of pain.

"Read this, Deoris."

Obediently but without interest the girl glanced at the traced figures, then suddenly bent over them and began to read with furious concentration, her lips moving, her small fingers gripping the parchment so tightly that Domaris thought for a moment it would tear across. Then Deoris flung herself forward, her head pillowed on the scroll, in a passion of wild weeping.

Domaris watched with puzzled consternation, for she—even she—did not wholly understand the girl's terrible fear and its sudden release; even less could she know of that single night Deoris had hoarded apart like a treasure in her memory, when

Riveda had been not Adept and teacher, but lover
. . . Still, intuition prompted her to take Deoris
very gently into her arms again, holding her with
tender concern, not speaking a word, hardly breathing, while Deoris sobbed and wept until she could
weep no more.

Domaris was relieved beyond telling: grief she
could understand, but Deoris's childlike, dazed
lethargy, the fits of furious rage which alternated
with apathy, had frightened the older woman more
than she knew. Now, as Deoris lay spent on her
shoulder, her eyes closed and her arm around
Domaris's neck, it was for a moment almost as if
all the years had rolled back and they were again
what they had been before Micon's coming. . . .

With a flash of inner, intuitive sight, Domaris
knew what had been wrought of love; and some
touch of her own loss and grief returned, trans-
figured. *Micon, Riveda—what matter? The love and
bereavement are the same.* And to the depths of her
being Domaris was glad—glad that after so long,
Deoris could at last weep for Riveda.

II

But Deoris was dry-eyed again, sullen and rigidly polite, when she was confronted with Reio-ta
outside the hall where they must go before the
Vested Five. Her memory of him was still that of a
mad chela ghosting cat-footed after the dark Adept—
this handsome, self-possessed young Priest startled her. For a moment she actually did not know
who he could be. Her voice stumbled as she said,
formally, "Prince Reio-ta of Ahtarrath, I am grateful for this kindness."

Reio-ta smiled faintly without raising his eyes to her. "There is no d—debt, Deoris, I am y—yours to command in all things."

She kept her eyes fixed upon the blue hem of her loose, ungainly garment, but she did take his offered hand, touching him with scared hesitation. Her face burned with shame and misery as she felt his eyes study her awkward body; she did not raise her own to see the sadness and compassion in his gaze.

The ceremony, though very brief, seemed endless to Deoris. Only Reio-ta's strong hand, tightly clasped over her own, gave her the courage to whisper, faintly, the responses; and she was shaking so violently that when they knelt together for the benediction, Reio-ta had to put his arm around her and hold her upright.

At last Ragamon put the question: "The child's name?"

Deoris sobbed aloud, and looked in appeal at Reio-ta, meeting his eyes for almost the first time.

He smiled at her, and then, facing the Vested Five, said quietly, "The stars have been read. This daughter of mine I name—Eilantha."

Eilantha! Deoris had climbed high enough in the priesthood to interpret that name. *Eilantha*—the effect of a sown cause, the ripple of a dropped stone, the force of karma.

"Eilantha, thy coming life is acknowledged and welcome," the Priest gave answer—and from that moment Deoris's child was Reio-ta's own, as if truly begotten of him. The sonorous blessing rolled over their bent heads; then Reio-ta assisted the woman to rise, and although she would have drawn away from him, he conducted her ceremoniously to the doorway of the hall, and retained her fingers for a moment.

"Deoris," he said gravely, "I would not b—burden you with cares. I know you are not well. Yet a few things must be said be—between us. Our child . . ."

Again Deoris sobbed aloud and, violently wrenching her hands away from his, ran precipitately away from the building. Reio-ta called after her sharply in hurt puzzlement, then started to hasten after the fleeing girl, fearful lest she should fall and injure herself.

But when he turned the corner, she was nowhere to be seen.

III

Deoris came to rest finally in a distant corner of the Temple gardens, suddenly realizing that she had run much further than she had intended. She had never come here before, and was not certain which of the out-branching paths led back toward the house of Mother Ysouda. As she turned hesitantly backward and forward, trying to decide precisely where she was and which way to go, a crouching form rose up out of the shrubbery and she found herself face to face with Karahama. Instinctively Deoris drew back, resentful and frightened.

Karahama's eyes were filled with a sullen fire. *"You!"* the Priestess spat contemptuously at Deoris. *"Daughter of Light!"* Karahama's blue garment was rent from head to foot; her unkempt, uncombed hair hung raggedly about a face no longer calm but congested and swollen, with eyes red and inflamed, and lips drawn back like an animal's over her teeth.

Deoris, in an excess of terror, shrank against the wall—but Karahama leaned so close that she touched the girl. Suddenly, with awful clarity, Deoris knew: Karahama was insane!

"Torturer of children! Sorceress! Bitch!" A rabid wrath snarled in Karahama's voice. "Talkannon's proudest daughter! Better I had been thrown to die upon the city wall than see this day! And you for whom I suffered, daughter of the high lady who could not stoop to see my poor mother—and what of Talkannon now, Daughter of Light? He will wish he had hanged himself like Demira when the priests have done with him! Or has the proud Domaris kept *that* from you, too? Rend your clothing, Talkannon's daughter!" With a savage gesture, Karahama's clawed hands ripped Deoris's smock from neck to ankle.

Screaming with fright, Deoris caught the torn robe about her and sought to twist free—but Karahama, leaning over her, pressed Deoris back against the crumbling wall with a heavy, careless hand against her shoulder.

"Rend your clothing, Daughter of Light! Tear your hair! Daughter of Talkannon—who dies today! And Domaris sought to shelter you from that! Domaris, who was cast out like a harlot, cast out by Arvath for the barren stalk she is!" She spat, and shoved Deoris violently back against the wall again. "And you—*my sister, my little sister!*" There was a vague, mocking hint of Domaris's intonation in the phrase, a sing-song eeriness, an echo like a ghost. "And your own womb heavy with a sister to those children you wronged!" Karahama's tawny eyes, lowered between squinting lashes, suddenly widened and she looked at Deoris through dilated pupils, flat and beast-red, as she shouted, "May slaves and the daughters of harlots attend your bed! May you give birth to monsters!"

Deoris's knees went lifeless under her and she collapsed on the sandy path, crouching against the stones of the wall. "Karahama, Karahama, curse me not!" she implored, "The Gods know—*The Gods know I meant no harm!*"

"She meant no harm," Karahama mocked in that mad, eerie sing-song.

"Karahama, the Gods know I have loved you, I loved your daughter, curse me not!"

Suddenly Karahama knelt at her side. Deoris cringed away—but with easy, compassionate hands, the woman lifted her to her feet. The mad light had quite suddenly died from her eyes, and the face between the dishevelled braids was sane again, and sorrowful.

"So, once, was I, Deoris—not innocent, but much hurt. Neither are you innocent! But I curse you no more."

Deoris sobbed in relief, and Karahama's face, a mask of pain, swam in a ruddy light through her tears. The crumbling stones of the garden wall were a rasping pain against her shoulders, but she could not have stood, unsupported. Suddenly she could hear the low, insistent lapping of the tide, and knew where she was.

"You are not to blame," said Karahama, in a voice hardly louder than the waves. "Nor he—nor I, Deoris! All these things are shadows, but they are very black. I bid you go in peace, little sister

. . . your hour is upon you, and it may be that you will do a bit of cursing yourself, one day!"

Deoris covered her face with her hands—and then the world went dark about her, a dizzy gulf opened out beneath her mind, and she heard herself screaming as she fell—fell for eternities, while the sun went out.

Chapter Eleven

VISIONS

I

When Deoris failed to return, Domaris slowly grew anxious, and finally went in search of her sister—a search that was fruitless. The shadows stretched into long, gaunt corpses, and still she sought; her anxiety mounted to apprehension, and then to terror. The words Deoris had flung at her in anger years ago returned to her, a thundering echo in her mind: *On the day I know myself with child, I will fling myself into the sea . . .*

At last, sick with fright, she went to the one person in all the Temple precincts on whom Deoris now had the slightest claim, and implored his assistance. Reio-ta, far from laughing at her formless fears, took them with an apprehension that matched her own. Aided by his servants, they sought through the night, through the red and sullen firelight of the beaches, along the pathways and in the thickets at the edge of the enclosure. Near morn-

ing they found where she had fallen; a section of
the wall had given way, and the two women lay
half in, half out of the water. Karahama's head
had been crushed by fallen stones, but the scarred,
half-naked form of Deoris was so crumpled and
twisted that for sickening minutes they believed
that she, too, was lifeless.

They carried her to a fisherman's hut near the
tide-mark, and there, by smoldering candlelight,
with no aid save the unskilled hands of Domaris's
slave-girl, was born Eilantha, whose name had
been written that same day upon the rolls of the
Temple. A tiny, delicately-formed girl-child, thrust
two months too soon into an unwelcoming world,
she was so frail that Domaris dared not hope for her
survival. She wrapped the delicate bud of life in
her veil and laid it inside her robes against her own
breast, in the desperate hope that the warmth would
revive it. She sat there weeping, in reborn grief
for her own lost child, while the slave-girl tended
Deoris and aided Reio-ta to set the broken arm.

After a time the infant stirred and began feebly
to wail again, and the thin sound roused Deoris.
Domaris moved swiftly as she stirred, and bent
over her.

"Do not try to move your arm, Deoris; it is
broken at the shoulder."

Deoris's words were less than a whisper. "What
has happened? Where?" Then memory flooded back.
"Oh! Karahama!"

"She is dead, Deoris," Domaris told her gently—
and found herself wondering, in a remote way,
whether Deoris had flung herself over the wall
and Karahama had been killed in attempting to
prevent it—whether they had simply fallen—or

whether Karahama had thrust her sister over the wall. No one, not even Deoris, was ever to know.

"How did you find me?" Deoris asked, without interest.

"Reio-ta helped me."

Deoris's eyes slipped wearily shut. "Why could he not . . . attend to his own affairs . . . this one last time?" she asked, and turned her face away. The child at Domaris's breast began its whimpering wail again, and Deoris's eyes flickered briefly open. "What is . . . I don't . . ."

Cautiously, Domaris lowered the infant toward her sister, but Deoris, after a momentary glimpse at the little creature, shut her eyes again. She felt no emotion except faint relief. The child was not a monster—and in the wrinkled, monkey-like face she could discern no resemblance whatever to Riveda.

"Take it away," she said tiredly, and slept.

Domaris looked down at the young mother, with despair in her face which lightened to a haunted tenderness. "Thy mother is tired and ill, little daughter," she murmured, and cradled the baby against her breasts. "I think she will love thee— when she knows thee."

But her steps and her voice dragged with exhaustion; her own strength was nearly gone. Domaris had never fully recovered from the brutal treatment she had received at the hands of the Black-robes; moreover, she dared not keep this a secret for long. Deoris was not, as far as Domaris could judge, in physical danger; the child had been born easily and so swiftly that there had been no time even to summon help. But she was suffering from exposure and shock.

Domaris did not know if she dared to take any

further responsibility. With the baby still snuggled inside her robes, she sat down on a low stool, to watch and think. . . .

II

When Deoris awoke, she was alone. She lay unmoving, not asleep, but heavy with weariness and lassitude. Gradually, as the effect of the drugs began to weaken, the pain stole back, a slow pulsing of hurt through her torn and outraged body. Slowly, and with difficulty, she turned her head, and made out the dim outline of a basket of reeds, and in the basket something that kicked and whimpered fretfully. She thought dully that she would like to hold the child now, but she was too weak and weary to move.

What happened after that, Deoris never really knew. She seemed to lie half asleep through all that followed, her eyes open but unable to move, unable even to speak, gripped by nightmares in which there was no clue to what was real—and afterward there was no one who could or would tell her what really happened on that night after Riveda's child was born, in the little hut by the sea. . . .

It seemed that the sun was setting. The light lay red and pale on her face, and on the basket where the baby squirmed and squalled feebly. There was a heat-like fever in Deoris's hurt body, and it seemed to her that she moaned there for a long time, not loudly but desolately like a hurt child. The light turned into a sea of bloody fire, and the chela came into the room. His dark, wandering glance met hers . . . He wore bizarrely unfamiliar clothing, girt with the symbols of a strange priesthood, and for a moment it seemed to be Micon who stood before her, but a gaunt, younger Micon, with un-shaven face. His secret eyes rested on Deoris for a long time; then he went and poured water, bending, holding the cup to her parched lips and support-ing her head so gently that there was no hurt. For an instant it seemed Riveda stood there, nimbused in a cloud of the roseate sunset, and he bent down and kissed her lips as he had done so rarely in her life; then the illusion was gone, and it was only the solemn young face of Reio-ta looking at her gravely as he replaced the cup.

He stood over her for a minute, his lips moving; but his voice seemed to fade out over incredible distances, and Deoris, wandering in the vague si-lences again, could not understand a word. At last he turned abruptly and went to the reed-basket, bending, lifting the baby in his arms. Deoris, still gripped by the static fingers of nightmare, watched as he wandered about the room, the child on his shoulder; then he approached again, and from the pallet where Deoris was lying he lifted a long loose blue shawl, woven and fringed deeply with knots— the garment of a Priestess of Caratra. In this he carefully wrapped the baby, and, carrying her clum-sily in his hands, he went away.

The closing of the door jarred Deoris wholly awake, and she gasped; the room was lurid with the dying sunlight, but altogether empty of any living soul except herself. There was no sound or motion anywhere save the pounding of the waves and the crying of the wheeling gulls.

She lay still for a long time, while fever crawled in her veins and throbbed in her scarred breasts like a pulsing fire. The sun set in a bath of flames, and the darkness descended, folding thick wings of silence around her heart. After hours and hours, Elis (or was it Domaris?) came with a light, and Deoris gasped out her dream—but it sounded delirious even in her own ears, all gibberish and wild entreaties. And then there were eternities where Domaris (or Elis) bent over her, repeating endlessly, "Because you trust me . . . you do trust me . . . do this because you trust me . . ." There was the nightmare pain in her broken arm, and fever burning through her veins, and the dream came again and again—and never once, except in her unquiet slumber, did she hear the crying of the small and monkey-like child who was Riveda's daughter.

She came fully to her senses one morning, finding herself in her old rooms in the Temple. The feverish madness was gone, and did not return.

Elis tended her night and day, as gently as Domaris might have; it was Elis who told her that Talkannon was dead, that Karahama was dead, that Domaris had sailed away weeks before for Atlantis, and that the chela had disappeared, no one knew where; and Elis told her, gently, that Riveda's child had died the same night it was born.

Whenever Deoris fell asleep she dreamed—and always the same dream: the dark hut where her child had been born, and she had been dragged unwillingly back from death by the chela, whose face was bloodied by the red sunlight as he carried away her child, wrapped in the bloodstained fragments of Karahama's priestly robes. . . . And so she came at last to believe that it had never happened. Everyone was very kind to her, as to a child orphaned, and for many years she did not even speak her sister's name.

Book III
TIRIKI

"When the Universe was first created out of
nothing, it at once fell apart for lack of cohesion.
Like thousands of tiny tiles that have no apparent
meaning or purpose, all the pieces are identical in
shape and size, though they may differ in color
and pattern; and we have no picture of the intended mosaic to guide us. No one can know for
sure what it will look like, until the last tile is
finally fitted into place ... There are three tools
for the task: complete non-interference; active control over each and every movement; and inter-
change of powers until a satisfactory balance is
achieved. None of these methods can succeed,
however, without consent of the other two; this we
must accept as a fundamental principle—else we
have no explanation for what has already transpired.

"The problem is, as yet, unsolved; but we proceed, in waves. An advance in general knowledge is followed by a setback, in which many things are lost—only to be regained and excelled in the next wave of advancement. For the difference between that mosaic and the Universe is that no mosaic can ever become anything more than a picture in which motion has ended—a picture of Death. We do not build toward a time when everything stands still, but toward a time when everything is in a state of motion pleasing to all concerned—rock, plant, fish, bird, animal and man.

"It has never been, and never will be, easy work. But the road that is built in hope is more pleasant to the traveler than the road built in despair, even though they both lead to the same destination."

from *The Teachings of Micon of Ahtarrath*, as taken down by Rajasta the Mage

Chapter One

THE EXILE

I

It was deep dusk, and the breeze in the harbor was stiffening into a western wind that made the furled sails flap softly and the ship rise and fall to the gentle rhythm of the waves. Domaris stared toward the darkening shores, her body motionless, her white robes a spot of luminescence in the heavy shadows.

The captain bowed deeply in reverence before the Initiate. "My Lady—"

Domaris raised her eyes. "Yes?"

"We are about to leave the port. May I conduct you to your cabin? Otherwise, the motion of the ship may make you ill."

"I would rather stay on deck, thank you."

Again the captain bowed, and withdrew, leaving them alone again.

"I too must leave you, Isarma," said Rajasta, and stepped toward the rail. "You have your letters and your credentials. You have been provided for. I wish . . ." He broke off, frowning heavily. At last, he said only, "All will be well, my daughter. Be at peace."

She bent to kiss his hand reverently.

Stooping, Rajasta clasped her in his arms. "The Gods watch over thee, daughter," he said huskily, and kissed her on the brow.

"Oh, Rajasta, I can't!" Domaris sobbed. "I can't bear it! Micail—my baby! And Deoris . . ."

"Hush!" said Rajasta sternly, loosing her pleading, agonized hands; but he softened almost at once, and said, "I am sorry, daughter. There is nothing to be done. You *must* bear it. And know this: my love and blessings follow you, beloved— now and always." Raising his hand, the Guardian traced an archaic Sign. Before Domaris could react, Rajasta turned on his heel and swiftly walked away, leaving the ship. Domaris stared after him in astonishment, wondering why he had given her—an exile under sentence—the Sign of the Serpent.

A mistake? No—Rajasta does not make such mistakes.

After what seemed a long time, Domaris heard the clanking of anchor-chains and the oar-chant from the galley. Still she stood on the deck, straining her eyes into the gathering dusk for the last sight of her homeland, the Temple where she had been born and from which she had never been more than a league away in her entire life. She remained there, motionless, until long after night had folded down between the flying ship and the invisible shore.

II

There was no moon that night, and it was long before the woman became conscious that someone was kneeling at her side.

"What is it?" she asked, tonelessly.

"My Lady—" The flat, hesitant voice of Reio-ta was a murmuring plea, hardly audible over the sounds of the ship. "You must come below."

"I would rather remain here, Reio-ta, I thank you."

"My Lady—there is—something I m-must show thee."

Domaris sighed, suddenly conscious of cold and of cramped muscles and of extreme weariness, although she had not known it until now. She stumbled on her numb legs, and Reio-ta stepped quickly to her side and supported her.

She drew herself erect at once, but the young priest pleaded, "No, lean on me, my Lady . . ." and she sighed, allowing him to assist her. She thought again, vaguely and with definite relief, that he was nothing at all like Micon.

The small cabin allotted to Domaris was lighted by but a single, dim lamp, yet the slave-woman— strangers, for Elara could not be asked to leave her husband and newborn daughter—had made it a place of order and comfort. It looked warm and inviting to the exhausted Domaris: there was a faint smell of food, and a slight pungent smoke from the lamp, but all these things vanished into the perimeter of her consciousness, mere backdrop to the blue-wrapped bundle lying among the cushions on the low bed . . . clumsily wrapped in frag-

ments of a stained blue robe, it squirmed as if
alive . . .

"My most revered Lady and elder sister," Reio-ta
said humbly, "I would b-beg you to accept the
care of my acknowledged daughter."

Domaris caught her hands to her throat, swaying;
then with a swift strangled cry of comprehension
she snatched up the baby and cradled it against
her heart. "Why this?" she whispered. *"Why this?"*

Reio-ta bent his head. "I—I—I grieve to take her
from her m-mother," he stammered, "but it was—it
was—you know as well as I that it would be death
to leave her there! And—it is my right, under the
Law, to take my d-daughter where it shall please
me"

Domaris, wet-eyed, held the baby close while
Reio-ta explained simply what Domaris had not
dared to see . . .

"Neither Grey-robe nor Black—and mistake not,
my Lady, there are Black-robes still, there will
be Black-robes until the Temple falls into the
sea—and maybe after! They would not let this
child live—they b-believe her a child of the Dark
Shrine!"

"But . . ." Wide-eyed, Domaris hesitated to ask
the questions his words evoked in her mind—but
Reio-ta, with a wry chuckle, divined her thought
easily.

"To the Grey-robes, a sacrilege," he murmured.
"And the B-Black-robes would think only of her
value as a sacrifice! Or that—that she had b-been
ruined by the Light-born—was not the—the incarnation of the—" Reio-ta's voice strangled on the
words unspoken.

For another moment, Domaris's tongue would

not obey her, either; but at last she managed to say, half in shock, "Surely the Priests of Light . . ."

"Would not interfere. The Priests of Light—" Reio-ta looked at Domaris pleadingly. "They cursed Riveda—*and his seed!* They would not intervene to save her. But—with this child gone, or vanished— Deoris too will be safe."

Domaris buried her face in the torn robe swathed about the sleeping infant. After a long minute, she raised her head and opened tearless eyes. "Cursed," she muttered. "Yes, this too is karma. . . ." Then, to Reio-ta, she said. "She shall be my tenderest care—I swear it!"

Chapter Two

THE MASTER

The soft, starlit night of Ahtarrath was so still that the very steps of their bare feet on the grass could be heard. Reio-ta gave Domaris his hand, and she clutched at his fingers with a grip that betrayed her emotion before this ordeal; but her face was serene in its lovely, schooled calm. The man's eyes, brooding secretly under dark lashes, flashed a swift, approving look at her as his other hand swept aside the heavy sacking curtain that screened the inner room. Her hand was cold in his, and a sense of utter desolation seemed to pass from her to him. She was calm—but he was fleetingly reminded of the moment when he had led the trembling Deoris before the Vested Five.

Full realization suddenly welled over Reio-ta, lashing him with almost unbearable self-loathing. His remorse was a living thing that sprang at him and clawed at his vitals; a lifetime, a dozen lifetimes could never wipe out anything he had done! And this sudden insight into the woman beside him,

the woman who should have been his sister, was a
further scourge. She was so desperately, so utterly
alone!

With a gentle, deprecatory tenderness, he drew
her into the austere inner chamber, and they faced
a tall, thin-faced old man, seated on a plain wooden
bench. He rose at once and stood quietly surveying
them. It was not until many months later that
Domaris learned that the ancient Priest Rathor
was blind, and had been so from birth.

Reio-ta dropped to his knees for the ancient's
blessing. "Bless me, Lord Rather," he said humbly,
"I bring n-news of Micon. He died a hero—and to
a noble end—and I am not blameless."

There was a long silence. Domaris, at last,
stretched imploring hands to the old man; he
moved, and the movement broke the static pattern
of self-blame in the younger Priest's face. Reio-ta
continued, gazing up at the aged Rathor, "I b-bring
you the Lady Domaris—who is the mother of
Micon's son."

The ancient master raised one hand, and breathed
a single sentence; and the softness of his voice
stayed with Domaris until the moment of her death.
"All this I know, and more," he said. Raising Reio-ta,
he drew him close and kissed the young Priest
upon the forehead. "It is karma. Set your heart
free, my son."

Reio-ta struggled to steady his voice. "M-Master!"

Now Domaris also would have knelt for Rathor's
blessing, but the ancient prevented her. Deliberately, the master bent and touched his lips to the
hem of her robe. Domaris gasped and quickly raised
the old man to his feet. Lifting his hand, Rathor
made a strange Sign upon her forehead—the same

Sign Domaris had yielded to Micon at their first meeting. The ancient smiled, a smile of infinite benediction ... then stepped back and re-seated himself upon his bench.

Awkwardly, Reio-ta took her two hands in his own. "My Lady, you must not cry," he pleaded, and led her away.

Chapter Three

LITTLE SINGER

With the passing of time, Domaris grew somehow accustomed to Ahtarrath. Micon had lived here, had loved this land, and she comforted herself with such thoughts; yet homesickness burned in her and would not be stilled.

She loved the great grey buildings, massive and imposing, very different from thc low, white-glcaming structures in the Ancient Land, but equally impressive in their own fashion; she grew to accept the terraced gardens that sloped down everywhere to the shining lakes, the interlacing canopies of trees taller than she had ever seen—but she missed the fountains and the enclosed courts and pools, and it was many years before she could accustom herself to the many-storied buildings, or climb stairs without the sense that she violated a sacred secret meant for use in temples alone.

Domaris had her dwelling on the top floor of the building which housed the unmarried Priestesses; all the rooms which faced the sea had been set aside for Domaris and her attendants—and for one other from whom she was parted but seldom, and never for long.

She was instantly respected and soon loved by everyone in the New Temple, this tall quiet woman with the white streak in her blazing hair; they accepted her always as one of themselves, but with the reserve and honor accorded to one who is a little strange, a little mysterious. Ready always to help or heal, quick of decision and slow of anger, and always with the blond and sharp-featured little girl toddling at her heels—they loved Domaris, but some strangeness and mystery kept them at a little distance; they seemed to know instinctively that here was a woman going through the motions of living without any real interest in what she was doing.

Only once did Dirgat, Arch-priest of the Temple— a tall and saintly patriarch who reminded Domaris slightly of Ragamon the Elder—come to remonstrate with her on her apparent lack of interest in her duties.

She bowed her head in admission that the rebuke was just. "Tell me wherein I have failed, my father, and I will seek to correct it."

"You have neglected no iota of your duty, daughter," the Arch-priest told her gently. "Indeed, you are more than usually conscientious. You fail us not—but you fail yourself, my child."

Domaris sighed, but did not protest, and Dirgat, who had daughters of his own, laid his hand over her thin one.

"My child," he said at last, "forgive me that I call you so, but I am of an age to be your grandsire, and I—I like you. Is it beyond your power to find some happiness here? What troubles you, daughter. Open your heart. Have we failed to give you welcome?"

Domaris raised her eyes, and the tearless grief in them made the old Arch-priest cough in embarrassment. "Forgive me, my father," she said. "I sorrow for my homeland—and for my child—my children."

"Have you other children, then? If your little daughter could accompany you, why could not they?"

"Tiriki is not my daughter," Domaris explained quietly, "but my sister's child. She was daughter to a man condemned and executed for sorcery—and they would have slain the innocent child as well. I brought her beyond harm's reach. But my own children . . ." She paused a moment, to be sure that her voice was steady before she spoke. "My oldest son I was forbidden to bring with me, since he must be reared by one—worthy—of his father's trust; and I am exiled." She sighed. Her exile had been voluntary, in part, a penance self-imposed; but the knowledge that she had sentenced herself made it no easier to bear. Her voice trembled involuntarily as she concluded bleakly, "Two other children died at birth."

Dirgat's clasp tightened very gently on her fingers. "No man can tell how the lot of the Gods will fall. It may be that you will see your son again." After a moment he asked, "Would it comfort you to work among children—or would it add to your sorrow?"

Domaris paused, to consider. "I think—it would comfort me," she said, after a little.

The Arch-priest smiled. "Then some of your other

duties shall be lightened, for a time at least, and you shall have charge of the House of Children."

Looking at Dirgat, Domaris felt she could weep at the efforts of this good and wise man to make her happy. "You are very kind, father."

"Oh, it is a small thing," he murmured, embarrassed. "Is there any other care I can lighten?"

Domaris lowered her eyes. "No, my father. None." Even to her own attendants, Domaris would not mention what she had known for a long time; that she was ill, and in all probability would never be better. It had begun with the birth of Arvath's child, and the clumsy and cruel treatment she had received—no, cruel it had been, but not clumsy. The brutality had been far from unintentional.

At the time, she had accepted it all, uncaring whether she lived or died. She had only hoped they would not kill her outright, that her child might live. . . . But that had not been their idea of punishment. Rather it was Domaris who should live and suffer! And suffer she had—with memories that haunted her waking and sleeping, and pain that had never wholly left her. Now, slowly and insidiously, it was enlarging its domain, stealing through her body—and she suspected it was neither a quick nor an easy death that awaited her.

She turned back her face, serene and composed again, to the Arch-priest, as they heard tiny feet—and Tiriki scampered into the room, her silky fair hair all aflutter about the elfin face, her small tunic torn, one pink foot sandalled and the other bare, whose rapid uneven steps bore her swiftly to Domaris. The woman caught the child up and pressed her to her heart; then set Tiriki in her lap, though the little girl at once wriggled away again.

"Tiriki," mused the old Arch-priest. "A pretty name. Of your homeland?"

Domaris nodded ... On the third day of the voyage, when nothing remained in sight of the Ancient Land but the dimmest blue line of mountains, Domaris had stood at the stern of the ship, the baby folded in her arms as she remembered a night of poignant sweetness, when she had watched all night under summer stars, Micon's head pillowed on her knees. Although, at the time, she had hardly listened, it seemed now that she could hear with some strange inward ear the sound of two voices blended in a sweetness almost beyond the human: her sister's silvery soprano, interlaced and intermingled with Riveda's rich chanting baritone ... Bitter conflict had been in Domaris then, as she held in her goose-fleshed arms the drowsing child of the sister she loved beyond everything else and the only man she had ever hated—and then that curious trick of memory had brought back Riveda's rich warm voice and the brooding gentleness in his craggy face, that night in the star-field as Deoris slept on his knees.

He truly loved Deoris at least for a time, she had thought. *He was not all guilty, nor we all blameless victims of his evil-doing. Micon, Rajasta, I myself—we are not blameless of Riveda's evil. It was our failure too.*

The baby in her arms had picked that moment to wake, uttering a strange little gurgling croon. Domaris had caught her closer, sobbing aloud, "Ah, little singer!" And Tiriki—*little singer*—she had called the child ever since.

Now Tiriki was bound on a voyage of exploration: she toddled to the Arch-priest, who put out a hand to pat her silky head; but without warning she opened her mouth and her little squirrel teeth closed, hard, on Dirgat's bare leg. He gave a most undignified grunt of astonishment and pain—but before he could chide her or even compose himself, Tiriki released him and scampered away. As if his leg had not been hard enough, she began chewing on a leg of the wooden table.

Dismayed but stifling unholy laughter, Domaris caught the child up, stammering confused apologies.

Dirgat waved them away, laughing as he rubbed his bitten leg. "You said the Priests in your land would have taken her life," he chuckled, "she was only bearing a message from her father!" He gestured her last flustered apologies to silence. "I have grandchildren and great-grandchildren, daughter! The little puppy's teeth are growing, that is all."

Domaris tugged a smooth silver bangle from her wrist and gave it to Tiriki. "Little cannibal!" she admonished. "Chew on this—but spare the furniture, and my guests! I beg you!"

The little girl raised enormous, twinkling eyes, and put the bangle to her mouth. Finding it too large to get into her mouth all at once—although she tried—Tiriki began to nibble tentatively on the rim; tumbled down with a thump on her small bottom, and sat there, intent on chewing up the bracelet.

"A charming child," Dirgat said, with no trace of sarcasm. "I had heard that Reio-ta claimed paternity, and wondered at that. There's no Atlantean blood in this blonde morsel, one can see it at a glance!"

"She is very like her father," said Domaris quietly. "A man of the Northlands, who sinned and was— destroyed. The chief Adept of the Grey-robes— Riveda of Zaiadan."

The Arch-priest's eyes held a shadow of his troubled thoughts as he rose, to take his departure. He had heard of Riveda; what he had heard was not good. If Riveda's blood was predominant in the child, it might prove a sorry heritage. And though Dirgat said nothing of this, Domaris's thoughts echoed the Arch-priest's, as her glance rested on Riveda's daughter.

Once again, fiercely, Domaris resolved that Tiriki's heritage should not contaminate the child. *But how can one fight an unseen, invisible taint in the blood—or in the soul?* She snatched Tiriki up in her arms again, and when she let her go, Domaris's face was wet with tears.

Chapter Four

THE SPECTRE

The pool known as the Mirror of Reflections lay dappled in the lacy light filtering through the trees, repeating the silent merging of light with darkness that was the passing of days, and then of years.

Few came here, for the place was uncanny, and the pool was credited with having the ability to collect and reflect the thoughts of those who had once gazed into its rippling face, wherever they might be. In consequence the place was lonely and forsaken, but there was peace there, and silence, and serenity.

Thither came Deoris, one day, in a mood of driving unrest, the future stretching blank and formless before stormy eyes.

The whole affair had been, after all, something like using a bullwhip to kill a fly. Riveda was dead. Talkannon was dead. Nadastor was dead, his disciples dead or scattered. Domaris was in exile. And Deoris herself—who would bother to

sentence her, now that the child of sacrilege was
dead? More, Deoris had been made an Initiate of
the highest Mystery in the Temple; she could not
be simply left to her own devices after that. When
she had recovered from her illness and her injuries,
she had entered upon a disciplinary period of
probation; there had been long ordeals, and a period of study more severe than any she had ever
known. Her instructor had been none other than
Maleina. Now that time, too, was ended—but what
came after? Deoris did not know and could not
guess.

Throwing herself down on the grassy margin of
the pool, she gazed into the depths that were stained
a darker blue than the sky, thinking lonely, bitter
thoughts, yearning rebelliously for a little child of
whom she had scarcely any conscious recollection.
Tears gathered and slowly blurred the bright
waters, dripping unheeded from her eyes. Tasting
their salt on her lips, Deoris shook her head to
clear her vision, without, however, taking her intent,
introspective gaze from the pool.

In her mood of abstraction, of almost dreamy
sorrow, she saw without surprise the features of
Domaris, looking upward at her from the pool: a
thinner face, the fine boning distinct, and the expression a look of appeal—of loving entreaty. Even
as she looked, the lips widened in the old smile,
and the thin arms were held out, in a compelling
gesture, to fold her close . . . How well Deoris knew
that gesture!

A vagrant wind ruffled the water and the image
was gone. Then, for an instant, another face formed,
and the pointed, elfin features of Demira glinted

delicately in the ripples. Deoris covered her face with her hands, and the sketched-in ghost vanished. When she looked again, the ripples were ruffled only by lifting breezes.

Chapter Five

THE CHOSEN PATH

In these last years, Elis had lost her old prettiness, but had gained dignity and mature charm. In her presence, Deoris felt a curious peace. She took Elis's youngest child, a baby not yet a month old, in her arms and held him hungrily, then handed him back to Elis and with a sudden, despairing move, she flung herself to her knees beside her cousin and hid her face.

Elis said nothing, and after a moment Deoris lifted her eyes and smiled weakly. "I am foolish," she admitted, "but—you are very like Domaris."

Elis touched the bent head in its coif of heavy dark plaits. "You yourself grow more like her each day, Deoris."

Deoris rose swiftly to her feet as Elis's older children, led by Lissa—now a tall, demure girl of thirteen—rushed into the room. Upon seeing the woman in the blue robes of an Initiate of Caratra, they stopped, their impulsive merriment checked and fast-fading.

Only Lissa had self-possession enough to greet her. "*Kiha* Deoris, I have something to tell you!"

Deoris put her arm around her cousin's daughter. Had she ever carried this sophisticated little maiden as a naughty toddler in her arms? "What is this great secret, Lissa?"

Lissa turned up excited dark eyes. "Not really a secret, *kiha* ... only that I am to serve in the Temple next month!"

A dozen thoughts were racing behind Deoris's calm face—the composed mask of the trained priestess. She had learned to control her expressions, her manner—and almost, but not quite, her thoughts. She, Initiate of Caratra, was forever barred away from certain steps of accomplishment. Lissa—Lissa would surely never feel anything like her own rebellion ... Deoris was remembering; she had been thirteen or fourteen, about Lissa's age, but she could not remember precisely *why* she had been so helplessly reluctant to enter the Temple of Caratra even for a brief term of service. Then, in the relentless train of thought she could never halt or slow once it had begun in her mind, she thought of Karahama ... of Demira ... and then the memory that would not be forced away. If her own daughter had lived, the child she had borne to Riveda, she would have been just a little younger than Lissa—perhaps eight, or nine—already approaching womanhood.

Lissa could not understand the sudden impetuous embrace into which Deoris pulled her, but she returned it cheerfully; then she picked up her baby brother and went out on the lawns, carefully shepherding the others along before her. The woman watched, Elis smiling with pride, Deoris's smile a little sad.

"A young priestess already, Elis."

"She is very mature for her age," Elis replied. "And how proud Chedan is of Lissa now! Do you remember how he resented her, when she was a baby?" She laughed reminiscently. "Now he is like a true father to her! I suppose Arvath would be glad enough to claim her now! Arvath generally decides what he wants to do when it is too late!"

It was no secret anymore; a few years ago Arvath had belatedly declared himself Lissa's father and made an attempt to claim her, as Talkannon had done with Karahama in a similar situation. Chedan had had the last word, however, by refusing to relinquish his stepdaughter. Arvath had undergone the strict penances visited on an unacknowledged father, for nothing—except, perhaps, the good of his soul.

A curious little pang of memory stung Deoris at the mention of Arvath; she knew he had been instrumental in pronouncing sentence upon Domaris, and she still resented it. He and Deoris did not meet twice in a year, and then it was as strangers. Arvath himself could advance no further in the priesthood, for as yet he had no child.

Deoris turned to take her departure, but Elis detained her for a moment, clasping her cousin's hand. Her voice was gentle as she spoke, out of the intuition which had never yet failed her. "Deoris—I think the time has come for you to seek of Rajasta's wisdom."

Deoris nodded slowly. "I shall," she promised. "Thank you, Elis."

Once out of her cousin's sight, however, Deoris's

countenance was a little less composed. She had evaded this for seven years, fearing the condemnation of Rajasta's uncompromising judgment ... Yet, as she went along the paths from Elis's home, her step hurried.

What had she been afraid of? He could only make her face herself, know herself.

II

"I cannot say what you must do," Rajasta told her, rigid and unbending. "It is not what I might demand of you, but what you will demand of yourself. You have set causes into motion. Study them. What penalties had been incurred on your behalf? What obligations devolve upon you? Your judgment of yourself will be harsher than mine could ever be—but only thus can you ever be at peace with your own heart."

The woman kneeling before him crossed her arms on her breast, in strict self-searching.

Rajasta added a word of caution. "You will pronounce sentence upon yourself, as an Initiate must; but seek not to meddle again with the life the Gods have given you three times over! Death may not be self-sentenced. It is Their will that you should live; death is demanded only when a human body is so flawed and distorted by error that it cannot atone, until it has been molded into a cleaner vehicle by rebirth."

Momentarily rebellious, Deoris looked up. "Lord Rajasta, I cannot endure that I am set in honor, called Priestess and Initiate—I who have sinned in my body and in my soul."

"Peace!" he said sternly. "This is not the least of

your penance, Deoris. Endure it in humility, for this too is atonement, and waste is a crime. Those wiser than we have decided you can serve best in that way! A great work is reserved for you in rebirth, Deoris; fear not, you will suffer in minute, exact penance for your every sin. But sentence of death, for you, would have been the easy way! If you had died—if we had cast you out to die or to fall into new errors—then causes and crimes would have been many times multiplied! No, Deoris, your atonement in this life shall be longer and more severe than that!"

Chastened, Deoris turned her eyes to the floor.

With a hardly audible sigh, Rajasta placed a hand upon her shoulder. "Rise, daughter, and sit here beside me." When she had obeyed, he asked quietly, "How old are you?"

"Seven-and-twenty summers."

Rajasta looked at her appraisingly. Deoris had not married, nor—Rajasta had taken pains to ascertain it—had she taken any lover. Rajasta was not certain that he had been wise in allowing this departure from Temple custom; a woman unmarried at her age was a thing of scorn, and Deoris was neither wife nor widow. . . . He thought, with a creeping sorrow that never left him for long, of Domaris. Her grief for Micon had left her emotions scarred to insensitivity; had Riveda so indelibly marked Deoris?

She raised her head at last and her blue eyes met his steadily. "Let this be my sentence," she said, and told him.

Rajasta looked at her searchingly as she spoke; and when she was finished he said, with a kindness that came nearer to unnerving her than anything in many years, "You are not easy on yourself, my daughter."

She did not flinch before him. "Domaris did not spare herself," Deoris said slowly. "I do not suppose I will ever see my sister again, in this life. But . . ." She bent her head, feeling suddenly almost too shy to continue. "I—would live, so that when we meet again—as our oath binds us to do in a further life—I need not feel shame before her."

Rajasta was almost too moved to speak. "So be it," he pronounced at last. "The choice is your own—and the sentence is—just."

Chapter Six

WITHOUT EXPECTATIONS

I

In the eleventh year of her exile, Domaris discovered that she could no longer carry on her duties unaided, as she had done for so long. She accepted this gracefully, with a patient endurance that marked everything she did; she had known for a long time that she was ill, and would in all probability never be better.

She went about those duties which remained with an assured serenity which gave justice to all—but the glowing confidence was gone, and all the old sparkling joy. Now it was a schooled poise that impressed her personality, a certain grave attention that lived in the present moment, refusing equally the past and the future. She gave respect and kindness to all, accepting their honor with a gentle reserve; and if this homage ever struck at her heart with a sorrowful irony, she kept it hidden in her heart.

But that Domaris was more than a mere shell, no one could doubt who saw her in the quiet moments of the Ritual. Then she lived, and lived intensely; indeed she seemed a white flame, the very flesh of her seemed to glow. Domaris had not the slightest idea of her impact on her associates, but she felt then a strange, passive happiness, a receptivity—she never quite defined it, but it was compounded of a lively inner life that touched mystery, and a sense of Micon's nearness, here in his own country. She saw it with his eyes, and though at times the gardens and still pools roused memories of the enclosed courts and fountains of her homeland, still she was at peace.

Her Guardianship was still firm and gentle, but never obtrusive, and she now reserved for herself a period of each day which she devoted to watching the harbor. From her high window she gazed, with a remote and terrible loneliness, and every white sail which left the harbor laid a deeper burden of solitude on her heart. The incoming ships lacked, for her, the same poignant yearning that washed over her as she waited, quiescent, for something— she did not know what. There was a doom upon her, and she felt that this interval of calm was just that—an interval.

She was seated there one day, her listless hands still, when her serving woman entered and informed her, "A woman of nobility requests audience, my Lady."

"You know that I see no one at this hour."

"I informed her of that, Lady—but she insisted."

"Insisted?" Domaris expostulated, with an echo of her old manner.

"She said she had travelled very far, and that the matter was one of grave importance."

Domaris sighed. This happened, now and again—usually some barren woman in search of a charm that would produce sons. Would they never cease to plague her? "I will see her," she said wearily, and walked with slow dignity to the ante-room.

Just at the door she stopped, one hand clutching at the door-frame, and the room dipped around her. *Deoris! Ah, no—some chance resemblance, some trick of light—Deoris is years away, in my homeland, perhaps married, perhaps dead.* Her mouth was suddenly parched, and she tried, unsuccessfully, to speak. Her face was moonlight on white marble, and Domaris was trembling, not much, but in every nerve.

"Domaris!" And it was the loved voice, pleading, "Don't you recognize me, Domaris?"

With a great gasp, Domaris reached for her sister, stretching out her arms hungrily—then her strength failed, and she fell limp at Deoris's feet.

Crying, shaking with fright and joy, Deoris knelt and gathered the older woman in her arms. The change in Domaris was like a blow in the face, and for a moment Deoris wondered if Domaris was dead—if the shock of her coming had killed her. Almost before she had time to think, however, the grey eyes opened, and a quivering hand was laid against her cheek.

"It *is* you, Deoris, it is!" Domaris lay still in her sister's arms, her face a white joy, and Deoris's tears fell on her, and for a time neither knew it. At last Domaris stirred, unquietly. "You're crying—but there is no need for tears," she whispered, "not now." And with this she rose, drawing Deoris up with her. Then, with her kerchief, she dried the other's tears and, pinching the still-saucy nose, said, elder-sisterly, "Blow!"

II

When they could speak without sobbing, or laughing, or both, Domaris, looking into the face of the beautiful, strange, and yet altogether familiar woman her sister had become, asked shakily, "Deoris, how did you leave—my son? Is he—tell me quickly—is he well? I suppose he would be almost a man now. Is he much like—his father?"

Deoris said very tenderly, "You may judge for yourself, my darling. He is in the outer room. He came with me."

"O merciful Gods!" gasped Domaris, and for a moment it seemed she would faint again. "Deoris, my baby—my little boy . . . ."

"Forgive me, Domaris, but I—I had to have this one moment with you."

"It's all right, little sister, but—oh, bring him to me *now!*"

Deoris stood and went to the door. Behind her Domaris, still shaking, crowded to her side, unable to wait even a moment. Slowly and rather shyly, but smiling radiantly, a tallish young boy came forward and took the woman in his arms.

With a little sigh, Deoris straightened herself and looked wistfully at them. There was a little pain in her heart that would not be stilled as she went out of the room . . . and when she returned, Domaris was seated on a divan and Micail, kneeling on the floor at her feet, pressed a cheek already downy against her hand.

Domaris raised happy, questioning eyes at Deoris, startled by seeing. "But what is this, Deoris? *Your* child? How—who—bring him here, let me see," she said. But her glance returned again and again to her son, even as she watched Deoris unwrapping the swaddling bands from the child she had carried in. It was partly pain to see Micail's features; Micon was so keenly mirrored in the dark, young, proud face, the flickering half-smile never absent long from his lips, the clear storm-blue eyes under the bright hair that was his only heritage from his mother's people . . . Domaris's eyes spilled over as she ran her thin hand over the curling locks at the nape of his neck.

"Why Micail," she said, "you are a man, we must cut off these curls."

The boy lowered his head, suddenly shy again.

Domaris turned to her sister again. "Give me your baby, Deoris, I want to see—him, her?"

"A boy," said Deoris, and put the yearling pink lump into Domaris's arms.

"Oh, he is sweet, precious," she cooed over him lovingly, "but . . .?" Domaris looked up, hesitant questions trembling on her lips.

Deoris, her face grave, took her sister's free hand and gave Domaris the only explanation she was ever to receive. "Your child's life was forfeited— partly through my fault. Arvath was debarred from rising in the priesthood because he had no living son. And the obligation, which you had—failed— could be said to pass to me . . . and . . . Arvath was not unwilling."

"Then this is—Arvath's son?"

Deoris seemed not to hear the interruption, but continued, quietly, "He would even have married me, but I would not tread on the hem of your robe. Then—it seemed a miracle! Arvath's parents are here, you know, in Ahtarrath, and they wished to have his son to bring up, since Arvath is not—has not married again. So he begged me to undertake this journey—there was no one else he could send— and Rajasta arranged that I should come to you and bring Micail, since when he comes to manhood he must claim his father's heritage and his place. So—so I took ship with the children, and . . ." She shrugged, and smiled.

"You have others?"

"No. Nari is my only child."

Domaris looked down at the curly-headed child on her knee; he sat there composed and laughing, playing with his own thumbs—and now that she knew, Domaris fancied she could even see the resemblance to Arvath. She looked up and saw the expression on her sister's face, a sort of wistfulness. "Deoris," she began, but the door bounced open and a young girl danced into the room, stopping short and staring shyly at the strangers.

"*Kiha* Domaris, I am sorry," she whispered, "I did not know you had guests."

Deoris turned to the little maiden: a tall child, possibly ten years old, delicate and slender, with long straight fine hair loosely falling about her shoulders, framing a pointed and delicate little face in which glimmered wide, silver-blue eyes in a fringe of dark lashes . . .

"Domaris!" Deoris gasped, "Domaris, *who is she?* Who is that child? *Am I mad or dreaming?*"

"Why, my darling, can't you guess?" Domaris asked gently.

"Don't, Domaris, I can't bear it!" Deoris's voice broke on a sob. "You—never saw Demira—"

"Sister, look at me!" Domaris commanded. "Would I jest so cruelly? Deoris, it is your baby! Your own little girl—Tiriki, Tiriki darling, come here, come to your mother—"

The little maiden peered shyly at Deoris, too timid to advance, and Domaris saw dawning in her sister's face a hope almost too wild for belief, a crazy half-scared hope.

"But Domaris, my baby died!" Deoris gasped, and then the tears came, hurt, miserable sobs, lonely floods she had choked back for ten years; the tears she had not been able to shed then; the nightmarish misery. *"Then it wasn't a dream!* I dreamed Reio-ta came and took her away—but later they told me she died—"

Deoris put the little boy down and went swiftly to her sister, clasping the dark head to her breast. "Darling, forgive me," Domaris said, "I was distracted, I did not know what to say or do. I said that to some of the Temple people to keep them from interfering while I thought what I might do; I never believed it would—oh, my little sister, and all those years you thought . . ." She raised her head and said, "Tiriki, come here."

The little girl still hung back, but as Deoris looked longingly at her, still only half daring to believe the miracle, the child's generous small heart went out to this beautiful woman who was looking at her with heartbreaking hope in her eyes. Tiriki came and flung her arms around Deoris in a tight hug, looking up at the woman timidly.

"Don't cry—oh, don't!" she entreated, in an earnest little voice that thrust knives of memory into Deoris's heart. *"Kiha* Domaris—*is* this my mother?"

"Yes, darling, yes," she was reassured—and then Tiriki felt herself pulled into the tightest embrace she had ever known. Domaris was laughing—but she was half crying, too; the shock or joy had been almost too great.

Micail saved them all. From the floor, holding Deoris's baby with a clumsy caution, he said in a tone of profound boyish disgust:

"Girls!"

Chapter Seven

THE UNFADING FLOWER

Domaris laid aside the lute she had been playing and welcomed Deoris with a smile. "You look rested, dear," she said, drawing the younger woman down beside her. "I am so happy to have you here! And—how can I thank you for bringing Micail to me?"

"You—you—what can I say?" Deoris picked up her sister's thin hand and held it to her own. "You have already done so much. Eilantha—what is it you call her—*Tiriki*—you have had her with you all this time? How did you manage?"

Domaris's eyes were far away, dim with dreamy recollection. "Reio-ta brought her to me. It was his plan, really. I did not know she was in such terrible danger. She would not have been allowed to live."

"Domaris!" Shocked belief was in the voice and the raised eyes. "But why was it kept secret from me?"

Domaris turned her deep-sunken eyes on her

sister. "Reio-ta tried to tell you. I think you were—
too ill to understand him. I was afraid you might
betray the knowledge, or . . ." She averted her eyes.
"Or try to destroy her yourself."

"Could you think . . .?"

"I did not know *what* to think, Deoris! It is a
wonder I could think at all! And certainly I was
not strong enough to compel you. But, for varying
reasons, neither Grey nor Black-robes would have
let her live. And the Priests of Light . . ." Domaris
still could not look at her sister. "They cursed
Riveda—*and his seed.*" There was a moment of
silence; then Domaris dismissed it all with a wave
of her hand. "It is all in the past," she said steadily.
"I have had Tiriki with me since then. Reio-ta has
been a father to her—and his parents love her very
much." She smiled. "She has been terribly spoilt,
I warn you! Half priestess, half princess . . ."

Deoris kept her sister's white hand in hers, looking at her searchingly. Domaris was thin, thin
almost to gauntness, and only lips and eyes had
color in her white face; the lips like a red wound,
the eyes sometimes feverishly bright. And in Domaris's burning hair were many, many strands of
white.

"But Domaris! You are ill!"

"I am well enough; and I shall be better, now
that you are here." But Domaris winced under her
scrutiny. "What do you think of Tiriki?"

"She is—lovely." Deoris smiled wistfully. "But I
feel so strange with her! Will she—love me, do you
think?"

Domaris laughed in gentle reassurance. "Of
course! But she feels strange, too. Remember, she
has known her mother only two days!"

"I know, but—I want her to love me now!" There was more than a hint of the old rebellious passion in Deoris's voice.

"Give her time," Domaris advised, half-smiling. "Do you think Micail really remembered *me?* And he was much older. . . ."

"I tried hard to make him remember, Domaris! Although I saw little of him for the first four or five years. He had almost forgotten me, too, by the time I was allowed to be with him. But I tried."

"You did very well." There was tearful gratitude in her eyes and voice. "I meant that Tiriki should know of you, but—she has had only me all her life. And I had no one else."

"I can bear it, to have her love you best," Deoris whispered bravely, "but only just—bear it."

"Oh my dear, my dear, surely you know I would never rob you of that."

Deoris was almost crying again, although she did not weep easily now. She managed to still the tears, but in her violet-blue eyes there was an aching *acceptance* which touched Domaris more deeply than rebellion or grief.

A childish treble called, "*Kiha* Domaris?" and the women, turning, saw Tiriki and Micail standing in the doorway.

"Come here, darlings," Domaris invited, but it was at her son she smiled, and the pain in her heart was a throbbing agitation, for she saw Micon looking at her. . . .

The boy and girl advanced into the room valiantly, but with a shyness neither could conquer. They stood before their mothers, clinging to one another's hands, for though Tiriki and Micail were still nearly strangers, they shared the same puzzle-

ment: everything had become new to both. All his
life Micail had known only the austere discipline
of the priesthood, the company of priests; in truth
he had never completely forgotten his mother—but
he felt shy and awkward in her presence. Tiriki,
though she had known hazily that Domaris had
not actually borne her, had all her life been petted
and spoiled by Domaris, idolized and given such
complete and sheltering affection that she had never
missed a mother.

The strangeness welled up again, and Tiriki
dropped Micail's hand and ran to Domaris, clinging jealously to her and hiding her silver-gilt hair
in Domaris's lap. Domaris stroked the shining head,
but her eyes never left Micail. "Tiriki, my dearest,"
she admonished softly, "don't you know that your
mother has longed for you all these years? And
you do not even greet her. Where are your manners,
child?"

Tiriki did not speak, hiding her eyes in bashful-
ness and rebellious jealousy. Deoris watched, the
knife thrusting into her heart again and again. She
had outgrown her old possessiveness of Domaris,
but a deeper, more poignant pain had taken its
place; and now, overlaid upon the scene it seemed
she could almost see another silver-gilt head resting upon her own breast, and hear Demira's mournful voice whispering, *If Domaris spoke kindly to me,
I think I would die of joy . . .*

Domaris had never seen Demira, of course; and
despite what Deoris had said to comfort the little
saji girl, Domaris would have treated Demira with
arrogant contempt if she had seen her. *But really,*
Deoris thought with sadness and wonder, *Tiriki is
only what Demira would have been, given such*

*careful, loving fosterage. She has all Demira's heed-
less beauty, her grace, and a poised charm, too, which
Demira lacked—a sweetness, a warmth, a—a confidence!* Deoris found herself smiling through her
blurry vision. *That is Domaris's work,* she told
herself, *and perhaps it may be all for the best. I
could not have done so much for her.*

Deoris put out her hand to Tiriki, stroking the
bright, feathery hair. "Do you know, Tiriki, I saw
you but once before you were taken from me, but
in all these years there has been no day when you
were absent from my heart. I thought of you always as a baby, though—I did not expect to find
you almost a woman. Maybe that will make it—
easier, for us to be friends?" There was a little
catch in her voice, and Tiriki's generous heart could
not but be moved by it.

Domaris had beckoned Micail to her, and apparently forgotten their existence. Tiriki moved closer
to Deoris; she saw the wistful look in the violet-
blue eyes, and the tact so carefully instilled by her
beloved Domaris did not fail her. Still timidly, but
with a self-possession that surprised Deoris, she
slipped her hand into the woman's.

"You do not seem old enough to be my mother,"
she said, with such sweet graciousness that the
boldness of the words was not impertinent; then,
on impulse, Tiriki put her arms about her mother's
waist and looked up confidingly into her face . . .
At first, Tiriki's only thoughts had been, *What would
Kiha Domaris want me to do? I must not make her
ashamed of me!* Now she found herself deeply af-
fected by Deoris's restrained sorrow, her lack of
insistence.

"Now I have a mother and a little brother too,"

the little girl said, warmly. "Will you let me play with my little brother?"

"To be sure," Deoris promised, still in the same restrained manner. "You are almost a woman yourself, so he will grow up to believe he has two mothers. Come along now, if you like, and you shall watch the nurse bathe and dress him, and afterward you shall show us the gardens—your little brother and me."

This, it soon became clear, had been exactly the right thing to say and do; the right note to strike. The last reserve dropped away quickly. If Tiriki and Deoris were never really to achieve a mother-and-daughter relationship, they did become friends —and they remained friends through the long months and years that slipped away, virtually without event.

Arvath's son grew into a sturdy toddler then a healthy lad: Tiriki shot up to tallness and lost the last baby softness in her face. Micail's voice began to change, and he too grew tall; at fifteen the resemblance to Micon had become even more pronounced; the dark-blue eyes sharp and clear in the same way, the face and slender strong body animated with the same intelligent, fluid restlessness . . .

From time to time Micon's father, the Prince Mikantor, Regent of the Sea Kingdoms, and his second wife, the mother of Reio-ta, claimed Micail for a few days; and often they earnestly besought that their grandchild, as heir to Ahtarrath, might remain at the palace with them.

"It is our right," the aging Mikantor would say somberly, time and again. "He is Micon's son, and must be reared as befits his rank, not among

women! Though I do not mean to demean what
you have done for him, of course. Reio-ta's daughter,
too, has place and rank with us." When saying
this, Mikantor's eyes would always fix Domaris
with patient, sorrowful affection; he would willingly have accepted her, too, as a beloved daughter—but her reserve toward him had never softened.

On each occasion that the subject arose, Domaris,
with quiet dignity, would acknowledge that Mikantor was right, that Micon's son was indeed heir
to Ahtarrath—but that the boy was also her son.
"He is being reared as his father would wish, that
I vow to you, but while I live," Domaris promised,
"he will not leave me again. While I live—" Her
voice would dwell on the words. "It will not be
long. Leave him to me—until then."

This conversation was repeated with but a few
variations every few months. At last the old Prince
bowed his head before the Initiate, and ceased
from importuning her further . . . though he continued his regular visits, which became if anything
more frequent than before.

Domaris compromised by allowing her son to
spend a great deal of time with Reio-ta. This ar-
rangement pleased all concerned, as the two rap-
idly became intimate friends. Reio-ta showed a
deep deference to the son of the older brother he
had adored and betrayed—and Micail enjoyed the
friendliness and warmth of the young prince. He
was at first a stiff, unfriendly boy, and found it
difficult to adjust to this unrestricted life; Rajasta
had accustomed him, since his third year, to the
austere self-discipline of the highest ranks of the
Priest's Caste. However, the abnormal shyness and

reserve eventually melted; and Micail began to display the same open-hearted charm and joyfulness that had made Micon so lovable.

Perhaps even more than Reio-ta, Tiriki was instrumental in this. From the first day they had been close, with a friendliness which soon ripened into love; brotherly and unsentimental love, but sincere and deep, nonetheless. They quarrelled often, to be sure—for they were very unlike: Micail controlled, calm of manner but proud and reserved, inclined to be secretive and derisive; and Tiriki hot-tempered beneath her poise, volatile as quick silver. But such quarrels were momentary, mere ruffles of temper—and Tiriki always regretted her hastiness first; she would fling her arms around Micail and beg him, with kisses, to be friends again. And Micail would pull her long loose hair, which was too fine and straight to stay braided for more than a few minutes, and tease her until she begged for mercy.

Deoris rejoiced at their close friendship, and Reio-ta was altogether delighted; but both suspected that Domaris was not wholly pleased. Of late, when she looked into Tiriki's eyes, an odd look would cross her face and she would purse her lips and frown a little, then call Tiriki to her side and hug her penitently, as if to make up for some unspoken condemnation.

Tiriki was not yet thirteen, but already she seemed altogether womanly, as if something worked like yeast within her, awaiting some catalyst to bring sudden and complete maturity. She was a fey, elfin maiden, altogether bewitching, and Micail all too soon realized that things could not

long continue as they were; his little cousin fascinated him too greatly.

Yet Tiriki had a child's innocent, impulsiveness,
and when it came it was very simple; a lonely
walk along the seashore, a touch, a playful kiss—
and then they stood for several moments locked
tight in one another's arms, afraid to move, afraid
to lose this sudden sweetness. Then Micail very
gently loosed the girl and put her away for him.
"Eilantha," he whispered, very low—and Tiriki,
understanding why he had spoken her Temple
name, dropped her eyes and stood without attempting to touch him again. Her intuition set a final
seal on Micail's sure young knowledge. He smiled,
with a new, mature responsibility, as he took her
hand—only her hand—in his own.

"Come, we should return to the Temple."

"O Micail!" the girl whispered in momentary
rebellion, "now that we have found each other—
must we lose this again so quickly? Will you not
even dare to kiss me again?"

His grave smile made her look away, confused.
"Often, I hope. But not here or now. You are—too
dear to me. And you are very young, Tiriki—as am
I. Come." His quiet authority was once again that
of an older brother, but as they mounted the long
terraced path toward the Temple gateway, he re-
lented and turned to her with a quick smile.

"I will tell you a little story," he said with soft
seriousness, and they sat down on the hewn steps
together. "Once upon a time there was a man who
lived within a forest, very much alone, alone with
the stars and the tall trees. One day he found a
beautiful gazelle within the forest, and he ran toward her and tried to clasp his arms around her

slender neck and comfort his loneliness—but the gazelle was frightened and ran from him, and he never found her again. But after many moons of wandering, he found the bud of a lovely flower. He was a wise man by then, because he had been alone so long; so he did not disturb the bud where it nodded in the sunshine, but sat by it for long hours and watched it open and grow toward the sun. And as it opened it turned to him, for he was very still and very near. And when the bud was open and fragrant, it was a beautiful passion-flower that would never fade."

There was a faint smile in Tiriki's silver-grey eyes. "I have heard that story often," she said, "but only now do I know what it means." She squeezed his hand, then rose and danced up the steps. "Come along," she called merrily. "They will be waiting for us—and I promised my little brother I would pick him berries in the garden!"

Chapter Eight

DUTY

That spring the illness Domaris had been holding at bay finally claimed her. All during the spring rains and through the summer seasons of flowers and fruits, she lay in her high room, unable to rise from her bed. She did not complain, and turned away their solicitude easily; surely she would be well again by autumn.

Deoris watched over her with tender care, but her love for her sister blinded her eyes, and she did not see what was all too plain to others; and, too often, neither Deoris nor any other could help the woman who lay there so patiently, powerless, through the long days and nights. Years had passed since anyone could have helped Domaris.

Deoris learned only then—for Domaris was too ill to care any longer about concealment—how cruelly her sister had been treated by the Blackrobes. Guilt lay heavy on the younger woman after that discovery—for something else came out that Deoris had not known before: just how seriously

Domaris had been injured in that strange, dream-like interlude which even now lay shrouded, for Deoris, in a dark web of confused dreams—the illusive memory of the Idiot's Village. What Domaris at last told her not only made clear exactly why Domaris had been unable to bring Arvath's first child to term, it made it amazing that she had even been able to bear Micon's.

Prince Mikantor finally got his dearest wish, and Micail was sent to the palace; Domaris missed her son, but would not have him see her suffering. Tiriki, however, would not be so constrained, but defied Deoris and even Domaris, for the first time in her life. Childhood was wholly behind her now; at thirteen, Tiriki was taller than Deoris, although slight and immature, as Demira had been. Also, like Demira, there was a precocious gravity in the greyed silver of her eyes and the disturbed lines of her thin face. Deoris had been so childish at thirteen that neither sister noticed, or realized, that Tiriki at that age was already grown; the swifter maturity of the atavistic Zaiadan type escaped their notice, and neither took Tiriki very seriously.

Everyone did what they could to keep her away on the worst days; but one evening when Deoris, exhausted from several days almost without sleep, napped for a moment in the adjoining room, Tiriki slipped in to see Domaris lying wide-eyed and very still, her face was white as the white lock in her still-shining hair.

Tiriki crept closer and whispered, "*Kiha*—?"

"Yes, darling," Domaris said faintly; but even for Tiriki she could not force a smile. The girl came closer yet, and picked up one of the blue-threaded hands, pressing it passionately to her cheek, kissing the waxen fingers with desperate adoration. Domaris tiredly shifted her free hand to clasp the little warm ones of the child. "Gently, darling," said Domaris. "Don't cry."

"I'm not crying," Tiriki averred, raising a tear-less face. "Only—can't I do anything for you, *Kiha* Domaris? I—you—it hurts you a lot, doesn't it?"

Under the child's great-eyed gaze, Domaris only said, quietly, "Yes, child."

"I wish I could have it instead of you!"

The impossible smile came then and flickered on the colorless mouth. "Anything rather than that, Tiriki darling. Now run away, my little one, and play."

"I'm not a baby, *Kiha!* Please, let me stay with you," Tiriki begged, and before the intense en-treaty Domaris closed her eyes and lay silent for a space of minutes.

I will not betray pain before this child! Domaris told herself—but a drop of moisture stood out on her lower lip.

Tiriki sat down on the edge of the couch. Domaris, ready to warn her away—for she could not bear the lightest touch, and sometimes, when one of the slave-women accidentally jarred her bed, would cry out in unbearable torture—realized with amaze-ment that Tiriki's movements had been so delicate that there was not the slightest hurt, even when the girl bent and twined her arms around Domaris's neck.

Why, Domaris thought, *she's like a little kitten, she could walk across my body and I would feel no hurt! At least she's inherited* something *good from Riveda!*

For weeks now, Domaris had borne no touch

except her sister's, and even Deoris's trained hands
had been unable to avoid inflicting torment at
times; but now Tiriki ... The child's small body
fitted snugly and easily into the narrow space at
the edge of the couch, and she knelt there with her
arms around her foster-mother for so many minutes that Domaris was utterly dumbfounded.

"Tiriki," she rebuked at last—reluctantly, for the
child's presence was curiously comforting—"you
must not tire yourself." Tiriki only gave her an
oddly protective, mature smile, and held Domaris
closer still. And suddenly Domaris wondered if she
were imagining it—*no, it was true:* the pain was
gradually lessening and a sort of strength was surging through her worn body. For a moment, the
blessedness of relief was all Domaris could understand, and she relaxed, with a long sigh. Then the
relief disappeared in sudden amazement and apprehension.

"Are you better now, *Kiha?*"

"Yes," Domaris told her, resolving to say nothing.
It was absurd to believe that a child of thirteen
could do what only the highest Adepts could do
after lengthy discipline and training! It had been
but a fancy of her weakness, no more. Some remnant of caution told her that if it were true, then
Tiriki, for her own safety, must be kept away ...
But keeping Tiriki away was easier to resolve than
to do.

In the days that followed, though Tiriki spent
much time with Domaris, taking a part of the
burden from the exhausted Deoris, Domaris main-
tained a severe control over herself. No word or
movement should betray her to this small woman-
child.

Ridiculous, she thought angrily, *that I must guard myself against a thirteen-year-old!*

One day, Tiriki had curled up like a cat beside her. Domaris permitted this, for the child's closeness was comforting, and Tiriki, who had been a restless child, never fidgeted or stirred. Domaris knew she was learning patience and an uncanny gentleness, but she did not want the girl to overtax herself, so she said, "You're like a little mouse, Tiriki. Aren't you tired of staying with me?"

"No. Please don't send me away, *Kiha* Domaris!"

"I won't, dear, but promise me you will not tire yourself!"

Tiriki promised, and Domaris touched the flaxen hair with a white finger and lay still, sighing. Tiriki's great grey cat's eyes brooded dreamily . . . *What can the child be thinking about? What a little witch she is! And that curious—healing instinct. Both Deoris and Riveda had had something like that,* she remembered, *I should have expected as much* . . . But Domaris could not follow the train of thought for long. Pain was too much a part of her now; she could not remember what it was like to be free of it.

Tiriki, her small pointed face showing, faintly, the signs of exhaustion, came out of her reverie and watched, helpless and miserable; then, in a sudden surge of protectiveness she flung her arms lightly around Domaris and pressed gently to her. And this time it was not a fancy: Domaris felt the sudden quick flow of vitality, the rapid surging ebb of the waves of pain. It was done unskillfully, so that Domaris felt dizzy and light-headed with the sudden strength that filled her.

The moment she was able, she sharply pushed

Tiriki away. "My dear," she said in wonder, "you mustn't . . ." She broke off, realizing that the girl was not listening. Drawing a long breath, Domaris raised herself painfully up on one elbow. "Eilantha!" she commanded shortly. "I am serious! You must never do that again! I forbid it! If you try—I will send you away from me altogether!"

Tiriki sat up. Her thin face was flushed and a queer little line was tight across her brow. "*Kiha*," she started, persuasively.

"Listen, precious," Domaris said, more gently, as she lay herself on her pillow again, "believe me, I'm grateful. Someday you will understand why I cannot let you—rob yourself this way. I don't know how you did it—that is a God-given power, my darling . . . but not like this! And not for me!"

"But—but it's *only* for you, *Kiha!* Because I love you!"

"But—little girl—" Domaris, at a loss for words, lay still, looking up into the quiet eyes. After a long moment, the child's dreamy face darkened again.

"*Kiha*," Tiriki whispered, with strange intentness, "when—where—where and when was it? You said—you told me . . ." She stopped, her eyes concentrated in an aching search of the woman's face, her brows knitted in a terrible intensity. "Oh, *Kiha*, why is it so hard to remember?"

"Remember what, Tiriki?"

The girl closed her eyes. "It was you—you said to me—" The great eyes opened, haunted, and Tiriki whispered, "Sister—and more than sister— here we two, women and sisters—pledge thee, Mother—where we stand in darkness." Her voice thickened, and she sobbed.

Domaris gasped. "You don't remember, you can't! Eilantha, you cannot, you have been spying, listening, you could not . . ."

Tiriki said passionately, "No, no, it was *you*, Kiha! It was! I remember, but it's like—a dream, like dreaming about a dream."

"Tiriki, my baby-girl—you are talking like a mad child, you are talking about something which happened before . . ."

"It did happen, then! It did! Do you want me to tell you the rest?" Tiriki stormed. "Why won't you believe me?"

"But it was before you were born!" Domaris gasped. *"How can this be?"*

White-faced, her eyes burning, Tiriki repeated the words of the ritual without stumbling—but she had spoken only a few lines when Domaris, pale as Death, checked her. "No, no Eilantha! Stop! You mustn't repeat those words! Not ever, ever— until you know what they mean! What they imply . . ." She held out exhausted, wasted arms. *"Promise me!"*

Tiriki subsided in stormy sobs against her foster-mother's breast; but at last muttered her promise.

"Some day—and if I cannot, Deoris will tell you about it. One day—you were made Devotee, dedicated to Caratra before your birth, and one day . . ."

"You had better let me tell her now," said Deoris quietly from the doorway. "Forgive me, Domaris; I could not help but hear."

But Tiriki leaped up, raging. "You! You had to come—to listen, to spy on me! You can never let me have a moment alone with *Kiha* Domaris, you are jealous because I can help her and you cannot! I hate you! I hate you, Deoris!" She was sobbing furiously, and Deoris stood, stricken, for Domaris had beckoned Tiriki to her and her daughter was crying helplessly in her sister's arms, her face hidden on Domaris's shoulder as the woman held her with anxious, oblivious tenderness. Deoris bent her head and turned to go, without a word, when Domaris spoke.

"Tiriki, hush, my child," she commanded. "Deoris, come here to me—no, there, close to me, darling. You too, baby," she added to Tiriki, who had drawn a little away and was looking at Deoris with resentful jealousy. Domaris laid one of her worn, wax-white hands in Tiriki's and stretched out her other hand to Deoris. "Now, both of you," Domaris whispered, "listen to me—for this may be the last time I can ever talk to you like this—the last time."

Chapter Nine

THE SEA AND THE SHIP

As summer gave way to autumn, even the children abandoned the hope and pretense that Domaris might recover. Day after day she lay in her
high room, watching the sun flicker on the white
waves, dreaming. Sometimes when one of the high-
bannered *wing-bird* ships slid over the horizon, she
wondered if Rajasta had received her message . . .
but not even that seemed important anymore. Days,
then months slipped over her head, and with each
day she grew paler, more strengthless, worn with
pain brought to the point beyond which even pain
cannot go, weary even with the effort of drawing
breath to live.

The old master, Rathor, came once and stood for
a long time close to her bedside, his hand between
her two pale ones and his old blind eyes bent upon
her worn face as if they saw not some faraway and
distant thing, but the face of the dying woman.

As the year turned again, Deoris, pale with long
nights and days of nursing her sister, was com-

manded unequivocally to take more rest; much of
the time, now, Domaris did not know her, and
there was little that anyone could do. Reluctantly,
Deoris left her sister to the hands of the other
Healer-priestesses, and—one morning—took her
children to the seashore. Micail joined them there,
for since his mother's illness he had seen little of
Tiriki. Micail was to remember this day, afterward,
as the last day he was a child among children.

Tiriki, her long pale hair all unbraided, dragged
her little brother by the hand as she flew here and
there. Micail raced after them, and all three went
wild with shouting and splashing and rowdy
playing, chasing in and out of the sloshing waves
on the sand. Even Deoris flung away her sandals
and dashed gaily into the tidewaters with them.
When they tired of this, Tiriki began to build in
the sand for her little brother, while Micail picked
up shells at the high-water mark and dumped them
into Tiriki's lap.

Deoris, sitting on a large sun-warmed rock to
watch them, thought, *They are only playing at being
children, for Nari's sake and mine. They have grown
up, those two, while I have been absorbed in Domaris. . . .* It did not seem quite right, to Deoris,
that a boy of sixteen and a gril of thirteen should
be so mature, so serious, so adult—though they
were acting, now, like children half their age!

But they quieted at last, and lay on the sand at
Deoris's feet, calling on her to admire their sand-
sculpture.

"Look," said Micail, "a palace, and a Temple!"

"See my pyramid?" little Nari demanded shrilly.

Tiriki pointed. "From here, the palace is like a
jewel set atop a green hill . . . Reio-ta told me,

once. . . ." Abruptly she sat up and demanded, "Deoris, did I ever have a real father? I love Reio-ta as if he truly were my father, but—you and *Kiha* Domaris are sisters; and Reio-ta is the brother of Micail's father . . ." Breaking off again, she glanced unquietly at Micail.

He understood what she meant immediately, and reached out to tweak her ear—but his impulse changed, and he only twitched it playfully instead.

Deoris looked soberly at her daughter. "Of course, Tiriki. But your father died—before you could be acknowledged."

"What was he like?" the girl asked, reflectively.

Before Deoris could answer, little Nari looked up with pouting scorn. "If he died before 'nowledging her, how could he *be* her father?" he asked, with devastating small-boy logic. He poked a chubby finger into his half-sister's ribs. "Dig me a hole, Tiriki!"

"Silly baby," Micail rebuked him.

Nari scowled. "Not a baby," he insisted. "My father was a Priest!"

"So was Micail's, Nari; so was Tiriki's," Deoris said gently. "We are all the children of Priests here."

But Nari only returned to the paradox he had seized on with new vigor. "If Tiriki's father died *before* she was born, then she don't have a father because he wasn't live to be her father!"

Micail, tickled by the whimsy of Nari's childish innocence, grinned delightedly. Even Tiriki giggled—then sobered, seeing the look on Deoris's face.

"Don't you want to talk about him?"

Again pain twisted oddly in Deoris's heart. Sometimes for months she did not think of Riveda at all—then a chance word or gesture from Tiriki would bring him back, and stir again that taut, half-sweet aching within her. Riveda was burned on her soul as ineradicably as the *dorje* scars on her breasts, but she had learned calm and control. After a moment she spoke, and her voice was perfectly steady. "He was an Adept of the Magicians, Tiriki."

"A Priest, like Micail's father, you said?"

"No, child, nothing like Micail's father. I said he was a Priest, because—well, the Adepts are like Priests, of a sort. But your father was of the Grey-robe sect, though they are not regarded so highly in the Ancient Land. And he was a Northman of Zaiadan; you have your hair and eyes from him. He was a Healer of great skill."

"What was his name?" Tiriki asked intently.

For a moment, Deoris did not answer. It occurred to her than Domaris had never spoken of this, and since she had raised Tiriki as Reio-ta's daughter, it was her right not to . . . At last Deoris said, "Tiriki, in every way that matters, Reio-ta is your father."

"Oh, I know, it isn't that I don't love him!" Tiriki exclaimed, penitantly—but as if drawn by an irresistible impetus, she went on, "But tell me, Deoris, because I remember, when I was only a baby—Domaris spoke of him to another Priestess —no, it was a Priest—oh, I can't remember, really, but . . ." She made a strange little helpless gesture with her hands.

Deoris sighed. "Have it as you will. His name was Riveda."

Tiriki repeated the name curiously. "Riveda. . . ."

"I did not know that!" Micail broke in, with sudden disquiet. "Deoris, can it be the same Riveda I heard talk in the Priest's Court as a child? Was he—the sorcerer, the heretic?" He stopped short at the dismay in Deoris's eyes, her pained mouth.

Nari raised his head and clamored, "What's a heretic?"

Micail, immediately repenting his rash outburst, unfolded his long legs and hoisted the little boy to his shoulder. "A heretic is one who does wicked things, and I will do a wicked thing and throw you into the sea if you do not stop plaguing Deoris with foolish questions! Look, I think that ship is coming to anchor, come, let's watch it; I'll carry you on my shoulder!"

Nari crowed in shrill delight, and Micail galloped off with him. Soon they were little more than tiny figures far along the beach.

Deoris came out of her daydream to find Tiriki slipping her hand into hers, saying with a low voice, "I did not mean to trouble you, Deoris. I—I only had to be sure that—that Micail and I were not cousins twice over." She blushed, and then said, entreatingly, "Oh, Deoris, you must know why!" For the first time, of her own will, Tiriki put up her face for her mother's kiss.

Deoris caught the slender child in her arms. "Of course I know, my little blossom, and I am very happy," she said. "Come—shall we go and see the ship too?" Hand in hand, close together, they followed the trail of Micail's hurrying feet through the sand until all four stood together again.

Deoris picked up her son (Nari at least was hers alone, for a time at least, she was thinking) and listened smiling as Micail, his arm around Tiriki, talked of the *wing-bird* which was gliding to harbor. The sea was in his blood as it had been in his father's; on the long voyage from the Ancient Land he had been mad with joy.

"I wonder if that ship is from the Ancient Land?" Tiriki said curiously.

"I would not be surprised," Micail answered wisely. "Look—they're putting out a boat from the ship, though; that's strange, they don't usually land boats here at the Temple, usually they go on to the City."

"There is a Priest in the first boat," Tiriki said as the small craft beached. Six men, common sailors, turned away along the lower path, but the seventh stood still, glancing up toward where the Temple gleamed like a white star atop the hill. Deoris's heart nearly stopped; it was . . .

"Rajasta!" Micail cried out, suddenly and joyously; and, forgetting his new-found dignity, he sped swiftly across the sands toward the white-robed man.

The Priest looked up, and his face glowed as he saw the boy. "My dear, dear son!" he exclaimed, clasping Micail in his arms. Deoris, following slowly with her children, saw that the old Guardian's face was wet with tears.

His arm about Micail, Rajasta turned to greet the others; Deoris would have knelt, but he embraced her with his free arm. "Little daughter, this is a lucky omen for my mission, though it is not a mission of joy," he told her. To her own surprise, Deoris discovered that she was weeping. Rajasta held her close, with a sort of dismayed embarrassment, comforting her awkwardly as she sobbed, and little Nari tugged at his mother's skirt.

"You'd spank *me* for that, D'ris," he rebuked shrilly.

Deoris laughed at this, recovering her composure somewhat. "Forgive me, Lord Rajasta," she said, flushing deeply, and drew Tiriki forward. "A miracle befell me, my father, for when I came here I found—my own small daughter, in Domaris's care."

Rajasta's smile was a benediction. "I knew of that, my daughter, for Reio-ta told me of his plan."

"You knew? And all those years . . . ?" Deoris bent her head. It had, indeed been wisest that she learn to think of her child as lost to her forever.

Tiriki clung to Deoris, bashfully, and Rajasta laid his hand on her silky head. "Do not be frightened, little one; I knew your mother when she was younger than you, and your father was my kinsman. You may call me Uncle, if you wish."

Nari peeped from behind his sister. "*My* father is a Priest!" he said valiantly. "Are you my Uncle too, Lord Guardian?"

"If you like," said Rajasta mildly, and patted the tangled curls. "Is Domaris well, my daughter?"

Deoris paled in consternation. "Did you not receive her letter? *You do not know?*"

Rajasta, too, turned pale. "No, I have had no word—all is confusion at the Temple, Deoris, we have had no letters. I have come on Temple business, though indeed I had hoped to see you both. What—what has befallen her?"

"Domaris is dying," Deoris said unsteadily.

The Priest's pale cheeks looked haggard—for the first time in her life, Deoris realized that Rajasta was an old, old man. "I feared—I felt," the Guardian said, hoarsely, "some premonition of evil upon her. . . ." He looked again at Micail's thin, proud face. "You are like your father, my son. You have his eyes . . ." But Rajasta's thoughts went on beyond his words: *He is like Domaris, too.* Domaris, whom he loved as more than a daughter—no one begotten of his own flesh had ever been half so dear to Rajasta; and Deoris said she was dying! *But the essential part of Domaris*, he reminded himself sternly and sadly, *has long been dead. . . .*

They dismissed the children as they neared the dormitory of the Priestesses. Alone together, Rajasta and Deoris climbed the stairs. "You will find her very changed," Deoris warned.

"I know," said Rajasta, and his voice held a deep sorrow; he leaned heavily on the young woman's offered arm. Deoris tapped gently on the door.

"Deoris?" a faint voice asked from within, and Deoris stepped aside for the Guardian to precede her. She heard her own name again, raised questioningly, then a glad cry: "Rajasta! Rajasta—my father!"

Domaris's voice broke in a sob, and Rajasta hastened to her side. Domaris tried to raise herself, but her face twisted with pain and she had to fall back. Rajasta bent and clasped her gently in his arms, saying, "Domaris, my child, my lovely child!"

Deoris very quietly withdrew and left them alone.

Chapter Ten

KARMA

I

Standing on the terrace, listening for the shouts of the Temple children in the lower gardens, Deoris heard a quiet step behind her, and looked up into Reio-ta's smiling eyes.

"The Lord Rajasta is with Domaris?" he asked.

Deoris nodded; her eyes grew sad. "She has been living only for this. It will not be long now."

Reio-ta took her hand and said, "You must not grieve, Deoris. She has been—less than living—for many years."

"Not for her," Deoris whispered, "but only for myself. I am selfish—I have always been selfish— but when she is gone I shall be alone."

"No," said Reio-ta, "you will not be alone." And, without surprise, Deoris found herself in his arms, his mouth pressed to hers. "Deoris," he whispered at last, "I loved you from the first! From the moment I came up out of a—a maelstrom that had drowned me, and saw you lying on the floor of a Temple I did not recognize, at the feet of—a Greyrobe whose name I did not even know. And the terrible burns on you! I loved you then, Deoris! Only that gave me the strength to—to defy . . ."

Matter-of-factly, Deoris supplied the name that, after so many years, his tongue still stumbled on. "To defy Riveda. . . ."

"Can you care for me?" he asked passionately. "Or does the past hold you still too close?"

Mutely Deoris laid her hand in his, warmed by a sudden confidence and hope, and knew, without analysing it, that it was for this that she had waited all her life. She would never feel for Reio-ta the mad adoration she had known for Riveda; she had loved—no, worshipped Riveda—as a suppliant to a God. Arvath had taken her as a woman, and there had been friendship between them and the bond of the child she had given him in her sister's place— but Arvath had never touched her emotions. Now, in full maturity, Deoris found herself able and willing to take the next step into the world of experience. Smiling, she freed herself from his arms.

He accepted it, returning her smile. "We are not young," he said. "We can wait."

"All time belongs to us," she answered gently. She took his hand again, and together they walked down into the gardens.

II

The sun was low on the horizon when Rajasta called them all together on a terrace near Deoris's apartments. "I did not speak of this to Domaris," he told them soberly, "but I wished to say to you tonight what I mean to tell the Priests of this Temple tomorrow. The Temple in our homeland— the Great Temple—is to be destroyed."

"Ah no!" Deoris cried out.

"Aye," said Rajasta, with solemn face. "Six months ago it was discovered that the great pyramid was sinking lower and lower into the Earth; and the shoreline has been breached in many places. There have been earthquakes. The sea has begun to seep beneath the land, and some of the underground chambers are collapsing. Ere long—ere long the Great Temple will be drowned by the waves of the sea."

There was a flurry of dismayed, confused questions, which he checked with a gesture. "You know that the pyramid stands above the Crypt of the Unrevealed God?"

"Would we did not!" Reio-ta whispered, very low.

"That Crypt is the nadir of the Earth's magnetic forces—the reason the Grey-robes sought to guard it so carefully from desecration. But ten years and more ago ..." Involuntarily Rajasta glanced at Tiriki, who sat wide-eyed and trembling. "Great sacrilege was done there, and Words of Power spoken. Reio-ta, it seems, was all too correct in his estimation, for we still had not rooted out the worms at our base!" For a moment Rajasta's eyes were stark and haunted, as if seeing again some horror the others could not even guess at. "Later, spells even more powerful than theirs were pronounced, and the worst evils contained, but—the Unrevealed God has had his death-wound. His dying agonies will submerge more than the Temple!"

Deoris covered her face with her hands.

Rajasta went on, in a low, toneless voice, "The Words of Power have vibrated rock asunder, disrupted matter to the very elements of its making; and once begun at so basic a level the vibrations cannot be stilled until they die out of their own. Daily about the Crypt, the Earth trembles—and the tremors are spreading! Within seven years, at the most, the entire Temple—perhaps the whole shoreline, the city and the lands about for many and many a mile—will sink beneath the sea—"

Deoris made a muffled, choking sound of horror.

Reio-ta bowed his head in terrible self-abasement. "Gods!" he whispered, "I—I am not guiltless in this."

"If we must speak of guilt," Rajasta said, more gently than was his habit, "I am no less guilty than any other, that my Guardianship allowed Riveda to entangle himself in black sorceries. Micon shirked the begetting of a son in his youth, and so dared not die under torture. Nor can we omit the Priest who taught him, the parents and servants who raised him, the great-great—grandsire of the ship's captain who brought Riveda's grandmother and mine from Zaiadan . . . no man can justly apportion cause and effect, least of all upon a scale such as this! It is karma. Set your heart free, my son."

There was a long pause. Tiriki and Micail were wide-eyed, their hands clasped in the stillness, listening without full understanding. Reio-ta's head remained bowed upon his clasped hands, while Deoris stood as rigid as a statue, her throat clasped shut by invisible hands.

Finally, dry-eyed, pale as chalk, she ran her

tongue over dry lips and croaked, "That—is not all, is it?"

Rajasta sadly nodded agreement. "It is not," he said. "Perhaps, ten years from now, the edges of the catastrophe will touch Atlantis as well. These earthquakes will expand outwards, perhaps to gird the world; this very spot where we now stand may be broken and lie beneath the waters some day— and it may be, also, there is nowhere that will be left untouched. But I cannot believe it will come to that! Men's lives are a small enough thing—those whose destiny decrees that they should live, will live, if they must grow gills like fishes and spend their days swimming unimaginable deeps, or grow wings and soar as birds till the waters recede. And those who have sown the seeds of their own death will die, be they ever so clever and determined . . . but lest worse karma be engendered, the secrets of Truth within the Temple must not die."

"But—if what you say is so, how can they be preserved?" Reio-ta muttered.

Rajasta looked at him and then at Micail. "Some parts of the earth will be safe, I think," he replied at last, "and new Temples will rise there, where the knowledge may be taken and kept. The wisdom of our world may be scattered to the four winds and vanish for many an age—but it will not die forever. One such Temple, Micail, shall lie beneath your hand."

Micail started. "Mine? But I am only a boy!"

"Son of Ahtarrath," Rajasta said sternly, "usually it is forbidden that any should know his own destiny, lest he lean upon the Gods and, knowing, forbear to use all his own powers . . . yet it is necessary that you know, and prepare yourself!

Reio-ta will aid you in this; though he is denied high achievement in his own person, the sons of his flesh will inherit Ahtarrath's powers."

Micail looked down at his own slight, strong hands—and Deoris suddenly remembered a pair of tanned, gaunt, twisted hands lying upon a table-top. Then Micail flung back his head and met Rajasta's eyes. "Then, my father," he said, and put out his hand to Tiriki, "we would marry as soon as might be!"

Rajasta gazed gravely at Riveda's daughter, reflecting. "So be it," he said at last. "There was a prophecy, long ago when I was still young—*A child will be born, of a line first risen, then fallen; a child who will sire a new line, to break the father's evils forever.* You are young . . ." He glanced again into Tiriki's child-face; but what he saw there made him incline his head and add, "But the new world will be mostly to the young! It is well; this, too, is karma."

Shivering, Tiriki asked, "Will only the Priests be saved?"

"Of course not," Rajasta chided gently. "Not even the Priests can judge who is to die and who is to live. Those outside the Priesthood shall be warned of danger and told where to seek shelter, and assisted in every way—but we cannot lay compulsion on them as on the Priesthood. Many will disbelieve, and mock us; even those who do not may refuse to leave their homes and possessions. There will be those who will trust to caves, high mountains, or boats—and who can say, they may do well, or better than we. Those who will suffer and die are those who have sown the seeds of their own end."

"I think I understand," said Deoris quietly, "why did you not tell Domaris of this?"

"But I think she knows," Rajasta replied. "She stands very close to an open door which views beyond the framework of one life and one time." He stretched out his hands to them. "In other Times," he said, in the low voice of prophecy, "I see us scattered, but coming together again. Bonds have been forged in this life which can never separate us—any of us. Micon, Domaris—Talkannon, Riveda—even you, Tiriki, and that sister you never knew, Demira—they have only withdrawn from a single scene of an ending drama. They will change—and remain the same. But there is a web—a web of darkness bound around us all; and while time endures, it can never be loosed or freed. It is karma."

III

Since Rajasta had left her, Domaris had drifted in dreamless reverie, her vague thoughts bearing no relation to the pain and weakness of her spent body. Micon's face and voice were near, and she felt the touch of his hand upon her arm—not the frail and careful clasp of his maimed hands, but a strong and vital grip upon her wrist. Domaris did not believe that there was immediate reunion beyond death, but she knew, with serene confidence, that she and Micon had forged bonds of love which could not fail to draw them together again, a single bright strand running through the web of darkness that bound them one to another. Sundered they might be, through many lives, while other bonds were fulfilled and obligations discharged;

but they would meet again. Nor could she be parted from Deoris: the strength of their oath bound them one to the other, and to the children they had dedicated from life to life forever. Her only regret was that in this life she would not see Micail grow to manhood, never know the girl he would one day take to wife, never hold his sons. . . .

Then, with the clarity of the dying, she knew she need not wait to see the mother of Micail's children. She had reared her in her lonely exile, sealed her unborn to the Goddess they would all serve through all of Time. Domaris smiled, her old joyous smile, and opened her eyes upon Micon's face . . . *Micon?* No—for the dark smile was crowned with hair as flaming bright as her own had once been, and the smile that answered hers was young and unsteady as the clasp of his still-bony young hand upon hers. Beyond him, for an instant, she saw Deoris; not the staid Priestess but the child of dancing, wind-tangled ringlets, merry and sullen by turns, who had been her delight and her one sorrow in her carefree girlhood. There, too, was Rajasta, smiling, now benevolent, now stern; and the troubled, hesitant smile of Reio-ta.

All my dear ones, she thought, and almost said it aloud as she saw the pale hair of the little *saji* maiden, the child of the *no-people,* who had slipped away from Karahama's side to lead Domaris to Deoris that day in the Grey Temple—but no; time had slid over them. It was the face of Tiriki, flushed with sobbing, that swam out of the light. Domaris smiled, the old glorious smile that seemed to radiate into every heart.

Micon whispered, "Heart of Flame!" Or was it Rajasta who had spoken the old endearment in his shaking voice? Domaris did not see anything in particular now, but she sensed Deoris bending over her in the dim light. "Little sister," Domaris whispered; then, smiling, "No, you are not little any more . . ."

"You look—so very happy, Domaris," said Deoris wonderingly.

"I *am* very happy," Domaris whispered, and her luminous eyes were wide twin stars reflecting their faces. For a moment a wave of bewilderment, half pain, blurred the shining joy; she stirred, and whispered rackingly, *"Micon!"*

Micail gripped her hand tight in his own. "Domaris!"

Again the joyous eyes opened. "Son of the Sun," she said, very clearly. "Now—it is beginning again." She turned her face to the pillow and slept; and in her dreams she sat once more on the grass beneath the ancient, sheltering tree in the Temple gardens of her homeland, while Micon caressed her and held her close, murmuring softly into her ear . . .

IV

Domaris died, just before dawn, without waking again. As the earliest birds chirped outside her window, she stirred a little, breathed in her sleep, "How still the pool is today—" and her hands, lax-fingered, dropped over the edge of the couch.

Deoris left Micail and Tiriki sobbing helplessly in each other's arms and went out upon the balcony, where she stood for a long time motionless, looking out on greyish sky and sea. She was not consciously thinking of anything, even of loss and grief. The fact of death had been impressed on her so long ago that this was only confirmation. *Domaris dead? Never!* The wasted, wan thing, so full of pain, was gone; and Domaris lived again, young and quick and beautiful . . .

She did not hear Reio-ta's step until he spoke her name. Deoris turned. His eyes were a question—hers, answer. The words were superfluous.

"She is gone?" Reio-ta said.

"She is free," Deoris answered.

"The children—?"

"They are young; they must weep. Let them mourn her as they will."

For a time they were alone, in silence; then Tiriki and Micail came, Tiriki's face swollen with crying, and Micail's eyes bloodshot above smeared cheeks—but his voice was steady as he held, "Deoris?" and went to her. Tiriki put her arms around her foster-father and Reio-ta held her close, looking over her shining hair at Deoris. She in turn looked silently from the boy in her arms to the girl who clung to the Priest, and thought, *It is well. These are our children. We will stay with them.*

And then she remembered two men, standing face to face, opposed in everything yet bound by a single law throughout Time—as she and Domaris had been bound. Domaris was gone, Micon was gone, Riveda, Demira, Karahama—gone to their places in Time. But they would return. Death was the least final thing in the world.

Rajasta, his old face composed and serene, came out upon the balcony and began to intone the morning hymn:

> *"O beautiful upon the horizon of the East,*
> *Lift up thy light unto day, O Eastern Star,*
> *Day-Star, awaken, arise!*

Lord and giver of Life, awake!
Joy and giver of Light, arise!"

A shaft of golden light stole over the sea, lighting the Guardian's white hair, his shining eyes, and the white robes of his priesthood.

"Look!" Tiriki breathed. "The Night is over."

Deoris smiled, and the prism of her tears scattered the morning sun into a rainbow of colors. "The day is beginning," she whispered, "the new day!" And her beautiful voice took up the hymn, that rang to the edges of the world:

"O beautiful upon the horizon of the East,
Day-Star, awaken, arise!"